The Slayer's Magic

The Slayer's Magic

BOOK 1 OF BEADS OF BONE

C.J. Hosack

Space Wizard Science Fantasy
Raleigh, NC
www.spacewizardsciencefantasy.com

Cover art by Amy Maker
Editing by Courtney Brooks
Book Layout © 2015 BookDesignTemplates.com
"Gesta Praediana" by Lehonti A. Pérez Ovalle
Luc's Poem by Praedo's Scribe by Emily Gearheart Lim

The Slayer's Magic/C.J. Hosack.— 1st ed.
ISBN 978-1-960247-19-3

Author's website: https://cjhosack.com/

For
Lorenzo
The original and my inspiration.
And
Linda
My first writing cheerleader. I miss you so much.

CONTENTS

Chapter One

Before the Dragon Slayer came and left his magic to the Ancestors, those who were adopted may have had an easier time. Now, heredity is everything and those without bloodlines have no value in society.

— Lyv de Dico. "Ancestral Culture and its Effect on Youth." *Journal of Mind Magic Medicine*. Ancestral Library Periodicals Section, Second Floor, Shelf 100, Box 2.

With the force of pent-up frustration, Ryn chucked a stone across the glittering surface of the river. Bouncing twice, it sank instead of skipping nicely across the water. The flower-shaped note wiggled and squirmed in her hand. She picked up another rock. Smooth, flat and round, this rock was perfect. This one would fly. The paper pushed at her fingers, blooming back into shape, fighting to take up space. Instead of skipping the rock, she threw it as hard as she could across the river. Grabbing another, apple-sized rock, she pitched it hard at the water. It landed with a satisfying plop and splash. She opened her hand for the flower note to show off, flaunting its petals. She strangled it.

A dark shape brushed past Ryn's hair. She sucked in a startled breath, as she swatted at whatever was next to her head. A bird came to rest on the embankment next to her. Ryn jumped back, pressing her hand against her fast-beating heart. The bird stretched its wings then folded them, head tilting as one eye examined Ryn. The robin had a red breast, but the shimmering gold-tipped feathers hinted this was no ordinary bird.

The bird grew, morphing, changing shape, transforming itself into a lanky girl with long brown hair that glistened in the sun—smooth...except for a few feathers sticking out of it.

"What the...Yll! You scared me half to death!"

Yll laughed. "Sorry, you should see the look on your face though!"

"Not funny." Ryn attempted to crush the note again, but it fought against her. "I didn't know you were back," she said.

"I thought it would be fun to surprise you. Check it out!" Yll showed off the Ancestor bead on a cord around her neck. "Can you believe, six years of waiting, but I'm finally not an Ordinary anymore!"

"Yeah, it's so great." Ryn hid her flat tone by picking up a stone, head bowed to examine it for a moment before she skipped it several times across the water.

Yll stood and placed her hand on Ryn's arm. "This changes nothing. You're still my best friend."

Ryn took the flower note and pressed it into Yll's hand. Her eyes flashed up at Ryn before opening the folded paper and reading. Ryn didn't need to see it again, as the words had been seared into her memory.

Ryn,
Ancestor blood should never be sullied by an Ordinary. My parents and I refuse to let my friends be in a situation that could lead to ruining our purebred family lines. Now that we are of age you shouldn't mix with the rest of the village—you should go live in Waatch with the rest of the Ordinary urchins. It would be easy for my father to make life difficult for you and your odd family.
Prym de Vivus

Yll's fingers pressed to her lips as she read. When she finished the paper folded itself neatly back into a flower. Ryn snatched it, pitching it into the water.

Summer air spun around Ryn's feet, and the smell of warmed cedar worked to sooth her anger.

"I'm so sorry, Ryn." Yll looked at the ground, fingers fiddling with the bead at her throat.

Ryn's hand went to the necklace she wore. Her fingers slid along the row of beads, twelve in all. They weren't real.

They weren't made of Ancestor bone, but stone, lovingly carved by her brother to represent a bead from each type of Ancestor magic. She wasn't sure how her brother had made them, as it had been a surprise for her eighth birthday, but they had brought her much happiness. In the past they had presented an opportunity to imagine and pretend she could be one of them. Now she fought the urge to rip them off and throw them into the river.

Being adopted meant she didn't know who her Ancestors were. She could be anyone—who knew? The thought thrilled her, but also tore at her heart. The uncertainty was a large missing piece of who she was. Until recently, Yll had been in the same boat, because she was adopted as well. She hadn't known her Ancestry, but lucky for her, Yll's mother was Madame Curator of the Library who spent years researching to find Yll's family and, of course, her magic. Ryn's mother, on the other hand, didn't seem to approve of family history research.

Ryn sighed, "You were gone for a long time."

"Yeah, there wasn't a boat home for a moon. I had the chance to get to know the people of Muto a bit and start my lessons with the Ancestor."

Ryn picked out the feathers stuck in Yll's hair.

Yll blushed. "Yeah, it needs work."

"It's amazing you can shape shift after only one moon." Ryn made an attempt to smile.

"Well, I'm coming to it much older than most, so the lessons go pretty fast. Have to be done by the time I'm eighteen," Yll said.

"Good." Ryn tried to earnestly feel the words she was saying. "Good for you."

Yll, her oldest friend whom she had known since they were toddlers, gave her a look that said she didn't believe it.

"I don't know what to say," Yll said. "If I could find your Ancestors and give you your beads I would do it."

"I know." Ryn watched the flower note swirl in an eddy, then float down the river.

"If only there was a way to access the Library and do family research ourselves," Yll said.

Ryn sat on the embankment. "We can't. We're not students, and we certainly don't work for the Library. Do you think they would believe we're traveling researchers?"

Giggling, Yll sat next to her. "Right up until mother catches us."

Yll's gaze shifted down the river in the direction the note floated off. "It's not fair. My mother is head of the Library. You would think that would give us certain privileges."

"Library rules are hard and fast. Even your mother can't get around them."

"It's so frustrating! If there was one place to find the records to prove where you came from it would be in that Library. Everyone sends their records there," Yll said.

"I can't even apply to work for the Library until I'm sixteen. Which would only leave me two years to find my Ancestors before I'm too old. In the meantime-—" Ryn gestured down the river in the direction the note had floated.

They sat in silence for a bit until Ryn noticed Yll looking uncomfortable.

Ryn's eyes narrowed. "Prym invited you to the party, didn't she?"

Yll's face flushed as she turned away.

Ryn saw it all in that moment. They had both longed to belong in the village, to be accepted. They never had been, but they had each other and that was all that mattered. Now Yll belonged, and Ryn didn't. She was alone in ways she never had been before.

"It's fine, you should go," Ryn heard herself say in a detached way. "It's what you've always wanted."

"Don't be angry, Ryn."

Ryn forced a smile. "Why would I be angry? This is a happy day."

For Yll, but not for Ryn.

***

Ryn's heart lightened at the sight of her family's cottage and the smell of bacon cooking. Her stomach grumbled.

She had left the cottage early. The rising summer sun was difficult to sleep through, so she had gotten up early to wander down by the river.

The flower note had been waiting on the porch for her.

It was gone now. Good riddance.

She took the door latch in her hand and tried to banish all the gloominess of seeing Yll with magic. Ryn still had her family. Her brother had magic from his father, but her mother was Ordinary, like her. At least there was one person left who knew what it felt like.

Plastering a smile on her face, she pushed the door open. Her mother was bustling around the hearth frying eggs and making biscuits. Ryn loved it when her mother cooked a big breakfast.

"Ryn sweetheart, will you take the biscuits off the fire for me? I think they're about to burn." Her mother gestured with her head toward the iron pot over the fire.

"Sure." Ryn used a towel to swing it away from the heat.

"Jett, will you get mugs for tea please?" Ryn's mother called to her brother, who was absorbed in a staring contest with Abby the cat. Ryn wasn't sure how spirit magic worked exactly, but Jett enjoyed how it helped him commune with animals.

The kettle started to whistle, so Ryn pulled that off too. Jett stood, stretching, then pulled the mugs from the top shelf that was hopelessly out of Ryn's reach.

Once everything was on the table, they took their seats.

Jett touched two fingers to his forehead. "Thanks be to the Ancestors," he said.

Ryn's mother frowned at him. She always did that when he prayed. Ryn's mother didn't come from the Ancestors, so she didn't feel inclined to worship them. Jett's father was of Ancestor blood. Her mother's second marriage was to Ryn's father, who was also of Ancestor blood. Both fathers had encouraged the behavior during their respective times in the household.

The thought of Ancestors brought Ryn's mind back to her predicament—no longer being welcome in the village, and her best friend slipping away. Her face must have revealed something, because her mother glared at Jett in a way that meant he was in for a long discussion later. She reached across the table to take Ryn's hand.

"Ryn, sweetheart, remember that we don't need Ancestors or magic to be happy. I'm happy being far away from all of that. There are so many greater talents than magic."

"But everyone here does magic. I'm the only one who doesn't."

"The village is not the whole wide world, and most people out there don't do magic. Look at Clayr, she's Madame Curator of the Library, the most powerful institution there is, and she doesn't do magic. You don't need it," her mother said.

"But Clayr's different, everyone else in the Library does magic," Ryn started.

"Not everyone, Clayr has been working hard to change that." Her mother took both of Ryn's hands into hers. "Did you know I always wanted to have a little girl but could never have one?"

Oh no—here it comes, Ryn fought to keep her eyes from rolling, she'd lost count of the number of times she'd heard this. It was something she'd always known.

"I was overjoyed to bring you home to be mine! You were such a tiny thing. My greatest fear has always been that someone will take you from me."

"But knowing where I come from wouldn't change that. *And* I'd have magic!"

Ryn's mother released her hands. "Eat up, we have lots of chores to do today."

Jett and Ryn both groaned at the same time.

***

After a morning of sweeping and dusting and mucking out chickens, Ryn sank down onto her bed. The painting on her wall loomed over her. Her mother probably spent too much on it, money Ryn was sure they didn't have, but her mother loved it. It must be hard for her mother to make ends meet on her own without Ryn's father to help. He had left them a few years ago. Her parents hadn't really fought, not that Ryn had noticed, but they had clearly grown apart. Her father simply spent more and more time away from the house until it was decided it was best he leave. Ryn, always attached to her mother, didn't struggle with it too much, but there were times when she missed him.

Now she lay staring at the painting of the little flower girl. The girl stood in the snow barefoot with knobby knees, red from the cold. A breeze blew at her dress, ragged and patched. Her face delighted at the bright yellow flower she held in her hand. Snow swirled around her. Ryn wondered if her mother considered the painting a reminder of where Ryn could have ended up if her birth parents hadn't placed her in the orphanage. Staring at the tattered skirt Ryn could almost feel the cold wind blowing. Despite the warm summer afternoon, Ryn shivered and nestled deeper into the mattress till she drifted off to sleep...

***

Ryn found herself dreaming of cherry wood bookshelves, brimming with knowledge, and lining the walls of a room the size of her entire cottage. Drapery dripping with thousands of embroidered flowers, framed the windows overlooking rocky cliffs. The sound of waves rhythmically crashed against them. Crown molding spilled onto the ceiling, becoming complexly carved tiles. The smell of fresh polish drifted up from the dark wood flooring. The air in the room was charged with energy. She shivered with the thrill of it.

Her gaze was drawn to the end of a long, clawed-foot table. Her father stood there, intent on his study of a book. Heart leaping at the sight of him, a longing overtook her. She hadn't seen him for too long. Not since he'd left them. Shifting forward toward him she found she wore a heavily petticoated dress, of the kind they wore in the great Ancestral Houses. Her eyes took in the room again. Realization dawned that this *was* one of the Ancestral Houses. She wondered at how her brain could imagine something she had never seen before in such detail.

The swish of her skirts drew the attention of her father.

"Ryn! There you are. It's so good to see you. Come quick, I have something to show you." He gestured her forward.

Now that her eyes were locked on him, she couldn't look away. She hadn't realized how much she'd been longing for this moment. She rushed to the end of the table as fast as her legs, and skirts, would allow. Her passing almost knocking over a potted plant. When she reached him, he threw his arms around her.

"Oh, it's so good to see you!" he exclaimed.

Tears pricked her eyes. A million things she wanted to say, *I've missed you! Where have you been? When are you coming home?* but all she could do was hug him.

When at last he pulled back he turned her toward the book on the table. "What do you make of this?" he asked.

"You're the rare book expert," she said.

He put his thumb and forefingers to his chin, studying, but saying nothing. Ryn took a closer look.

She ran her hands over the impressive, tree patterned leather cover. Then opened the book and gasped—the first few pages were torn from the book. On the remaining pages there were entries—entries of when children arrived...and when they left.

"And look at this"—her father turned the pages of the book—"it mentions you..."

***

Bam! The bedroom door slammed closed.

Abby, who must have curled up next to Ryn to nap, jumped up and took off running.

Ryn stared at Jett through blurry eyes.

NO! No, no, no, no no! It had been right in front of her. The book had been right there—the record of where she came from!

"Why are you here?" Ryn croaked, rolling over to cover her face, struggling to hold the dream in her head. Maybe if she fell back to sleep it would continue.

"Clayr's here with some news. They kicked me out of the room," Jett said, plopping himself down on her bed.

"So go to your own room!"

Jett bent to pick up Abby and soothe her.

The evaporation of the dream spiked Ryn's annoyance with Jett. She wanted to throw him out, if only he wasn't twice her size. Grumbling, she rose to finish her chores.

"Where are you going?" Jett asked.

"To sweep the porch."

"Don't. They clearly want to be left alone." Jett rolled over and fluffed a pillow.

"Whatever. I'll be in and out, they won't even know I'm passing through."

Even so, Ryn cracked the door open to listen for a good pause in their conversation for the interruption.

"...came this morning to deliver the news," Clayr's voice said.

"What is he claiming is the purpose of his visit?" Her mother's voice was tense.

"Says he's working on some minor research project, and he wants to take on students." Clayr sighed.

Ryn's mother swore. Ryn tensed—her mother never swore. "Minor research project, my foot!"

"And taking on students out of term," Clayr added. "It means I'll have no choice but to hire at least one of them. Master Wes is a renowned researcher who never takes on students. The Board will expect me to hire his prized pupil—and they will be of his choosing. I won't be able to block them. Who knows what he'll bring in...and from where."

"You know that trip we keep putting off for me to pick up that packet of land records from Saarimuto?" Ryn's mother said. "I think it's time I went to retrieve them."

"Unfortunately, I agree, Ryette. It's best you make yourself scarce while Wes is around," Clayr said.

Her mother's gaze shifted to Ryn's door. Ryn shifted out of sight.

"What do I do with the children?" her mother asked.

"Jett and Ryn are plenty old enough to care for themselves," Clayr said. "Aren't you introducing them to Lar this evening? He can watch out for them when I'm not able."

The room got quiet. Ryn widened the crack just enough so she could see her mother now staring down into her cup with a distant look on her face.

"The boat that brought Yll back from Saarimuto is taking on supplies. It should leave on its return trip in a few days. You have time to think on it." Clayr rose.

"No, I need to go. It will be worse if I'm here," her mother said.

Clayr nodded. "I'll have your traveling papers and contract drawn up." She patted Ryn's mother on the shoulder. "It'll be fine. I've buried those records deep. He won't find them."

Ryn's mother put her hand on Clayr's and nodded.

Clayr moved toward the door. "We'll watch over the kids, don't worry. Gotta get back to chore day. Who knows where Yll has flitted off to in my absence. I'm beginning to regret having a shapeshifter in the house already." Opening the door to the cottage she added, "Have a wonderful dinner. Bye—love ya!" And she was gone.

Ryn watched her mother stand to grab the broom, then stop—staring into space. Closing her door, Ryn leaned against it, mind racing. What did she just hear? Master Wes, the world-renowned researcher coming here and taking on students? Why was that so upsetting? And why did it make her mother need to leave? What was going on? And who was this Lar and dinner tonight? Her mother had said nothing about it.

The ground seemed to be shifting beneath her and she was no longer sure where to find a solid place to stand.

Chapter Two

Over time, certain magics began to cling to one House bloodline or the other. The drive to keep bloodlines pure became strong, to little effect. Now certain Ancestral Houses seek outside means to restore themselves to their former magical glory.

— Ivy de Pentral. *Ancestor Magic and Its Dangers*. Ancestral Library, Second Floor, Cultural Room, Shelf 14, Shelfmark 68.

As the last flames left Zo's fingertips, he ran for the water pump. Learning to play with fire always made him thirsty.

It's not playing! Master Ignis' voice sounded in Zo's head.

"Whatever," Zo muttered.

Studying magic from a shade, a ghost of the Ancestor whose bead hung round Zo's neck, was always a bit strange. Master Ignis' lessons were strict and controlled—but fire, fire was so incredible. Fire made it all worth it. Fire didn't mind anger. Zo snapped his fingers and marveled at the flames dancing around them.

"Zo," his father called from the porch, "I thought you were cooking!"

Zo held up a hand full of flames. "Fire lesson."

An exasperated sigh came from his father.

The smile that wormed onto Zo's face refused to be suppressed. His father knew there was no choice. Once a lesson began there was no stopping it. Much to Zo's delight, it had gotten him out of many unpleasant tasks.

Zo forced his face as straight as possible as he jogged up the steps, pushing past his father into their cabin. "Don't worry, the chicken will get cooked. I already unpacked the spices last night. You go primp for our guests."

His father threw up his hands and stalked to his room, the only bedroom in the log cabin.

"Regg," Zo called up the loft he shared with his brother. "Come chop wood so I can cook."

Regg peered over the side of the railing with an open book in his hand.

"You were supposed to do that," Regg said, snapping his book closed.

"But I didn't, so now you get to." Zo headed for the table by the fire and the ingredients his father had laid out.

Regg growled in frustration.

"Hurry up, our guests will be here soon," Zo said, pulling on an apron and rolling up his sleeves. He loved cooking— mostly because it involved fire.

Regg stopped halfway to the door. "Guests? There are people in this Ancestor-forsaken village?"

"Oh, get out. I need space to work." Zo picked up a huge cleaver.

***

By the time Regg returned with an armload of split wood and kindling, Zo had all the pans bubbling, and chicken baking in a cast iron pot. Regg opened the wood box.

"There's plenty of wood in here." He glared at Zo.

Zo shrugged. "You needed something to do."

Regg rolled his eyes and dropped the wood next to the box.

Their father hurried into the room adjusting his sleeves and waistcoat. "Go get ready." He gestured with his head toward the loft. "I'll finish up."

Zo's eyes narrowed. "You'll ruin it."

"I can keep things from burning for a few minutes, go, go," his father snapped. He really was nervous about this meeting.

Zo threw off the apron and headed for the loft. Regg went out to wash up. Zo was back in a flash with an unbuttoned waistcoat over his loose-fitting shirt. His father gave him a disapproving look as a knock came at the door. Shaking a pointed finger at Zo's buttons, he crossed the room to open it.

A woman who seemed the perfect match for his father—with a mane of strawberry blond hair, and an air of knowing exactly what she was about—stood in the doorway.

"Ryette." His father took her hands and kissed her on the cheek. "Come in."

Zo had heard of her, of course, but hadn't met her. She was followed by a big mountain of a guy, dark haired and slightly taller than Zo, who seemed as friendly as an out-of-control fire. Big Mountain folded his arms. Zo found himself matching his stance. The meeting of the families, Zo hated this part. They were expected to become fast friends and family. In his observation, it never happened that way.

"My son, Jett." Ryette presented Big Mountain.

"Welcome! I'm Lar." Zo's father shook the large youth's hand.

From behind Big Mountain, a petite girl half Zo's size emerged. Her gaze turned up, taking in the high exposed beam ceiling. She clearly hadn't noticed Lar holding out his hand to her.

"My daughter, Ryn," Ryette said.

"Charmed." Zo's father took Petite Girl's hand and pressed it to his forehead.

Her eyes widened in surprise. The gesture was one a young person usually gave to their elders. It was a sign of high respect.

Lar led Ryn by her hand over to stand before Zo. "This is my oldest son, Zo."

His father gave him a pointed look, because of course he did. His father couldn't resist any opportunity to push a girl at him. Zo widened his eyes to keep from rolling them. Problem was, either his father was planning on adding these people as family, or he was presenting her as a potential love interest. Both prospects annoyed Zo. Still, there was something about her presence that felt warm and accepting. He wasn't falling for it though, not her as family, and definitely not her as an attraction. It wasn't right.

The door shut.

"And the one squeezing in behind you there is Regg," Lar said.

Regg nodded as he skirted the guests to stand next to Zo.

"It's so good to meet you," Ryette said.

She looked earnest. Zo was still skeptical.

Beardslee, Zo's cat, wandered over from under the table and sat almost on top of Zo's feet. His eyes told Zo it was dinner time.

"Chicken's almost finished. You'll have to wait, silly cat," Zo admonished him.

Scooping Beardslee up, he watched his father invite their guests to make themselves comfortable.

Ryn stayed by Zo. Looking down at her, she shifted from one foot to another, seeming hesitant about what to do next. Something about her awkwardness tugged at him.

"I have a cat," she said, putting out her hand so Beardslee could sniff her fingers. "She's got short multicolored hair and white paws though, nothing like this long gray fur."

Beardslee let Ryn pet him. The cat was used to traveling and took to new places and people well.

One of the pots bubbled over, liquid dripping and sizzling in the fire.

"Excuse me," Zo said, setting down the cat and hurrying over to the hearth.

Ryn followed.

"Can I help?" she asked.

As Zo passed the table, he picked up on Ryette's air of agitation, and his father's concern.

"What's wrong?" he overheard Lar whisper.

Ryette's eyes drifted over her children. Lar's head followed her gaze.

"Dinner's ready!" Zo said, using a potholder to lift the chicken off the fire.

"Great, I'm starving," Jett said, from the staring contest he seemed to have engaged Beardslee in.

Ryn appeared at Zo's side with a towel ready to help him move the boiling vegetables to the sideboard. He wasn't used to getting help. Hopefully he didn't trip over her.

Unfortunately, the prospect of dinner on the table wasn't the distraction for the parents' sudden distress Zo had hoped for. His father already had other ideas.

"Jett," Lar said, "we've just moved to the village, would you mind showing the boys around a bit?"

Jett froze in the middle of pulling out a chair at the table. "Wait—what?" Jett squinted at Lar.

"Please, Jett," Ryette said. It didn't sound like a request.

"My dinner's going to get cold," Zo complained.

Lar pointed at the pot with the chicken in it. "Cast iron pot—that'll stay hot for hours."

Regg's stomach growled. "I can't walk on an empty stomach."

Ryette stared down Jett, her lips pursed. Zo watched him crumble like cake.

"Fine," Jett huffed. "We'll walk through the village to Crystal Lake and back. Will that give you enough time?"

"What? No..." Zo started.

"Yes, thank you," Ryette said.

"You've got to be kidding me," Zo whispered under his breath.

He looked to his father who just waved him on. The smell of cooked chicken rumbled Zo's stomach.

His father gave him that "do as you're told or else I'll make you do chores all day tomorrow" look. As if Zo wasn't already the one who took care of the household.

Regg grabbed his arm. "Come on, maybe Jett knows some cute girls in the village."

Zo just glared at him.

Ryn followed her brother out the door. Her hunched-up shoulders stirred something protective in him. He followed the rest of them out, but not before giving his father one last glare that came straight from his stomach.

"What was that all about?" Jett asked, looking back at the closed cabin door.

"Mom's been acting weird since Clayr's visit," Ryn said. "I overheard her saying something about leaving on a job to avoid seeing somebody."

"Who would she be avoiding? She doesn't associate with anybody outside the village," Jett said.

Zo bent to pick up a rock. "Clearly, she does. She met my father."

They walked in silence for a while.

"What do people do here?" Regg asked. "It's so out of the way of anything."

Jett, hands in his pockets as he walked down the cabin's lane, shrugged. "Most everyone is an administrator of the Library. They don't have to be there every day, so they come here to get away from the craziness of the town."

Regg lifted an eyebrow. "So are there cute girls here in Sooke?"

Ryn's head jerked up. "Only stupid ones."

"My sister's adopted. Her ancestry is a mystery. She tends to hate people who have Ancestors." Jett grinned at them.

"Do not!" Ryn swatted her brother on the arm.

Zo glanced down at his open collar and the beads that hung there. Jett's open shirt revealed only one bead—the bead for spirit magic. The collar on Ryn's dress was in the fashion of what the native mainlanders wore—high and buttoned up. Mainlanders didn't have Ancestors to flaunt. Zo wondered what it would be like to grow up without magic. His fire magic was so much a part of him, he couldn't even imagine it. His finger touched his second bead, the one for healing magic... Well, with that one he would wish for something different.

Movement in the bushes caught Zo's eye in a flash of white, but when he looked closer, all he saw were trees and brambles. Throwing the rock he had been fiddling with into the forest, a tawny rabbit startled, crashing through the bushes.

"Come on," Jett said. "It's market day in the village. If we hurry, we might catch a couple vendors before they leave."

They picked up the pace and emerged from the lane into the outskirts of Sooke. It was an odd sort of village: not set on any major roads, in the middle of a forest, and with nothing but trees surrounding it. The square sat at its center with the buildings radiating out from it. Reminiscent of the design of Waatch.

"Regents and other Library officials built the village, but the baker has been known to attract customers from the surrounding area. His pastries are more delicate than the best bakers in Waatch." As they passed the bakery Jett sighed, "Unfortunately, it's too late in the day and the bakery is closed, but with the village on a hill, the square has a great view." Jett pointed toward the perfect view of the Dragon's Mountain in the distance.

Zo's stomach grumbled at the thought of fresh bread, but Jett was right, the view of snowcapped Dragon Mountain was crisp and clear from here.

"Look, the apple farmer's still here!" Ryn started off toward a group of carts at the edge of the square.

"Apples sound good," Zo said.

Actually, at this point anything edible sounded good.

They crossed the square, passing a statue of what looked like some random Ancestor set in the center of the square. At the base of the statue, a man sat lounging. He had an odd look about him, like he'd slept in the forest. Something about him didn't quite fit. Weird Forest-Man's eyes followed them across the square. Trying to ignore him, Zo lengthened his stride toward the apple cart.

An older woman was accepting coins from someone and handing them a bag of apples. Zo opened his mouth to ask what kind apples they had and stopped. A young man about Zo's age rounded the cart, muscles rippling as he carried a box of apples. In the summer heat he wore only a vest, his white-blond hair damp with sweat. Out of the corner of his eye, Zo saw Ryn sway a little.

"Can I help you?" the young man asked.

Zo cleared his throat.

"Four apples, please," Jett said.

"Certainly," said Apple Farmer. "These are new crop. We have a grove that bears fruit late summer instead of the fall." He wiped four apples with a rag, then handed one to Ryn with a flourish while she blushed furiously.

Zo gave Apple Farmer a coin, suppressing a shiver when their fingers touched.

"Thanks!" Regg said, taking an apple.

"Certainly, come back any time." Apple Farmer smiled a sweet smile as he deposited the coin in a money pouch.

Zo barely noticed the apple in his hand as they walked away. His eyes lingered on the apple farmer as long as they could.

Ryn released a long breath slowly.

"He likes you," Zo said, taking a bite of the apple.

"Oh, I doubt that. I'm short, everyone thinks I'm a kid— someone to pick up and throw in a waste bin or something." She took a bite of her apple. "Besides, I don't have any magic," she said around her mouth full of apple.

Zo shrugged. "He doesn't seem to care."

A sudden breeze blew through the square, causing a young lady to lose her scarf. Regg ran to retrieve it. When he returned it to her, she looked him over appraisingly. Staring at the beads displayed by his open collar, she smiled. The two began to flirt. Zo shook his head at the exchange, but Ryn stiffened.

"What's wrong?" Zo asked.

"Nothing," Ryn said, pointing with her chin at the girl as Regg wrapped the scarf around the girl's neck. "She's just the one person in the village who hates me the most."

Zo could see why. With her done up curls and fashionable clothes, the girl looked like the sort that only cared about status. He didn't have much use for those kinds of people. His mother was like that.

Zo gave a whistle. "Regg, let's go."

Regg bowed to kiss the girl's fingers then backed away, hurrying to catch up to the rest of them. "Alright, maybe this village isn't so Ancestor forsaken as I thought."

"That's Prym, she's one of the Regent's daughters. I would be careful with her," Jett said.

"I can be careful," Regg said.

Frowning, Ryn bowed her head. Zo wondered what the full story was there.

Jett led them the rest of the way across the square and down a path into the forest.

On the trail through the woods, Zo kept having a weird feeling they were being followed, but every time he looked back there was nothing. He had been on the move with his father and his brother since just after Regg received his beads. Sometimes thieves had followed them hoping to take advantage of them. He had that tingle at the back of his neck like something was not right, and there were flashes of something white in the underbrush, but he could never catch sight of anything definite. He shook it off. Now wasn't the time to get paranoid. It was probably just someone from the village headed toward wherever they were going.

The trail was a pleasant walk through the trees. Zo distracted himself by coaxing backstory out of Ryn and Jett. How they had lived here in Sooke their whole lives. That Ryn was somewhat fixated on wanting to do magic. That Jett was disappointed his mother didn't have magic to give him and, interestingly, that Ryn and Jett had different fathers. Jett's father was from House Pentral. Jett never found out what his father's mother's House was. Zo liked how Jett was experimenting with using spirit magic to communicate with animals. Ryn's father was from House Dico on his father's side, and Muto from his mother. Zo always found mind magic and shape shifting to be cool. Ryn was open about how her mother had married Jett's father young. They didn't know why that marriage fell apart, but she left Jett's father when Jett was just a baby. Shortly after that, she had married Ryn's father. It was her father who had found her at an orphanage and brought her home to a somehow newly barren Ryette. Though how they knew she was barren in such a short span of time was a mystery. Ryn seemed to think some physician had told her mother that.

The end of the trail opened up to a flat grassy area perfect for picnics. Jett explained it was a favorite gathering place for parties. It sat on the shores of the most pristine, beautiful lake with water of the purest blue Zo had ever seen. Late afternoon sun shimmered on the water making it so inviting he wanted to dive right in. The families swimming in the lake demonstrated that sentiment.

"Welcome to Crystal Lake," Ryn said.

Regg gasped. "It's beautiful."

Zo followed Regg's gaze. "Not the girls, you dork." Regg was clearly studying a girl in her swim things, sunning herself by the shore.

"Alright. I take it all back. I totally love this place," Regg said. Putting his hand on Zo's shoulder he whispered, "You should too. I know your preferences aren't as big a deal here on the mainland"—he nodded his head toward the sunbathing girl by the shore—"but finding yourself a girl would get Mom and Dad off your back."

"Who says I want to make them happy?" Zo said.

Regg shrugged. "Your funeral," he said, as strode off toward the girl.

Someone called to Jett, and he moved off to join them.

Zo watched a guy in the water splashing a couple of shrieking girls who sent a small wave back at him. One of the girls must have had water magic. The guy dove into the wave, startling the girl by scooping her up from beneath. Water dripped off his muscles as he carried her laughing and kicking to shore.

Zo sighed. Ryn flinched at the sound. Shifting his focus, he took a good look at her for the first time. She was short, but didn't carry herself like she was trying to make herself taller. In fact, she seemed to by trying to shrink further away into the ground. Her long brown hair glistened with a bit of red in the afternoon sun, but it was unadorned as if she didn't want to bring any attention to it. Her mouth was curled down in a frown that appeared unwelcoming, yet he felt comfortable in her presence.

"What are the best spots on the lake?" he asked.

Ryn pointed to where some kids were using a rope hanging from a tree branch to swing into the lake. Their mother called to them to come and dry off so they could go home for dinner.

"The rope swing is fun," she said, "but I have a favorite spot."

"Let's see it," he said.

She led him past the grassy picnic area. Following the shoreline, they climbed over rocks and a fallen tree to a small cove. The water was so clear he could see all the way to the rocks at the bottom of the lake. He knelt to put his hand in the water—and found it icy cold, even in the heat of late summer.

"Yikes," he said, shaking his hand out. "How do you swim in that?"

Ryn giggled. "You get used to it. Feels good on a really hot day." She picked up a rock and skipped it several times far out into the lake.

Zo felt challenged. His fingers closed on a perfect skipping stone just as the nearby bushes shifted. He glared at them for a while, but nothing appeared.

With little effort he sent his rock skipping across the water—not nearly as far as Ryn's.

"Not bad." She looked like she was suppressing a grin of triumph.

Her lifted mood had him casting about for something that would be even more fun. A pile of cedar bark gave him an idea.

"Hey, you've got a great throwing arm," he said, collecting the bark and bringing it closer to the water's edge. "Do you think you could throw a piece of bark for me to light on fire?"

Ryn's eyes got wide. "Isn't that playing with magic? I thought that was forbidden."

He couldn't resist rolling his eyes at that. "It's not playing, it's practicing. I need to practice." He handed her a piece of bark.

Ryn held the bark, skepticism written on her face.

"I've been learning to make a fireball. Toss it up and I'll see if I can hit it into the water."

Zo snapped his fingers, lighting them with fire. Ryn was still giving him that look, but she tossed it into the air. Zo pushed his fire out from his hands, but it barely left his hands before it curved down to the wet shore and extinguished.

"Again," he said, tossing her another piece.

This time when the bark went up into the air, he threw the fire with all his strength. It sailed underneath the bark and dropped into the lake.

"Close," Ryn said.

Just as Zo threw her another piece of bark something big and white streaked through the bushes growling toward them.

Zo turned and fired flames at it.

Chapter Three

Why eight and eighteen? Who chose those arbitrary ages? It certainly couldn't have been Praedo. He gave his bones to adults to pass on the magic. I have spent most of my life in the Library researching the reason for these ages, hoping to expand it. So far, the best explanation is the spirit of the Ancestors has chosen it. If only I could go back to my lessons of youth and ask them...

— Ivy de Pentral. *Ancestor Magic and Its Dangers*. Ancestral Library, Second Floor, Cultural Room, Shelf 14, Shelfmark 68.

Ryn's arm froze mid-throw as she watched Zo throw fire into a summer-heated dry bush that burst instantly into a roaring fire. Feet rooted to the ground, she couldn't move, her brain still processing how the forest was about to burn around them.

Zo swore, rushing to the water's edge and trying to splash water on the fire. The water wasn't reaching the flames.

From the corner of Ryn's eye, she saw the lake begin to swell into a giant wave.

"Water magic!" Ryn screamed before the wave broke over the both of them, slamming into them and sweeping them completely off their feet.

The freezing cold wave hit her, sucking the breath from her and sending her tumbling across the pebbled shore. As the water receded it forced its way up her nose, leaving her coughing and sputtering. She wiped water from her eyes, searching for Zo. He was nowhere in sight. She tried to call out to him, but all she could do was cough.

"Are you alright?"

Ryn looked up to find Jett crouching over her, his fingers brushing wet hair from her face.

No words came as her coughing fit continued. He pounded on her back.

Regg appeared scrambling over a boulder onto the rocky beach.

"Are you alright?" Jett asked again, eyebrows furrowed in worry.

Ryn at last stopped sputtering and nodded. She looked up to see Regg had found his brother. The wave had smashed him against a large log. Regg was pulling him out from under it. Ryn stood on shaky legs and stumbled over to the boys. Zo was coughing up water, his pant leg was torn, and his knee was bleeding.

Regg glanced at her, putting a reassuring hand on her arm. "He'll be fine, he can heal that right up—can't you Zo?"

Zo's face flushed red as he spit some water from his mouth. He tried to stand but collapsed back onto the rocks, wincing at the impact.

"Help me get him up," Regg said.

Jett helped Regg lift Zo so he was sitting on the log.

"How long does it take to heal?" Ryn asked, wishing she hadn't looked down at Zo's knee. The sight of the bloody gash made her queasy.

Regg shook his head. "Not long."

Zo's eyes shot daggers at his brother.

"Except when you're angry—then it doesn't work so well," Regg added.

Ryn's eyes followed the water as it receded across the pebbled shore returning to its natural banks.

Jett inspected the burnt bush, turning to give Zo a hard look.

"Were you playing with fire?" he asked.

"*Practicing*," Zo sputtered. "Practicing."

"Where'd the water magic come from?" Regg asked.

Zo coughed again. "No idea."

"Nelly was using her water magic by the park earlier," Ryn said.

"Oh. Yeah. I saw that," Zo said.

Jett frowned. "I was just with Nelly, wasn't her."

"This is taking forever. Let me heal it." Regg moved to put his hand on Zo's neck.

"I'm fine!" Zo slapped Regg's hand away.

Regg put his hands up in surrender.

"Let's get back to the cabin," Jett said. "I'm sure your dad will be interested in all of this."

"Naw," Zo said. "Practice is important."

Jett's eyes did that thing Ryn hated, the one that said he was going to make sure you understood the consequences of your actions.

Zo opened his mouth like he was going to further object, then shrugged and let Regg pull him to his feet. In the process of supporting Zo, Ryn noticed Regg had slipped his arm around Zo's back in such a way that his hand rested on Zo's neck. As they worked their way around the lake and through the woods, Zo gradually walked more and more on his own. Eventually, he had only a slight limp as they crossed the village square.

All the vendors were gone now. Ryn was disappointed the apple farmer was gone already. She knew it was silly, because he was far too handsome to be interested in her Ordinary self, but it was something to look forward to on market day. The apple farming family also had a daughter who was always kind to Ryn. Maybe because they were Ordinary like her, she felt like she fit in with them. Unfortunately, she could daydream all she wanted, but reality was the son would never ask her out. He was far too good looking to think much of her. Ordinary like her or not, he had already captured the attention of more than one village girl. Those girls had more to offer him than she did.

By the time they returned to the cabin, Zo's limp was less pronounced, but the cut was still visible. She watched him wince climbing the steps to the cabin door, but he was smooth as water gliding in through the doorway.

Her mother and Lar looked up from the table where they sat deep in conversation, Lar's hand gently resting on top of hers. At the sight of them her mother gasped, rushing to Ryn.

"What happened?" She inspected Ryn's wet clothes and disheveled hair. "Did you fall in the lake? Come over by the fire and let's get you dried off."

"I'm fine, Mother. The evening is still warm and I'm mostly dry."

"You're soaked to the bone—tell me what happened." Ryn's mother grabbed a towel from the cupboard and started drying her daughter's hair.

Ryn didn't know what to say. She didn't want to get Zo in trouble. As her mind whirred, Jett spoke up.

"Looks like someone was playing with fire, but don't worry, a wave of water magic put it out." Jett folded his arms and shifted his weight as if defying someone to contradict him.

"Practicing..." Zo muttered, "I'm supposed to practice, why does no one understand practicing?"

"Zo?" Lar asked.

Removing the lid from a pot Zo sniffed at the chicken. "This is barely warm enough."

"Zo!" Lar's voice raised.

Zo pushed his water-tousled locks out of his face and gave his father a defiant look.

"I learned how to make fire balls today. I was practicing," Zo said.

"You were throwing fire at the bushes?" Jett exclaimed.

"No—of course not."

"Then how did the bush get burned?" Jett asked.

Ryn piped in trying to help, "I saw this stranger in the woods on our walk. I think maybe he was in the bushes and..."

Zo held up his hands as if to stall an argument. "We were being followed from the village, I'm sure of it. I caught a glimpse of something—I was protecting us."

Lar went white and very still. "You threw fire at someone?" His voice was barely above a whisper.

Zo cracked his knuckles on the worktable in front of him. "Possibly, yeah."

Ryn's mother gasped. Lar paced.

"What's wrong?" Ryn asked.

"Throwing fire at people breaks all kinds of laws," Regg said, turning a chair around and sitting in it. The grin on his face made it clear he was enjoying watching his brother get into trouble.

Zo gave Regg a sharp look. "Not if you're defending yourself."

"Were you?" Lar asked. "Defending yourself?"

"Of course," Zo said, but his shrug looked a bit guilty.

"Were you seen?"

"No."

"Then who did the water magic?"

Silence settled on the room. Everything stopped.

Zo cleared his throat. "Dinner's getting cold. Let's eat." His voice came out a bit higher pitched than normal.

Like a spell lifting, sound and movement returned to the room.

Glowering, Lar pointed a finger at Zo. "Don't think we're done talking about this."

Ryn watched Zo roll his eyes when his father turned his back.

Her stomach became unsettled. She didn't want Zo to be in trouble because of her.

"I'll help you get the food onto the table." Ryn's mother moved to grab a pot with the towel she had in her hands.

The food was dished into bowls and set on the table. All was in readiness, so Lar directed where everyone was to sit. Ryn sat next to Zo, with Regg and Jett opposite them. Ryn's mother sat at one end of the table, while Lar took the other. Ryn suddenly realized they were sitting as if they were a family. She gave her mother a quizzical look. She reciprocated with a reassuring smile.

"Thank you for coming this evening," Lar said. "Despite the interruption earlier, this meeting has been a long time coming and Ryette and I hope that we will all enjoy each other's company." Lar's smile looked hopeful. "Please, eat."

"Thanks be to the Ancestors." Jett touched his fingers to his forehead.

"Praise be," said Regg, making the same gesture.

Zo grabbed a bowl and began to dish up the chicken. "It's not my best work. Don't judge."

"I'm sure it's fine," Ryn's mother said.

"So, what was the urgent problem, Mother? Did you figure it out?" Jett asked as he passed a bowl.

Ryn's mother hesitated for a minute before dishing up some roasted vegetables. "No problem. Clayr needs me to retrieve some important documents from Saarimuto. Lar and I just needed to discuss some logistics."

"You travel for Clayr all the time, what's the issue?" Jett asked.

Ryn's mother hesitated.

Lar accepted the bowl of chicken from Regg. "There's a big researcher coming to town taking on students. Clayr's going to be extra busy, she'll probably have to stay at the Library for a few weeks. Your mother was just concerned about who would watch over you while she's gone." Lar smiled as he passed the vegetables to Zo. "I told her I would be happy to help."

Jett scoffed. "I'm only a few moons away from being an adult. We don't need watching over. I'm perfectly capable."

Silence reigned.

Zo cleared his throat. "I've always wanted to see inside the Library."

"You'd probably burn it down," Regg muttered.

Ryn felt Zo kick his brother under the table.

"I want to study in the Library," Ryn said.

Keeping her head down, she pushed the food around her plate with her fork.

Once the thought was out of her mouth, she regretted saying it.

It was her mother's turn to go very still.

"You don't need to study at the Library, Ryn," her mother said. "They won't accept you there. You think the kids here in the village are harsh, Library workers are worse."

"But Clayr likes Ordinaries to work in the Library. She's an Ordinary—as *you* reminded me this morning," Ryn protested.

"Sweetheart." Her mother covered Ryn's hand with hers. "I've watched you struggle to fit in here in the village, and if it weren't for my work with Clayr, I would move us away. Ancestor politics is no place for you."

"But I could find my family," Ryn blurted out, then covered the mouth she couldn't seem to control. The hurt look that passed over her mother's face made her instantly regret what she'd said. "I mean, my magic."

Her mother gave a sad smile. "I know what you meant, and let me promise you—Clayr and I searched that Library from top to bottom and there is no record of your ancestry there." She squeezed Ryn's hand and let go. "There is nothing to find in that Library but more hurt. Please stay clear of it."

The quiet around the table was interrupted only by forks scraping on plates.

Regg cleared his throat. "So, there's this Debut party for this pretty blond girl in a few days. I managed to get an invite."

"Fantastic, son!" Lar said. "Zo, I want you to go with your brother."

Zo's fork stopped halfway to his mouth. "What? No."

"You need to get to know people in the village," Lar said.

"I don't do snobby, Ancestor types." Zo's fork finished its trip to his mouth.

"They're not snobby," Regg protested.

"They look down on Dad because he uses his fire magic to make a living instead of hoarding his magic like it's beneath them to be useful. They're snobs," Zo said, shoveling in another bite.

Ryn stared at Zo. She'd never met an Ancestor descendant who valued something other than magic. She was stunned. That made what Lar said next a dagger to her gut.

"Snobby or not, you need to find yourself a nice girl of Ancestor descendant. Bloodlines are everything Zo. I expect you to perpetuate the magic. The Ancestors demand it."

Ryn's jaw dropped, and her mother gasped.

Zo stood straight up, causing his chair to topple.

"I don't give a..." Zo glanced at Ryn and her mother. "I don't care what the Ancestors want."

Zo limped stiffly toward the door.

"Why haven't you healed yet?" Lar asked.

"Can't heal when you're angry," Regg called out.

Zo waved a rude gesture at his brother and slammed the door behind him.

Ryn felt tears well up in her eyes.

In the quiet that followed Zo's departure, Ryn whispered, "I was told I am not invited to that party, because they don't want me mixing my Ordinary blood with their Ancestry." Wiping her eyes with her napkin, she stood and followed Zo.

"Ryn..." But she shut the door on the rest.

The coolness of the evening air washed over her, feeling good after the heat of the cabin. It was fairly late, but on this side of the summer solstice it was only twilight—still light enough to see, but the days were getting shorter. Zo had removed his vest and was swinging an ax to split wood. Ryn watched him for a while, uncertain if she should approach. She had only just met him, and she didn't wish to make him angrier.

Eventually, when he paused gathering the wood to put into the small woodshed, he noticed her.

"Not hungry?" he asked. "I made a great dessert."

She shook her head, but he probably couldn't see it in the gathering gloom.

"I've never met anyone with Ancestor magic who didn't think they were the end all be all to this world's existence," she said.

He barked a bitter laugh. "Come to gawk at the oddity, have you?"

Ryn flushed with embarrassment. "No—I'm just used to being the oddity."

Zo gave her a sidelong look while he stacked the wood.

"I mean, I used to have my best friend, Yll. She was the only person who understood me, but now she has magic too." Ryn had thought her dress was getting dry, but the chill that came with the darkness made her put her arms around herself. "Prym sent me a note this morning saying she didn't want me at that party—I might contaminate their bloodlines."

Zo huffed. "Typical."

Ryn sank onto the porch bench.

"All my life I have been put down. Shunned. They tolerated my presence in classes we shared with tutors, or when playing at the lake. I was just the fun Ordinary they could practice their water magic on—and almost drowned me, like today. Or travel magic themselves in front of me to scare me. Or because I've grown up with them, they know me well enough to use their mind magic on me, telling everyone what boys I like—in front of the boys I like. The worst was when someone shapeshifted into a giant rat, chasing me out of the changing booth at the lake, naked in front of our whole swimming class. One of the boys I ran past grabbed me and..." Ryn shuttered at the memory. Embarrassed and ashamed, she hadn't told anyone about it—ever. Why was she telling a boy she had known for less than a day?

Zo slammed the axe head into the chopping block.

"Who was he?" Flames leapt into Zo's hands. "I'll make him eat flames!"

Ryn gasped at his intensity. This was exactly why she hadn't told anyone. It would only make her life here worse. The magic kids always found creative ways to get back at her. Ways that could never be traced back to them.

Shrinking from him she said, "It doesn't matter, it was too long ago to matter anymore."

His fingers continued to burn with flames.

"Ancestor power took my family from me." Zo's voice was so low she could barely hear him.

"What?" Ryn asked.

Zo shook out his hands, picked up a stray piece of wood and threw it toward the shed.

"That's why you don't want to go to the party," Ryn said.

He shrugged in the gloom. "That and I really can't abide their attitudes. My father works hard for a living. I help him on most jobs. There is a stigma attached to people who use magic to do actual work. Most Ancestor magic use is nearly forbidden, unless used for a 'noble cause'—whatever that is. House Ignis only uses fire to train for warfare. Lighting fires, cooking, burning fields after the harvest—those are all things you do if you're low class. I'm sick of being looked down on because we work for a living."

Ryn nodded absently, her mind racing. Was this someone with Ancestor magic that she could actually be friends with?

"I think it's a good idea," Zo said.

Ryn startled out of her thoughts. "What?"

"You should go study at the Library."

"But I thought you hated Ancestry people."

"Who said anything about Ancestry? Becoming a researcher is more powerful than doing magic," he said.

"I don't know about that. Plus, you heard what mother said—she forbade me from doing it."

"Did she, though?"

Zo climbed the steps and sat next to her.

An evening breeze tousled the treetops, the sound mimicking waves on the ocean.

"If only there was a way that I could show Prym and her friends what idiots they are," Ryn sighed.

Zo sat up straight. "There is."

"What?"

"We're going to that party."

"Yes, you are, your father already insisted on it," she said.

"No. *We're* going—you and me."

"What? No. They'll just make fun of me and throw me out. Prym's father is on the Board of Regents for the Library. I'll get in trouble."

Light from the cabin window flashed in Zo's eyes. "So, let's make it worth the trouble."

Chapter Four

The coming-of-age ceremony at sixteen years old is antiquated and needs to stop. The promising of someone from one house to another at an age when youth should be exploring the world and their magic is hideous. Not to mention the whole idea of betrothals. You would think we would have advanced beyond marrying for the creation of the best combination of magical powers.

— Lyv de Dico. "Ancestral Culture and its Effect on Youth." *Journal of Mind Magic Medicine*. Ancestral Library Periodicals Section, Second Floor, Shelf 100, Box 2.

"Let's *go*. We're supposed to meet Jett in the village square," Regg said, flaring out his coat tails to descend from the loft.

"Go ahead, I'll be along," Zo replied as he fiddled with his cufflinks. Doing up the right one with his left hand was a pain, but not as much as he pretended it was. He could have had it done a while ago.

Regg eyed him. "You're not getting out of going by stalling."

Zo sighed. "I know, I know. Go—I'll be there shortly."

"Better be," Regg said, descending the ladder.

Zo was going. In fact, he couldn't wait to get there, but for his and Ryn's plan to work they needed to wait till Regg and Jett were already at the party. Nobody knew Ryn was going, so he had to sneak her out of the house. Ryette was expected any minute, then he could go over and help Ryn get ready. If he left now he would be forced to go straight to the party.

"Where's Zo?" he heard his father ask Regg downstairs.

"Says he's coming," Regg's voice came, a little loud so Zo could hear.

"I'll make sure he does," Lar said. "You look good son. Have a great time."

"I most certainly will," Regg said.

"Not as much fun as I'm going to have," Zo said under his breath.

He finished the cufflink and fussed with his hair in the mirror. Not that it mattered. He would never meet someone among the Ancestor types.

A knock came at the door.

"Right on time," Zo whispered, grabbing his jacket from a chair.

Zo peeked over the railing just as Ryette entered the cabin. Lar took her by the hands and gave her a quick kiss. Her eyes gave the cabin a once-over, then she leaned into a deeper kiss. Zo resisted the urge to make frustrated noises as he sat on his bed to pull his shoes on, all the while keeping an eye on their progress. Just as he was wondering if it would be possible to sneak out while they were involved, they broke apart. Ryette put her head on Lar's shoulder, and he wrapped his arms around her.

"Wes will be here tomorrow. I leave in the morning," she said.

"I know," was Lar's quiet response.

"I want you to come with me," she said.

"I will gladly go with you."

Yes, please do, Zo thought.

"Clayr says Wes has three people with earth magic accompanying him," Ryette said. "Someone needs to stay to protect the children."

Lar stepped back and held her shoulders. "My earth magic will erase all traces of you and the kids. I will do it twice a day. No one will find them."

That was interesting. Zo didn't know earth magic could do that. He'd seen his father use it as a wayfinder and for tracking, but not to block those things.

"Let's go for a walk," Lar said. "It will help you relax."

Zo peaked over the bed to see Ryette nod, and to Zo's great delight they slipped out the door.

"Perfect," Zo said, grabbing his bag full of tricks and heading for the ladder. Everything was going smoothly so far.

***

As he approached Ryn's cottage his feet slowed. He'd been here a few times in the evening, but something about the late afternoon sun on the stone path to the porch made it idyllic. An old swing hanging from the branch of a tree spoke to how long they'd lived there. He wished he had that. A place to call home. A mother who worried more about what he needed, than about what she needed. Shaking his head, he mounted the stairs to the porch. He could see Ryn pacing inside. He knocked on the window and waved. She startled, then scurried to the door to let him in.

"You're ready already," Zo said.

"You took so long!" she said.

"The parents were downstairs, I had to wait till they left," he said. "You got the stuff?"

She held up a small bag.

"Great, let's go."

She gave him a long look. "You're sure they won't know it was us?"

"We'll be out before things start to happen. No one will suspect."

"Alright." She didn't sound convinced, but they were committed to it now, so off they went—even if it meant their doom. Zo chuckled to himself.

"You got a pocket?" Zo asked, holding up his bag.

Ryn pulled open a slit in her skirt, taking his bag and adding it with hers in the pocket tied at her waist. She settled her skirts closed. They were puffy enough the added bulk was invisible.

"Perfect," Zo said.

The sun was still fairly high as they walked down the lane toward the village. Zo regretted the formal occasion that called for him to wear a waistcoat and a jacket. Neither were embroidered after the current fashion, but they were of the right cut and style. Ryn's dress actually had a small dip in the front collar, but that dip was high, and not low enough to show off her collar bone. She would stand out, but hopefully they could enact their plan and leave before anyone paid too much attention. The steely blue of her dress actually matched his gray suit better than if they had planned it.

Like the clothes they wore, the past few days together plotting had shown how well they worked together. They often had the same idea at the same time. He'd only known her for a short time, but somehow, he felt he'd known her all his life. It was a strange thing, something he'd never experienced before. If he didn't know better, he'd almost wonder if Ryn could really be his sister. If he knew one thing about his father though, it was that he was faithful, loyal, and dedicated to taking care of people. There's no way Ryn was his sister—though it was fun to contemplate.

"Remember, try not to mingle with too many people before we set the plan into motion. I need to be introduced to everyone after you take care of the punch," Zo said.

"That shouldn't be hard. Nobody wants to talk to me anyway," she said.

The dejection in her voice flared his anger. He knew it was true, he'd seen it before in Ancestor types, but he needed control tonight so no one would suspect them.

"They're not worth talking to anyway." Zo forced a chuckle, trying desperately to lighten the mood.

Passing through the village they turned a corner and were greeted by a trellised archway framing the path to Crystal Lake. So many roses and other flowers festooned the arch, Zo wondered where they all came from. A long line was queued up, and two men, one skinny, and one burly with muscles Zo envied, were inspecting invitations. Ryn stopped in her tracks.

"They're not going to let me in," she said.

Zo pulled out his and Regg's invitation. He had made sure he was the one in possession of it.

"Don't worry, we'll get in." Zo held out his arm for Ryn to take.

He led her to the back of the line to wait. Putting his hand over hers, he held on tight so she couldn't bolt.

Steering them in front of the less intimidating thin man, he could hear Ryn swallow as they approached.

"The Ordinary is not allowed," Thin Man said.

Zo handed him the invite. "She's my guest."

Thin Man read the invitation. "Says here this is for a Zo and Regg of Ignis. She's not of anything."

Ryn tried to pull her hand away, but Zo gripped her tighter to his arm, while fighting down the urge to set the man's coattails on fire. They had a plan, he had to wait.

"My brother's not feeling well, the lady graciously accepted my invitation to take his place." Zo tried to sound as smooth as he could.

Thin man grunted. "I'll have to clear it." Then he disappeared down the trail.

Zo tried to look relaxed, with Ryn was stiff as a board and looking like she was going to faint.

"Don't lock your knees," Zo whispered to her.

"What?" she said, brow furrowing.

The line behind them shifted to Mister Biceps checking invitations. After letting the couple ahead of them through, Mister Biceps turned to them.

"I'm sorry, invitation please?" Mister Biceps asked.

Zo handed him the invitation.

One glance and he waved them through. "Welcome," he said.

Zo felt tension run out of him. A nervous giggle escaped from Ryn. He looked back over his shoulder, hoping the thin man wouldn't return till they were out of sight. When no shout for them to stop came, Zo slowed their pace.

"Upward and onward," Zo said.

There was another flower-strewn arch at the end of the path. The sweet smell of roses was heavy in the late afternoon as they wandered into a whole different lakeside from the one he'd seen a few days before. Formal tables were set out like the grass was a banquet hall. Pears, the fruit of House Vivus, layered with ribbons and flowers served as centerpieces. Lanterns were strung everywhere for when it got dark. A long row of flowered arches led from the center of the tables around the side of a lake to the tree line ending at another pathway. It was perfect for a spectacular entrance.

"Why does this Prym girl hate you so much?" Zo asked as they skirted the edges of the party trying to find a safe place to land.

"I don't know," Ryn said. "Why does anyone hate someone else? We played together fine when we were little, but as they all, one by one, turned eight and received their magics I started to stick out. Eventually, I was just a fun target, because I had no magic to defend myself with. I also tended to do better in our studies, which didn't seem to help."

"So, she's jealous," Zo said.

"I don't know why she would be. She has everything I don't—a big fancy house, powerful parents, loads of money... magic..."

"Hello, what have we here?" Zo interrupted.

Across the party, in the shade of a large oak tree, stood a young man laughing with a group of girls. The young man's eyes locked with Zo's. Turning his attention back to the girls, he said something that made them turn and glare at Zo and Ryn, then he wound his way through the party tables toward them.

"Oh no, oh no, oh no." Ryn shook her hands, trying to hide behind Zo's arm.

"What?" Zo asked, admiring how the cut of the young man's suit spoke of a very fit form, and how the gold embroidery on his jacket glimmered in the setting sun. "Is that a good 'oh no,' or a bad 'oh no'?"

He never got the answer. Golden Sparkle Boy stopped in front of Ryn, giving her a slight bow.

"Lady Ryn." He straightened, turning to Zo. "And who do we have here?"

Ryn's voice squeaked, and Zo glanced down to see her blushing furiously.

"Sorry," she said, "Iden of Dico, this is Zo of Ignis. Zo, Iden."

"Fire, huh?" Iden took Zo's hand in a firm grip, eyes searching at Zo's collar. "And healing. Interesting combination."

"My parents were an interesting couple," Zo said, examining Iden's necklace. "A mind reader hmmm—can you read my mind?"

"The magic doesn't work that way, but I don't think I need it tonight." Iden winked. "Are you new in the village?" he asked.

"Just moved in a few days ago," Zo said.

Two girls whose low-cut collars went a bit too far for Zo's taste rushed up from across the party. One of them grabbed Iden's arm.

"Have you heard the news?" the pink one in frills clutching Iden asked.

"A world-renowned researcher is coming to the Library," the one in yellow bows blurted out.

Pink frills continued, "And his top student will be offered an Assistant Researcher position! They could skip the toiling Docent job and go straight to a position of respect." She tipped her chin up.

"Are you going to apply?" Yellow Bows turned her face up hopefully to Iden.

"I hear Master Wes has opened applications to anyone," Iden said, looking straight at Ryn.

"That's just a rumor," Pink Frills sniffed. "Ordinaries need not apply. There's only five spots and they should go to those more deserving."

Zo watched Ryn shrink. He fought to keep flames from leaping to his fingertips. *Soon,* he consoled himself.

"Not interested," Iden said. "My parents devote everything to that place, why would I want to spend all *my* time there?"

Zo's heart leapt. Maybe there was someone here who would understand him after all.

A group of girls called from one of the nearby tables, "Oh Iden—come sit with us."

The waving and smiling and giggling was somewhat nauseating. Zo wondered how Iden took it with good humor.

Iden put his hand on Zo's arm and squeezed it. "We'll have to get together sometime. There's a fun little tea spot next to the bakery. You can find me there most mornings with a pastry and a teacup."

Iden's smile felt like it was meant for Zo alone, causing his insides to flip. Maybe he did understand the clamoring display of affection.

"I'll stop by sometime." It was Zo's turn to have his voice crack like he was some sort of silly preteen.

Pink Frills and Yellow Bows grabbed Iden's hands and started pulling him toward the girls' table.

"If you'll excuse me." Iden gave Zo a regretful look then let the girls pull him away.

Zo watched Iden for a few moments longer. Ryn slapped him on the arm.

"What?" Zo asked.

"How is it that we both keep liking the same boys?" she said.

Zo chuckled, "Little sister, that one ain't never going to like you, or any other girl, despite the act."

"I can see that!" she snapped. "*Now.*"

"Very curious in a community entirely filled with Ancestor magic types. How does he manage?"

Ryn held up her hands. "I don't know, everybody loves him."

"The Ancestor descendants I've known would have run him out of town. They take continuing their bloodlines seriously."

"People like your parents?" Ryn asked.

He opened his mouth to deny her statement, but found he couldn't.

He held her eyes for several heartbeats, then let it go. "How did you know?"

Ryn looked up at him and blushed a bright red. "I don't know. I suspected, but seeing Iden with you now—I just knew."

No one besides Regg had figured him out before. Everyone had always assumed he liked girls, and the way his father tended to set him up with a parade of them only supported that view. Irritated, he glanced down at her to find her gaze had drifted back to Iden.

His eyes narrowed. "You've liked him for a long time, haven't you?"

"How did you...? Since I was a little girl, I would...never mind. Shall we scope out the punch bowl?" She took his arm and started dragging him in that direction.

He let a chuckle break the tension their conversation had stirred up inside him and gave way to her pulling.

At an unoccupied table close to the punchbowl Zo stopped, pulling out a chair for Ryn. Her face turned up to him sharply, total surprise in her eyes. Had no one really shown her kindness and respect before? He was half tempted to change the plan and just burn the whole place to the ground, but he knew that wouldn't be helpful in the long run. Still, it would be so satisfying.

"I'll get us some punch," he said.

"Hopefully no one else has spiked it before us," Ryn joked.

"Naw—too early in the night."

As he approached the table that held the punch bowl and glasses, he couldn't help but think how this group was way too trusting. They should have a server here to pour the punch.

Oh well, makes the plan that much easier, Zo thought. He ladled up two glasses of punch and returned to sit next to Ryn.

"Let's see what flavor they've got going and how much our 'additive' will stand out," Zo said.

They both sipped while they scanned the party.

"Well?" Ryn asked.

"Tastes like berries and probably some apple juice, mixed with maybe some pear. The laxative will add some saltiness, but I think it will only enhance the flavor."

"Why salty?" she asked.

"It's made with seawater and lime," he said, noticing Regg surrounded by a group of girls as he showed off flames dancing around his fingers.

"How long till it takes effect?" Ryn asked.

"Depends upon when and how much they drink," Zo sipped at his punch. "Don't worry, I'll make them all *real* thirsty."

Ryn shifted in her seat. He needed to act quickly before she lost her nerve. The caterer adding more punch to the bowl was his cue.

"Now's our chance. You go spike the punch while I get Regg to start introducing me. By the time Miss Prym makes her grand entrance, the guests should start dropping like flies."

Ryn nodded and stood, taking her cup with her as if to refill her drink. Zo grabbed his cup and sauntered off with it. He needed people to see them drinking the punch. Hopefully it would deflect suspicion from them. If not, Ryn had a little something in her pocket to help misdirect an investigation.

Taking a deep breath, he plastered a smile on his face and headed toward his brother.

Chapter Five

Praedo must have expected a new dragon to be sent sooner, because it seems unlikely he anticipated the distillation of the magic through the family lines. Whereas his original beads granted all the powers, for centuries the power has been one per family or "House."

— Ivy de Pentral. *Ancestor Magic and Its Dangers*. Ancestral Library, Second Floor, Cultural Room, Shelf 14, Shelfmark 68.

Ryn took a deep breath, gripping her shaking hands as she walked away from Zo and their table. She couldn't believe she was going to spike the punch and make everyone desperate for a toilet. She'd never done anything like this before, couldn't think about hurting anyone, even though everyone here had hurt her in some way. As they had grown older, and the others in the village began to receive their beads, they had grouped themselves by their magics. Kids who could animate objects became a part of Prym's group. Jett had spent a lot of time when he was younger with the kids who did spirit magic. It also meant that Ryn and Yll had fewer and fewer friends until it was just the two of them.

Thinking of Yll made Ryn feel guilty for being at the party. Yesterday, despite having said earlier she didn't mind if Yll attended, she had made Yll promise not to. She hoped to keep her from their little prank...and from falling deeper in with Prym. Hopefully Ryn wouldn't be here for long, and Yll would never find out she had attended the party without her.

Ryn's job was simple: spike the punch, then hang back in the shadows while Zo gathered all the attention. Her biggest worry right now was someone would see her pour the laxative into the punch bowl.

She stood next to the table with the punch watching Zo approach his brother. Regg was all smiles introducing Zo to the group of girls clamoring around him. For Zo's plan to work, all Zo needed to do was shake their hands long enough to heat them up and make them all thirsty and running for the punch bowl. Ryn's heart sped up as she realized there were already a few girls looking sweaty.

Ryn slipped her hand into her pocket, while stirring the punch with the ladle. She held the bottle tight to conceal it within her hand as she extracted it from her pocket. The bottle slid so easily from its pouch. The cup in her hand was a good distraction as she pretended to refill it while discretely dumping the bottle's contents into the punchbowl. At first, the liquid didn't want to blend with the punch. Ryn's armpits became wet with sweat as she stirred the punch with the ladle, willing the two liquids to combine. She was so focused on mixing the punch she didn't hear anyone approach until a familiar voice came from right behind her.

"Ryn! What are you doing here?" Yll said.

Fumbling the ladle, Ryn fought to keep it from falling into the punch bowl. A shaking hand slipped the bottle into her pocket as she turned to face the one person she hoped not to see at the party.

Ryn's eyes narrowed. "What are *you* doing here?"

"I was invited," Yll mumbled, like she didn't really want to say the words.

"You promised me you wouldn't come," Ryn said.

Yll's lips pursed. She glanced away, then lifted her chin. "And you're not even invited to this party. You need to leave before Prym finds out and does something..."

Ryn planted her feet and folded her arms in her best attempt to convey how likely it was that she would leave now.

Yll took a deep breath, letting her eyes flutter shut briefly, before she cleared her throat. "Did you hear about Master Wes coming to teach at the Library?"

Ryn made a sharp gesture encompassing all of the party. "Of course."

Yll's face lit up like when they were kids and just received a new toy.

"Can you believe it? This is my chance to get into the Library without it looking like my mother got me the job! I never thought I'd have the opportunity. You know how long I've wanted to work in the Library, but I don't want everyone to resent me, or assume I'm there because of my mother. This is my chance to prove myself."

"How nice for you." Ryn tried to sound sincere, but it came out sarcastic.

Yll stepped closer to Ryn, taking her by elbow. "This is your chance too. You could finally gain access to the Library and do the research to find your birth family, and our moms wouldn't have to know anything about it. It could all be a part of your studies as a student."

It did sound appealing.

"Mother told me she has scoured the Library with your mom and found nothing. If your mom can't find it, how can I?"

Tammy, a village girl with illusion magic, came rushing up to the punch bowl. "Yll, I thought you shed this Ordinary. Come meet the two new guys. They are so hot. Literally—they do fire magic!" Tammy poured herself some punch. "So hot, I need a drink!" She gulped it down.

Yll's face lit up. "I know, the sandy-haired one is adorable! Shaking hands with the dark-haired one made me flush all over." Yll filled a cup and drank it down.

Weird, Ryn hadn't seen Yll with Zo and Regg, but then there was a whole gaggle of girls around them. The new boys seemed to be the life of the party.

"How is one of them light haired and one of them dark?" Tammy asked, eyes on the boys.

Yll giggled, "I asked if they had different fathers, but the light one showed off beads matching his brother and said 'No, different moods.'"

Ryn pointedly joined in by sipping her own, untainted punch.

Mary, another village girl, broke off from the group around Zo and Regg and made a beeline for the punch, fanning herself with a fluffy feathered fan. After gulping down her drink, she eyed Ryn.

"What is she doing here?" Mary pointed at Ryn. "Prym sent you a note to make sure you didn't come here. Get lost." Turning to Yll she said, "Get rid of the riff-raff or leave with her." Then she sniffed, staring at Yll and Ryn while sipping her punch.

That's right, Ryn's eyes narrowed, *just keep drinking*.

Yll turned to face Ryn.

Ryn refolded her arms, standing her ground, but her stomach had turned to ice.

"Hurry up Yll, we don't have all night, Prym's introduction and dance are about to start," Tammy said, sipping more punch.

Yll drew herself up and met Ryn's eyes.

"Leave." Their gazes locked for several heartbeats. "Find your Ancestors and you can join us."

Mary snorted. "As if we would take her," she murmured into her cup.

Yll held Ryn's eyes for a minute more then looked away.

Tammy snapped her fingers and an image of a huge bear appeared next to Ryn. Startled, Ryn stumbled backward, tripping over a tree root before falling on her rump.

The girls burst into laughter, then they linked arms with Yll, turning to rejoin the party.

Yll never looked back. Ryn sat with her tailbone throbbing and watched the one person who'd been her friend since she could barely walk, move further and further away from her. Her vision blurred. She hooded her eyes with one hand as she fought the hot tears threatening to escape down her cheeks. One deep breath followed another so no one would hear. This wasn't the time or place, so she fought for control. There was still one last bit she needed to do. With one hand beneath her, she struggled her way back to her feet, and from her pocket she pulled out the now empty bottle and the bag she had brought. It was a purse one of the Library managers had left at Ryn's house while visiting her mother. The plan was for Ryn to put the empty laxative bottle in it and leave it somewhere to be found. The hope was if someone was clever enough to figure out the punch had been spiked, the evidence would implicate the Library manager.

Ryn turned, bringing a napkin up to wipe her eyes so she could see better, then froze. Yll had left her purse on the table next to the punchbowl. Ryn would recognize it anywhere, as it had been a present from Yll's mother for her fourteenth birthday. It was beaded and sparkled in the glowing torchlight. Ryn's eyes immediately sought Yll in the crowd. She found her with Regg who was bowing to her with a flourish and kissing her hand. One of the girls whispered something in Yll's ear, making her laugh. Ryn poured all her will into making Yll look back at her, but she did not.

Anger bubbled up from deep inside Ryn. She shoved the Library manager's purse back into her pocket, opened Yll's purse, and deposited the bottle before pulling the drawstrings shut.

Another couple of girls left Zo and were racing for the punchbowl. Ryn hurried from the table before she could stop and think about what she had done. She skirted the edges of the party till she found an out-of-the-way spot close to the tree line. Here she would wait for Zo to finish, and the show to begin.

It didn't take too long. The sun was almost set, and it was growing dark. A horn blew and everyone at the party found their seats as Prym's father stepped up to the end of the arch tunnel.

"Children of the Ancestors, welcome and thank you for coming. It's hard to believe my little Prym is all grown up and ready to be presented to the world. I remember when she was just a streak of blond hair racing around my feet. She's always been so sweet—full of life and energy."

Oh gag, Ryn thought.

"I am proud to introduce my precious girl who is about to become a student of Master Wes, and the youngest

Assistant Researcher ever. I present to the world: Prym de Vivus."

A long low mournful sound came from a giant sea snail shell blown by a young man on the shores of the lake. It was an ancient type of horn, traditionally blown to announce and to gather. When the last of the sound bounced off the mountain wall on the far side of the lake, figures in midnight blue Ancestral robes, trimmed in gold, appeared at the end of the archway tunnel. They held torches aloft as they stood in two lines, the women of House Vivus on one side and the men of House Venti, her father's House, on the other. The procession proceeded through the arches. When all were under the arches, the line stopped. Two trumpets took up a jovial fanfare and Prym appeared with her brothers, one on each side of her, holding torches. The procession continued, and as Prym's extended family members exited the archway tunnel they split to surround the crowd in a large circle of glowing torches.

Ryn faded further into the bushes, hoping she wouldn't be caught in the torchlight.

Prym proceeded through the archway with her brothers, head held high. Her dress was the deep yellow of House Vivus, and her long, blond locks fell in cascading curls. She appeared as if a vision of the Ancestor Vivus herself.

When Prym and her brothers reached the end of the archway, the procession stopped.

One of the trumpeters tucked his instrument beneath his arm and stepped forward.

"We call upon all the Ancestral Houses. Those who control the elements: House Terr, House Mare, House Venti, House Ignis, and House Lux. Those who move us: House Viator, and House Pentral."

Ryn scoffed. If House Viator and House Pentral were ever together in one place war would break out. Those Houses hated each other.

"Those who inspire: House Dico, House Muto, House Vivus," The trumpet man gave a nod to Prym, "and House

Illusio. Lastly, the one that heals us, House Sano. Bring forth your best sons for the jewel of House Vivus."

The trumpeter bowed to Prym and her brothers who passed through the last arch. The crowd stood and applauded. Prym's brothers each took one of her hands and led her to the middle of the dance floor. Prym's father stepped up, bowing low to his daughter. The musicians began to play a full orchestra version of a traditional lullaby. Prym's father took her in his arms and danced with her, so loving and gentle, they swayed side to side. Both laughed as he spun her out and around, then took her back into his arms.

She watched him wipe a tear from his eye.

Ryn was just a few months away from being old enough for a "Debut Party," but with her father gone, she had no one to present her to the world, as well as no extended family to carry a torch for her, and well, no friends to invite to such a party. Her eyes drifted over to Yll surrounded by girls bending their heads together to chat and laugh. She turned away.

The music came to a soft close and Prym and her father bowed to the thunderous applause.

"And now," Prym's father pointed to a silver bucket of roses. "I present to you, my daughter. All eligible males are to come forward for a dance with my special rose."

Iden stepped forward, took a rose from the bucket, went to Prym in the middle of the dance floor, and presented the flower with a flourish only he was best at. The musicians began an old-fashioned dance song, and Iden and Prym danced. Ryn had to admit, Iden was very good at charming everyone. There were looks of envy on all the girls faces in the audience—and Ryn had to admit that included hers—as they watched Iden twirl Prym around the dance floor.

After a while another boy selected a rose, tapped Iden on the shoulder, and took his place. The bouquet of roses grew in her arms, as the boys took turns dancing with her. Ryn watched as her brother Jett stepped up to take his turn. She hadn't seen him the whole night and wondered where he had been hiding. The self-satisfied grin on his face was something she couldn't recall seeing on him before, and curiosity about where he'd been grew. Regg took a rose and tapped Jett out. Prym lit up and eagerly slipped her hand into his. As he danced her around the floor though, his eyes kept finding Yll in the audience.

At last, it was Zo's turn. By now Ryn could see people starting to rub their stomachs, or hold themselves in weird postures, like they were trying to hold something in. Ryn saw Tammy and Mary almost doubled over in the torchlight.

"Hurry up," Ryn whispered. "Enough already, we need to go." Zo couldn't hear her of course, but it helped her nervousness to say it out loud.

A branch snapped in the bushes behind her. She turned to peer into the gloom, but the bright light of the party made the woods impenetrable. When she turned back around, she gasped to find Jared, Prym's house help, who had taken their invitation and gone off to confirm if she should be at the party, standing right in front of her.

His hand clamped around her arm. "I've been told to show you what we do on Shimamare to party crashers."

A gasp came from the woods behind her.

Ryn tried to turn and look, but Jared gripped her arm tighter. "It involves an unpleasant amount of water."

"There you are!" Zo came up from behind Jared, twisting Ryn's arm from his grip. He held Jared's hand away from Ryn until Jared started to sweat. "We were just leaving."

Zo's voice left no room for question. He put Ryn's hand on his arm and made a beeline for the closest trail into the woods. Ryn watched Jared turn, sweating profusely, hurrying away toward the punchbowl. Relief flooded through her, she wasn't sure where this trail led, as long as it was away from the party.

A huge eruption of fire made her jump. Through the trees she caught a glimpse of two fire breathers spitting out fire as servants bearing large trays of fish, seafood and chicken entered the party through the archway.

"Ooo—fire breathers! I've never seen fire breathers in person before." Ryn slowed, fascinated.

Zo scoffed. "Why would you be impressed by people spitting firewater into flames when I can literally make my own fire?" Flames leapt to his palms, throwing out light to lead the way down the trail.

"Because it's awesome. I heard if they swallow that stuff they could die," Ryn said, trying to look back at the party, but Zo pulled her forward faster.

"Lame imitation of the real thing. Let's get out of here before the real show begins. People are already going down. I don't want to be anywhere near here when Prym starts pointing fingers."

Chapter Six

My magic will guide and protect your needs.
As long as it's used for the good of the land,
Ye shall hold great power within your hand.
Pass this gift down through each family line,
To guard this place throughout all of time.
So they crafted beads from his magical bones,
And wore them round necks like tiny white stones.

— Excerpt from Luc's Poem as recorded in *On the Legend of Luc,*
Praedo's Scribe. Ancestral Library, Third Floor Restricted Section.

Zo was completely lost and turned around in the woods, unable to see beyond the fire light in his palm,
"Do you know where we are?" he asked Ryn.
"Not really, this isn't a trail I take very often."
"Fantastic," he grumbled.
Ryn glanced back over her shoulder toward the party. "You're the one who chose this path."
"You could have told me no."
Zo was just as anxious as Ryn was to get her home. He was getting thirstier by the minute. His glass of untainted punch hadn't lasted long, and keeping a flame in his palm wasn't helping things. The worst part of the evening was sustaining the heat from his fire magic to dry out everyone he shook hands with. That constant heat had unsettled his stomach, and the punch hadn't been nearly enough to cool him off. Fortunately, tonight his goal of making everyone thirsty was motivation enough to keep going through the thirsty work.
Ryn paused. "Did you hear that?"
"Hear what?"
"Something's out there," her voice wavered a bit.
"Naw," he lied.

Something or someone had definitely been following them since they left the party, but he didn't want to panic Ryn while they were lost somewhere in the woods. The flash of white reminded him of their trip through the woods a few days ago. There was still the unexplained water magic from the first day by the lake. There had to have been someone close by that day.

Zo picked up their pace. He wasn't entirely sure he wanted to get in another fire fight in the middle of the woods. Downside—burn down the woods. Upside—it would definitely break up the party fast.

Their trail crossed a wider path and Ryn pulled him down it.

"I think I know where I am now," she said.

"How can you even tell which direction we're going in the dark?"

"I don't know. Just a feeling."

Zo was skeptical, but he let her take the lead, which he almost instantly regretted because she was so slow, he almost tripped over her. He felt like he was slogging through water just putting one foot in front of the other.

"Slow down, long legs," Ryn hissed when he accidentally kicked her heel.

"Walk faster."

"I'm going as fast as I can in this fancy dress and shoes," she growled.

Conversation between them stopped as they listened to the dark around them. In the quiet, Zo's mind drifted back to all the conversations he'd had meeting everyone in the village. Especially Iden. He definitely needed to get to the tea spot as soon as he could, and not just because pastries sounded delightful.

"You need to apply to study with Master Wes," he said. "Your mother is going to be out of town, she won't even know you've applied until you've already been accepted."

Ryn grunted. "You have an awful lot of confidence I'll be accepted. And mother will kill me when she gets back. Not to mention Yll and Prym are already planning to apply. Can you believe the arrogance of Prym's father telling everyone she would be the one chosen to get a Library position? She hasn't even applied yet! I suppose with him being on the Library Board of Regents he probably has some sway over Master Wes, but still—the nerve."

"That sounds like excuses. Do it Ryn. You know you want to. Your mom and whoever it was she mentioned can't possibly have looked through *all* the records in that Library. Have you seen how big that place is?"

She turned her face up at him, making the light from the flames in his palm play across her furrowed brow.

"Tonight was fun, but the best revenge you could have is to beat them at their own game," he grinned.

If she had a response to that she didn't say, because the trail opened into a clearing. He flared his flames to reveal Ryn's cottage, windows dark and still.

"Oh thank goodness she's not back yet," Ryn said, rushing across the yard and up the steps.

Before he could catch up, she was in the house. He found her fumbling around in the dark with a lantern.

"Here, let me." He lit the lantern for her.

"Thanks." She took the lantern with her to her room, leaving him to light another one, then dive for a pitcher of water. He had drunk half the pitcher before she returned, dressed in what looked like a comfy tunic and skirt.

"What do we do now?" Ryn glanced at the door like she was expecting a mob to come pound on it at any moment.

"Relax, find something to eat, and maybe play a game. We just need to look like we've been here most of the night." Zo sat in a chair drinking another glass of water. "You've got games, don't you?"

"Sure." Ryn paced.

Zo needed to distract her. If Ryette or anyone else found them looking nervous, there would be a lot of questions.

"What do you have to eat? Let's cook something." Zo stood and started looking through crocks and the cupboard.

Ryn's stomach growled. "I guess we didn't eat anything at the party. Here, Jett harvested some green beans yesterday."

"Perfect."

Zo removed his coat and waistcoat, rolled up his sleeves, and set about helping her make a fire to fry up the green beans with butter and onions. She found some potatoes to add to it.

They were at the table, stomachs full, playing a card game when a disheveled-looking Regg came bursting through the door.

"You!" He pointed at Zo.

"Meee?" Zo put his hand to his chest.

"You did this." Regg slammed the door behind him.

"Did what?" Zo leaned back, sipping his glass of water.

Regg crossed the room to stand in front of him, hands at his side opening and closing like he wanted to strangle Zo.

"I just spent the entire evening healing half the party's guests from stomach cramps and urgent cases of the runs. People who couldn't wait were just going in the woods. Then I was healing scratched bums from squatting over brambles. It was a nightmare. Nobody stayed to eat the food, everyone ran for home, most of them with soiled clothing. The smell was incredible." Regg's face had turned puffy and red.

Zo's eyes teared up as he fought to keep from bursting into laughter. Ryn choked on a giggle.

Zo carefully composed his face.

"I assure you I have no idea what you're talking about," Zo said, voice rising at the end as he fought to keep control.

"Like the blazing Ancestors you don't! You just can't leave well enough alone, can you?"

Zo turned his palms up. "What would I have done, and how would I have done it?"

"You did something to make everyone sick." Regg's focus shifted to Ryn. "I saw you standing at the punchbowl for an awfully long time."

Zo leaned forward to shift Regg's attention back to him. "You saw me drinking the punch, I haven't had any problems."

Ryn's face was red. "I was standing there so long because the girls had to remind me how unwelcome I am."

Zo had been so absorbed in his part of the plan, and drawing attention away from Ryn, that he had completely missed what happened. A stab of guilt went through him for exposing her to that situation.

Regg held Zo's gaze.

"I don't know how you did it, but I know you did. And now Prym is blaming me and Yll. She was one of the first to feel sick. We were dancing so I healed her, but since neither of us got sick everyone thinks we did it, even though I spent the rest of the night healing people and cleaning up the mess. Why would I do that to myself? It was a struggle too, because I knew you had to be the culprit, calming myself to heal everyone was difficult."

Zo watched Ryn's gaze shift from him to Regg, her face paled.

"Where's your proof that Zo did it?" Ryn shot Zo a worried glance.

"There are elixirs that help you poop," Regg said. "Dad keeps some for his stomach troubles."

"Wait." Ryn held up a hand. "Why would your dad need medicine for stomach problems? Doesn't he have you two to do that for him?"

Regg scoffed and pointed at Zo. "He has an anger problem and can't access his healing magic, and I hadn't worked intestinal issues...until now, when I spent a whole night mastering it."

"Practice!" Zo lifted his glass to him, grinning behind the cup.

Regg's hands balled into fists, and Zo prepared to block a blow from his brother.

"I was just getting to know everyone, and now I'm an outcast," Regg said through gritted teeth.

Zo shrugged. "Oh well."

Regg swung at Zo, who ducked it. Regg spun on his heels and stomped out, slamming the door behind him.

Ryn winced.

"He sure does enjoy slamming things," Zo said.

"Zo, if Regg figured it out..."

Jett burst through the door, gave them a dirty look, crossed to his room, and slammed the door.

"Aaand another one who enjoys slamming things," Zo said.

Lar and Ryette were close on Jett's heels.

"Oh boy." Zo rolled his eyes.

"What have you two been up to?" Ryette asked.

"Nothing," Zo said. "I went to the party. Met all the snooty Ancestor types. Danced with the spoiled brat host, then came here. Ryn and I cooked some food and we've been playing cards ever since."

Ryette and Lar crossed their arms at the same time. Zo fought to keep from laughing at how comically in sync they were.

"Is that true?" Ryette turned to Ryn.

Zo turned to Ryn, pouring all the pleading he could into his eyes. If Ryn caved and told the truth they were both dead.

He could see Ryn swallow hard before she answered. "Zo came, we cooked some food, and played some games."

Zo gave her what he hoped was a reassuring smile. It wasn't a blatant lie, it just left out the rest of the evening.

"I hope that is the truth, because Prym's family is looking for someone to blame for the disaster of her Debut party. If it turned out someone was at fault, they could have the responsible parties run out of the village." Ryette gave them a long hard look. "Nobody crosses a Library Regent."

The room grew very quiet and still. Ryn shifted in her seat while Zo cracked his knuckles on the table.

"Let's go." Lar waved at Zo. "We both have an early call in the morning,"

Zo paused. "Wait, why do I have to get up early?"

"Because you're coming with us to Waatch. I'm dropping Ryette at the docks and you at the Library. You've been apprenticed to the boiler master at the Library. I was going to let you settle in here a bit longer, and hopefully make some connections, but you clearly aren't interested in the village so you're leaving in the morning."

Zo stared at his father. He couldn't believe what he was hearing. "What?" he finally managed to croak out.

"You heard me. The events of tonight have made it clear that being settled in the village is not going to keep you busy enough. The boiler master will work you harder than I can."

"But I thought..."

"We'll discuss this at home," Lar cut him off.

Zo's eyes found Ryn seated across the table from him. She had gone still; her mouth was hanging slightly open.

"Let's go," Lar repeated.

"But—I met someone tonight and I have an appointment to see them in the morning for tea." Zo's mind was desperately searching for something to keep him here. Although he was proud of his father's work with magic, and he enjoyed the random seasonal work they did together, working everyday sounded horrible.

"The ship doesn't leave till after noon," Ryette interjected. "We could leave a little later in the morning," she offered, clearly trying to get on Zo's good side. Wasn't going to work for Zo though.

Lar grunted. "Fine. Meet with your new friend and we'll leave as soon as you get back, but we need to be in Waatch before noon," Lar said. "Now let's go, they need some together time tonight before Ryette leaves."

Zo bowed his head, tossed his cards on the table, then pushed himself out of the chair. Ryn surprised him by sliding back her chair and hurrying around the table. Awkwardly, she stopped in front of him, almost like she wasn't sure how he would react, then she threw her arms around him in a hug. He hugged her back, his eyes on the satisfied smiles on their parents' faces. He knew the parents wanted them to get along, especially if they were getting serious and had designs on making them all a family. For once, he didn't fight it. After only a few days, Ryn felt like the sister he didn't know he wanted. Calling her "sister" earlier this evening had rolled off his tongue in a way that rang true. Despite his usual optimism, he couldn't bring himself to tell her any platitudes, couldn't say it would be alright, so he let her go, and followed his father out the door. At least he had wrangled the morning out of his father, and a chance to meet with Iden. Hopefully Iden would be there tomorrow. If not, it would be a dismal day.

**

When the sunlight lightened the cabin the next morning, Zo crept silently around the loft getting dressed. The floorboards occasionally creaked, but Regg didn't stir. All that healing last night must have taken a lot out of him. He didn't snore, didn't roll over, he was just out. It might be too early, but Zo didn't want to miss Iden. He'd sit there sipping herbs all morning if that's what it took to see him.

Zo debated what to wear. He only had one formal coat, and he'd worn that last night. His everyday coat was plain, but it made him look more broad-shouldered and not so bean pole-ish. He chose one of Regg's shirts that exposed his neckline more than Zo usually liked to show off. Not that he was interested in flaunting his magic, just that showing more skin felt daring and bold.

Once dressed, he slipped as silently out the door as he could. The last thing he needed was his father following him out of curiosity to see who he was meeting with. Wandering down the sun-filled lane to the village, sure enough, Zo found the tea place right next to the bakery. More surprising was Iden sitting on the patio outside with a teacup reading the Waatch newspaper.

Zo approached his table and cleared his throat, "Is this seat taken?" he asked, trying to sound casual and not nervous.

Iden looked up from the paper and smiled. "It is now."

Zo thought for a minute about taking the chair and moving it to sit at another table as a joke, but time was precious, so he pulled out the chair and sat. Iden waved to a hostess who nodded and disappeared into the tea shop.

"I'm glad you accepted my invitation—and so quickly," Iden said, eyes twinkling as if he was drinking Zo in like a long-lost friend. "I was on the verge of moving to town to get away from this lot when you showed up."

"And I was prepared to absolutely hate it here, when I saw you across the party." Zo failed to keep the heat from rising to his face.

"A ray of hope and sunshine in this dismal place where we don't belong." Iden sat back as the hostess placed a teapot and cup in front of Zo.

"Anything else?" she asked.

"Do try a pastry, they are the best kept secret in Sooke." Iden winked.

"What kind would you like?" the hostess asked.

"Surprise me," Zo said.

"Daring, I like it." Iden poured more tea into his cup from his own teapot.

Zo grinned. "I just don't know what to order."

Iden sipped at his tea, the smell of mint drifted in the air to Zo.

"We should do this every morning." Iden grinned around his cup.

Zo accidentally inhaled the hot tea and started sputtering. Iden pounded him on the back.

"Something I said?" Iden asked.

"Actually, this is a hello and a goodbye. I've been apprenticed to the Library boiler, I'm leaving today." Zo coughed again trying to clear his lungs, or his painfully beating heart.

Iden grimaced. "That sounds like too much work." He sipped his tea again. "Tell me about yourself, what's Ignisapan like?"

"Don't know, never lived there," Zo said.

This time Iden choked on his tea. "What? But that's your father's House."

"My mother sits on the Board of Healers. She can't be drawn away from that, not even for her family." Zo feared his attempt to keep the bitterness from his voice failed.

"I see." Iden inspected the newspaper. "Were you and your friend the ones who spiked the punch last night?" He gave Zo a mischievous grin.

Zo hesitated. As much as he liked Iden, he could just be playing Zo for a confession. He also didn't want Iden to think he didn't trust him. He settled for giving Iden a shrug and a smile.

"You're lucky I didn't drink the punch last night or I might not find you so attractive right now."

This time Zo did flush furiously. He looked away across the village square. "Too bad I'll be living in Waatch starting today."

Iden pointed out a newspaper article about Master Wes' visit. "Perhaps I should apply to be a pupil of Master Wes. My parents will be thrilled," he laughed.

Zo's eyes snapped back to Iden. "Really? I thought you didn't want to have anything to do with the place."

"I like interesting places with interesting people, and the Library just became very interesting."

Zo laughed, relaxing back into his chair with his cup. The rest of the morning passed quickly, with Iden talking about what it was like growing up in Sooke with parents who spent more time in the Library than with him, and Zo talking about traveling around with his dad and his brother, working with fire magic and making a living at it. Iden was fascinated by all the places Zo had been, and the stories of the fires they had set. Especially the ones to back burn forest fires. Zo had some harrowing tales from fighting forest fires.

Zo scarcely noticed the time. The two of them were bent over the newspaper looking at the requirements to apply to study with Master Wes, when a chill passed over him as a shadow fell upon him.

"So, *this* is who you had to meet?" Lar shouted.

Startled, Zo jumped in his seat. Iden quickly withdrew the arm he had draped across Zo's chair. Lar searched the nearby tables as if to note who had seen them together.

"We're going." Lar's voice was low and menacing. "*Now.*"

Zo fought against his utter embarrassment. His face grew hot and all he wanted to do was tell his father to shove off.

He was still considering how to do that without making a scene in front of Iden, when Iden stood and shook Lar's hand. "Pleased to meet you. I'm Iden de Dico, promised to Prym de Vivus."

Zo's head whipped around to see Iden pull out a promise necklace from within his shirt. Zo had completely missed it, even when examining Iden's beads the night before.

Lar shifted his stance. One turned up corner of his mouth spoke to how he wished to be relieved Iden was committed, but didn't quite believe it.

"Congratulations," Lar said. "I'm afraid I still need to take Zo away as we're escorting Lady Ryette to her ship, and we need to go so she's not late."

Iden gave him a slight bow. "Not a problem." Turning to Zo he said, "I'll catch up with you later."

"Good luck with your girl," Lar said, as he hustled Zo away.

They walked across the square in silence. Zo's brain was reeling. It was the only way he was allowing his father to lead him away. How was Iden promised to Prym of all people? Why would he give in to his parents and this cursed village like that? And why wouldn't he have said something about it? Being promised to someone is huge—and Iden hadn't said a thing.

Once they passed the buildings on the other side of the village, Lar let loose.

"That better not have been what it looked like!" Lar's voice bounced off the sides of the shops.

"What did it look like?" Zo tried to sound innocent.

This was a game he and his father seemed to be playing a lot lately. Lar would heavily imply Zo had a preference the Ancestors wouldn't approve of, but would never come out and say it.

It was a game they apparently were still playing, because Lar's only reply was a choking noise of frustration. His father's hand grabbed his arm, stopping Zo in his tracks.

"There are lots of pretty Ancestor girls in Waatch. *Find one*," Lar said, releasing him.

Zo held back...something. He wasn't sure if he wanted to laugh or scream. Surrounding the Library there were lots of Ancestor descendants, as was evidenced by the population of Sooke, but the town of Waatch was populated mostly by Ordinaries from the mainland peninsula—and mainlanders could care less about perpetuating bloodlines. If his father wanted him to find a girl, Waatch didn't seem like the right place to trap him into a relationship with an Ancestor girl.

Chapter Seven

To aid his needs his friends gathered round.
Alas it was late, as his dying breath whispered,
They drew near to him to help and they heard.
Take ye my bones and turn them to beads...

— Excerpt from Luc's Poem as recorded in *On the Legend of Luc,*
Praedo's Scribe. Ancestral Library, Third Floor Restricted Section.

In the wee hours of the morning, Ryn's deep sleep shifted into something else. She was back in that fancy library. She found herself in a comfortable cushioned chair gazing out a window at the pre-dawn light turning the ocean purple, and the sky, shades of pink. Waves crashed on the cliffs below, sending sea spray up to rain down in loud plops on the rocks beneath the window. In the chair next to her sat her father, quietly watching the dawn break while sipping something that smelled of rose hips and lavender.

"It's beautiful, isn't it?" Her father asked.

"Uh huh," she agreed.

"I always loved this view."

It was the loveliest view from any window she had ever seen, but her eyes couldn't help wandering to the table behind her, searching for the book he'd shown her before.

"Where's the book?" she asked.

Her father set down his cup. "The Library," he said.

"We're in the library." Ryn's brow furrowed.

"Not this library, the great Ancestral Library."

"But you showed it to me in this library," Ryn insisted.

"Sorry, a bit of a cheat, dreams are fun for that."

"It can't be in the Library. Mother told me her and Clayr searched the Library and never found any records of me."

"Are those the words she used exactly?" her father held her gaze.

Ryn thought back. Was that what she had said? "Well, no. I suppose she said something about not finding any record of my ancestry."

"Yes, your ancestry is a whole different matter. Go to the Library, you will find what you need there," he said.

"Mother doesn't want me in the Library."

"Your mother wants a lot of things that ignore what we need." He took Ryn's hand. "Find a way. Get into the Library. You need to be there. I need you to..."

Abby jumped up on the bed, walked across Ryn's head, and sat on the pillow right in front of her face. Ryn rolled to her back, rubbing her nose full of cat fur. The place by the sea and her father faded until it was scattered to wherever dreams went during waking hours. She remembered her father's intense eyes. Maybe it was a memory and not the dream, but she was left with the overwhelming impression she needed to disobey her mother's wishes and find a way into the Library. That seemed unusual. Her parents had always been united in their parenting when she was little. Well, mostly—her father had a soft spot for Ryn and always downplayed her occasional mischief. Especially when he saw how scared she was when she was in trouble.

Now he was gone.

She rolled back over to another face full of fur. With a grunt, she pushed Abby away. The cat gave her a look of utter disapproval, then jumped down and sauntered out their door. Ryn thought about what her father had told her. Had her mother been lying about what was in the Library or did she just not know? And why was Ryn taking the word of a dream over her mother's? For some reason deep in her heart she felt what her father said was true, even if it was just a dream. If it was true, then she really did need to apply to study with Master Wes. She didn't understand at all what her mother and Clayr had been talking about the other day when Clayr came to visit. What could Master Wes be searching for at the Library that made her mother feel she needed to leave on a trip? He was just a researcher, and Ryn's family were just villagers, most of them Ordinary or half Ordinary. There was no good reason why Ryn shouldn't study in the Library. Even if her mother was right and there were no records to be found, at least Ryn would learn how to do research so she could travel to Ancestral House libraries and search them. She needed to learn. Her mother and Clayr weren't going to let her into the Library, but like Yll said last night, this was their chance to get in without their mothers' help.

The thought of Yll burned in Ryn's chest. She couldn't believe Yll had told her to come back when she found her Ancestors. That stung, more than anything that happened. She couldn't believe Yll would say something like that to her, not after all they'd been through together. Guilt about planting the bottle in Yll's purse crept in. Ryn shouldn't have done that to her oldest friend, but her anger had gotten the best of her. Probably no one would find the bottle anyway.

The smell of smoke tickled Ryn's nose. Her brother must have stoked the fire to make breakfast. She crept from bed and got dressed. She needed to see her mother off. More importantly, she needed to see Zo. Another pang of sadness hit her heart. For some reason the two of them just clicked. She couldn't recall meeting anyone else like that. Maybe Yll, but they had been so small when they met, how could they not grow to be close? Zo was something different. They led different lives, and he could do magic, but somehow, she trusted him. They became fast friends. Now he was leaving, and it was probably her fault for letting him talk her into going to that party and spiking the punch. Her gut twisted at the thought.

That left her with Jett, and he communicated more with animals than he did with people. It would be a lonely time while her mother was gone if she didn't get a position as one of Master Wes' students. Her mind was made up—one way or another she was going to get one of those spots.

***

Her mother's bag was packed and waiting by the doorway. Ryn had watched her mother the night before fill the bag with clothes and the equipment she would need to authenticate the documents she would collect. Wherever her mother was going it was a legitimate business trip for her. Ryn knew her mother wouldn't carry around all her official stamps and inks to certify documents for nothing. They were expensive and heavy.

Bag at her feet, her mother's eyes welled up with tears. "I wish I didn't have to go."

"We'll be fine Mom," Jett said.

Her mother solemnly took one of Ryn's hands and one of Jett's in her own. "I have a very big request and I need you to promise me you'll do it."

Ryn pursed her lips. She was afraid to ask what request her mother had, but they might as well be out with it.

"What?"

Jett nudged her like she shouldn't have asked.

Her mother frowned. "I need you two to stay close to the cottage. You can go to the market with Lar, but do not go down to the lake or wandering the woods." Her mother gave Ryn a pointed look. "I know you enjoy your log fort and the river..."

"Mother, I outgrew the log fort years ago," Ryn said.

"*And the river*," her mother repeated, "but while I'm gone, I need you to stay home."

"*What*?" Ryn and Jett said at the same time.

"The garden needs lots of tending this time of year as it is almost ready to harvest."

"But..." Ryn started.

"The tomatoes appear to be ripening in abundance this year, you two can preserve them for the winter."

"But..." Jett said.

Her mother released them, hands resting on their shoulders. "And we definitely need more wood for the winter."

"But summer is almost over!" Ryn protested. "By the time you get home, it *will* be over."

Jett's eyes narrowed at their mother. "You've never required us to stay at home before, what's going on?"

Her hands slid down their arms. "Nothing you need to worry about. As long as you are close to the cottage everything will be fine." She spent a long moment searching Ryn and Jett's eyes. "Promise me you will stay here."

Jett let out a long, exasperated breath.

They weren't really going to promise their mother, were they? If she promised to stay by the cottage she couldn't leave to study in the Library. Not without the sick gut feeling that her mother would find out and she would be in so much trouble.

Her mother's eyes pled with them. "Please. I wouldn't ask it if it wasn't important."

"If we don't need to worry, then we don't need to stay here?" Jett's eyes held their mother's.

Her back straightened and she did that thing with her mouth that said she meant business and she wasn't backing down.

"Fine," Jett finally growled. His concession seemed too quick, causing Ryn to wonder if it was genuine.

Ryn couldn't open her mouth to say it, her stomach churned. She managed a nod, then quickly looked away.

Her mother let out a sigh of relief, hugging each of them longer and tighter than ever before. She released Ryn, who pretended she didn't see the tear roll down her mother's nose.

"It's alright, you're going to be alright." She seemed to be talking more to herself than to them.

Jett picked up her bag for her.

"No. You two stay here, I'll meet Lar at the end of the lane," she said.

"I need to see Zo before he leaves," Ryn pleaded with her mother. "Please, it's important."

Her mother gave her a dubious look. "Stay with your brother. You can write Zo at the Library." She turned to take her bag from Jett.

He pulled it back. "Let us walk you to your meeting place. We'll be fine."

Ryn put on her most determined face.

Her mother looked them both over and relented. "Alright, I wouldn't mind a few more moments with you both before I leave."

Jett carried her bag for her. For once she let him, probably so she could put her arms around her children's waists and hold them close all the way down the lane. Ryn leaned into her mother. Despite everything, her mother was the only person who really understood Ryn. With Yll's bead acquisition, Ryn and her mother were the only two Ordinaries in the village now. She savored that closeness for one last moment. Her mother had always been Ryn's almost constant companion. The only time they were separated was when her mother traveled on business, and that had been sporadic until Ryn's father had left. Otherwise, they were nearly inseparable. It was a security Ryn needed—someone who didn't leave her.

At the end of the lane, Lar and Zo stood waiting by a carriage. Lar only had eyes for Ryn's mother. Zo stood with a bag over his shoulder, the air about him sizzled with energy.

Lar kissed her mother's cheek.

"A carriage is quite an expense. You shouldn't have." Ryn's mother tried to look stern, but failed.

"You should always leave in style," Lar grinned.

Ryn approached Zo carefully. The heat wave rolling off of him subsided a bit.

"Can I talk to you?" she asked.

Zo glanced at his father taking her mother's bag from Jett, then dropped his bag at his feet.

"Sure," he said.

Ryn eyed her mother as butterflies fluttered around in her stomach. There must have been something about the look on her face, because he pulled her around to the side of the carriage.

"What's up?" he asked.

Ryn glanced around making sure no one was close enough to overhear her.

"Can you get me an application to study with Master Wes?" her voice was barely above a whisper.

Zo's frown shifted into a toothy grin. "I will do that, and more. I was just reading in the newspaper about all the requirements. When I get to the Library, I'll find the best strategy for approaching Master Wes."

Ryn felt herself pale. "I need a strategy? I thought I just filled out the application."

"There's going to be stiff competition with only five spots, and who knows how many potential applicants."

Ryn swayed with anxiety.

"But don't worry, I'm going to be at the Library. I'll ask around. It's the buzz of Waatch, everyone is talking about it. Someone has to know what Master Wes is looking for in his students. We can make sure your application is perfect. You're going to land this thing, or we're going to die trying."

Zo's words invoked a weird image in her head of a bird, which happened to look a lot like the bird Yll transformed into, coming in for a landing and sliding across a slick floor, only to crash into a heap against a wall. Ryn giggled.

Zo looked smug, like he knew exactly what image he had put into Ryn's head.

Across the square a yellow streak came barreling toward them. Ryn turned to see Prym, red faced and huffing, looking like she was ready to take someone's head off.

"You!" Prym stopped in front of Ryn.

"Meee?" Zo stepped in closer.

Prym gave him a fiery flick of her eyes that rivaled the flames he could produce with a snap of his fingers.

"You ruined my party. I don't know how, but I'm going to prove it, and I'm going to have your horrible little family driven out of Sooke for good. Save yourself some trouble and just admit it now," Prym fumed.

"What did I do?" was the only thing Ryn could think of to say.

Prym ignored her and kept up her rant, "Jared searched everyone's bags and that horrible little half Ordinary friend of yours had an empty bottle of something in it. I know you were working together; Tammy saw you talking by the punchbowl. Once I prove it, I will bring the law down on your head."

"For a few sick people at a party? How is that a crime?" Zo asked.

Prym's nostrils flared. "It was my big night. You snuck in, uninvited, just so you could get back at me. I know it. Just wait..." Prym sputtered. "Just you wait!"

Someone whistled behind Prym.

"Darling, we're going to be late for your parents' luncheon." Prym turned slightly revealing Iden across the square, waving Prym over to him.

Prym huffed and stalked away. Iden threw Zo a wink.

Hmmm, Ryn thought, *they must have found some time together this morning.*

"Zo let's load up," Lar's voice came from around the carriage.

Ryn looked up at him and saw her one chance for a friend slipping away.

Zo took her by the shoulders. "You can do this. You're going to get one of those student spots. You are smart and capable."

Ryn folded her arms. "How do you know? We only just met."

Zo shrugged, "I know what I know. I'll send you the application as soon as I get to Waatch."

And with that he was stepping around the carriage with an air of determination. Ryn was glad she could give him purpose, but after one last hug from her mother she sadly watched them disappear in the cloud of dust the carriage kicked up.

Chapter Eight

Ordinary mainlanders claim the Ancestors stole their sacred site from them to build the Library. I haven't seen a lick of magic come out of a mainlander. Still, there is something about the spot the Library is built on. It repels everything magical. That presents a real problem in heating the Library. Fireplaces presented an inherent danger to Library collections. Someone clever discovered the beauty of radiant heating. Heat water and pump it through the floor. Safest way to do that was with magic, which required a boiler room far enough away it could be used.

— As quoted to Cheryl de Muto in Of Magic, Myth and Lore-Commentary and Anecdotes from the people of Waatch, the Library, and the Surrounding Area. Ancestral Library, First Floor, Lore Room, Shelf 29, Shelfmark 33.

The gradual descent from Sooke into Waatch provided Zo with a sweeping sight like no other. Towering over the center of town was the great Library. Its main turret was like a giant, watching over the puny buildings below, waiting for one of them to step out of line. From the Library, streets radiated out like spokes of a wheel. At this height it was so clearly wheel-like Zo imagined it spinning round and round on a cart, with the Library as its hub. All roads led to the Library, and everything flowed unto it. One glance at the town from here and there was no doubt where the center of the Ancestral world lay.

A breeze brought the smell of the ocean bay and a chill that sent a shiver down Zo's spine. Ducking his head back into the carriage, he instantly regretted it. Ryette and his father were in the opposite corner of the coach. The way they talked and touched was so intimate, Zo felt like an intruder. He was tempted to tell the driver he would walk the rest of the way...and then head back home, but he promised Ryn he would get that application. Besides, Lar would just drag him back here tomorrow. He might as well get on with it and get it over with. Maybe there was a way to get out of this apprenticeship. There had to be rules he could "accidentally" mess up and get himself dismissed. Then he could go back to burning fields at the end of harvest with his dad. He'd been helping his dad for a long time. It was familiar and comfortable, and there must be plenty of work here, or his father would never have chosen this place to settle.

They reached the spot where the road leveled off and joined the main road, leading to the north end of Waatch. Down this road, just past the north gate, was the harbor where they would leave Ryette. A deep, sad sigh from her brought Zo's attention to their conversation.

"If there's any trouble, send word through Gor and I'll return immediately," Ryette said.

Lar kissed her temple. "Everything will be fine. Wes will come, he won't find anything he's looking for, and he'll leave. It will be over before you know it."

"The kids are upset they have to stay at the cottage," she said.

"I'm sorry about that. If I had another person with earth magic to help me, I might be able to cover a wider area, but the cottage is all I can handle alone in a thorough manner." Lar pulled her in closer to him. "I also don't dare risk bringing in anyone else for fear of what they might discover."

Ryette tensed and glanced at Zo, like it was his fault he was overhearing their conversation.

"I know," was her clipped reply.

Zo hung his head out the window for the rest of the ride to the docks. He thought it was best not to get on her bad side any more than he already had. Plus, wearing a suit coat on a warm summer day inside a carriage was stifling.

When they rolled up to the docks, Zo was confused. The only boats moored there were small fishing crafts, none of them looked big enough to be a cargo ship to Muto. Yet Lar and Ryette stepped out of the carriage as if everything was exactly as it should be.

Lar lifted her bag off the top of the carriage. "Do you need help carrying it? I could come with you and carry it for you."

At the slow shake of her head, he leaned in, and they kissed a long-extended kiss that made Zo blush, glancing up and down the dock to see who was watching.

"Dad," Zo finally interrupted.

His father slowly brought the kiss to an end, handed Ryette her bag, then crushed her to him like he couldn't bear to let go. When they separated, Ryette wiped a tear from her eye. Squeezing his hand one last time, she slowly walked down the docks. Lar stood watching her go. Once she passed the harbor master's office a gust of wind blew up, swirling her hair. She turned behind the building and was gone.

Lar climbed into the carriage, and they pulled away toward Waatch.

The north gates were taller than his mother's mansion and thick as a house is wide. Lots of mainlander traffic bearing goods for the town, along with carriages displaying the colors of the great Ancestral houses, were coming and going, and leaving with the writs of power they needed. The Library was the place to get your lineage officiated. Without that official documentation the beads of Ancestral bone could not be bestowed.

Zo scarcely remembered his two ceremonies. He was barely eight, the earliest age for which you could receive your beads. His mother, a member of the Healing Council that oversaw all who used healing magic, had arranged for him to receive his healing bead on his eighth birthday. His entire extended family was at the after party his mother threw at her estate. The celebration went well into the night, his mother, the sparkling center of it all. After receiving his bead, everyone seemed to forget he was at his own party. His mother was in her glory though, mingling with all the guests, lamenting the fact that she was blessed by the Ancestors with two boys and no girls, yet declaring how Zo would someday join her on the Healing Council—

even though his patriarchal magic was fire, which traditionally meant it would be his focus in life. Bored by the adults, Zo wandered the party working on his newly given fire magic, practicing snapping his fingers to produce a flame. At some point early in the party, a relative from some distant healing school stepped on Zo at the same moment Zo snapped his fingers and actually made a flame pop up. The relative's coat wasn't on fire too long before someone put him out. After that, Zo's mother shoved him outside to wander the gardens alone. It was the night he began to resent his healing magic.

The memory made him frown at the House carriages trotting past his window, the buildings of Waatch rolling by proudly behind them. The street was lined with townhomes and other mansions that the workers and administrators of the Library occupied. Waatch on the north end also contained the fancier markets and craft shops. This was *the* entrance to Waatch, through which all dignitaries entered the town. The side streets were neat and tidy, the houses well kept. Though there was no room for lawns, there were plenty of well sculpted porches and pottery containing an abundance of summertime flowers. At the end of this grand promenade, was the Library. Beneath its shadow, everything about it spoke of grandeur, from its carved archways to the enormous stones from which it was built. The hair on Zo's arm stood up as the carriage rumbling through the Library gates onto the grounds. Power lay here—great and terrible in nature.

They drove through the stately Library gardens populated by researchers wandering in their black dresses and robes. At the far side of the Library, they reached a cluster of support buildings. The carriage rolled to a stop outside the biggest, most formidable looking of those buildings. Zo put his hand out, grabbing the door handle before his father could open it.

"Let's go home," Zo said. "You need my help. Fire season is already starting, you'll need every experienced firestarter you can get."

His father frowned at Zo's hand on the handle. "We'll manage without you this season."

There was a long pause.

When Lar looked into Zo's eyes, his stomach sank. "This is the Library, not some farming fire master. I've committed you to this." He pulled the apprenticeship documents from his lapel pocket. "If you don't fulfill the covenanted time of your apprenticeship, the Library can take legal action, which could include everything from fines to jail time for you and for me."

Zo felt the blood in his face join his stomach. He'd never heard of such harsh apprenticeship terms before.

"What the...why did you arrange this without asking me about it? How could you do this to me?"

Lar's mouth became a thin line, his face hard. "Because this is what you need. Do not mess up, I'd prefer not to spend the next few years of my life inside a jail cell."

With that, Lar tore Zo's hand from the handle and stepped out of the carriage.

Zo sat stunned. What was his father thinking? Zo was the one who did most of the cooking and the cleaning around the cabin. Regg was good only for having his nose in a book and chasing skirts. Did he just want Zo out of the way? Was he embarrassed by the son who wasn't interested in perpetuating the Ignis line? Something cold settled into the pit of his stomach that the heat of the carriage and his coat could not dispel.

"Zo!" his father called.

The contract had been made. There was no getting out of it, no messing up and getting himself dismissed. He shook his hand out, cracking his knuckles on his knee. Well, at least being here he would get Ryn a spot in that Master's class.

Taking a deep breath, Zo followed his father. A word to the guard at the door got them admitted to the building. The walls were as thick as the length of the carriage, which led Zo to hope it would be cooler inside, but the blast of heat emanating from a second door inside made Zo instantly start to sweat. That door opened to a maze of pipework, and flames—lots of flames.

"Purpose?" a man sitting at a desk next to the door asked.

"New apprenticeship," Lar said.

"Papers." Desk Guy held out his hand.

Lar handed him the papers he'd been gripping since he showed them to Zo. They were now crumpled.

Desk Guy grunted examining the papers. Turning, he yelled at a passing worker, "Get Master Nix for me."

The worker scurried off into the dark tangle of pipework.

Desk Guy signed, dated, and stamped Zo's paperwork.

"Thumb," Desk Guy demanded.

"What?" Zo asked, confused.

"Your hand, give it to me," Desk Guy grunted.

Zo tentatively held out his hand. Swiftly the man seized his thumb, pricking it with something sharp. Zo tried to jerk his hand back, but Desk Guy held it with an iron grasp, squeezing drops of blood from the prick. Then he forced Zo's thumb down onto the paper marking it with a bloody thumbprint before releasing his hand.

"Welcome to The Boiler," Desk Guy said, with a smile that did not look at all welcoming.

Just then a giant of a man came roaring around the corner of pipework. He made no sound, but his presence smelled of fire and sweat. He wore only a light vest and thin pants.

"Here you are." Desk Guy folded Zo's papers and gave them to the giant. "Master Nix, meet your new grunt."

Master Nix looked over the paperwork then handed them back to Desk Guy. He took Zo's hand. It was dry and leathery and HOT.

"Congratulations, you are now mine till I say otherwise. Get yourself over to the dorms, get checked in, changed, and back here within the hour." With that Master Nix turned and strode away, yelling at someone about water pressure.

Zo glared at his father, whose eyes were glued to Master Nix's retreating form, clearly refusing to glance in Zo's direction.

"Dorms and requisitions are two buildings over. Hustle it up!" Desk Guy gestured distractedly out the door as he resumed writing in a large ledger.

***

Outside, Lar pulled Zo's bag from the top of the carriage. "I know this seems harsh, but this is a better path for you than I can provide. Burning crops and clearing brush is not a life that will provide for a family. Library fire work is the highest paid fire magic without moving to Ignisapan. Unless you want to study warfare with the rest of the elites in House Ignis. Once you finish here, I have connections that could get you a position not on the front lines." Lar looked Zo in the eyes. "Or you could go to Eileansano and study healing with your mother. She would be thrilled."

Zo took his bag from his father. "No, thank you, Library dirty fire work is fine."

And with that he turned and walked away from his father. He tried to look nonchalant, but at the sound of the carriage pulling away, his heart sank. Was this really his life now? How did it all change in one night?

He should really learn to curb his brilliant ideas.

With help and direction from a fairly cute young Library guard, he was able to find the office that issued him clothes and assigned him a bunk in the dorm. He changed, stored his stuff in his assigned trunk, and got back to the boiler room building within the hour. As his hand rested on the latch to enter, he had a sudden flash of panic that this would be his entire life. He took a long, deep breath and lifted the latch.

Master Nix assigned him to the giant boilers in the main room. He said all grunts started there so he could keep an eye on them. After tossing him a waterskin the size of a small bucket, he told Zo to drink from it constantly, then showed him how to use his fire to heat the bottom of the boiler. Three grunts were assigned per boiler. Water flowed into the boilers from pipes entering through the walls. It was heated inside the great boiler vats, then several people with water magic directed the heated water through pipes that entered a tunnel below ground level.

"Why don't you just use wood to heat the boilers?" Zo asked.

"Fire magic is safer. Get to work!" With that Master Nix strode away.

It was hot and thirsty work. Zo drank his water as instructed, but soon his heart was racing, he was dizzy, and sick to his stomach. Desk Guy, whose name was actually Hal, led him outside to a cool water pool and put him in it, clothes and all. After he cooled off, they sent him back into the boiler room. The rest of the day went on like this, with Master Nix yelling at them, threatening them, and calling them names. When the whistle finally blew the signal to switch shifts, Zo thought he would collapse.

As he shuffled past Hal's desk with the rest of the grunts, Hal reached out and stopped him.

"You've been assigned graveyard shift, be back here after dinner."

Zo shook his head and tried to clear it, sweat spraying from his hair. He couldn't have possibly heard that right.

"What?"

"You heard me. Eat and come back. Your real shift starts in an hour."

Zo's anger flared. Normally that would have brought flames to his fingers, but he didn't even want to think about fire at the moment.

"But I just worked a shift," Zo argued.

Hal showed him an evil grin. "That was just your orientation, now the real work begins."

Stunned, all he could do was follow everyone else to the mess hall where they lined up for food. He was last in line until a girl with hair so blond it was almost white stepped in line behind him.

"You don't happen to have a relative who sells apples at local markets do you?" Zo quipped.

Blond girl's eyes grew wide. "My family are apple farmers. My mother and my brother sell at local markets."

Surprise made him stumble back. "Wow, small world. I met your brother a few days ago in Sooke. Good looking guy."

Blond girl shushed him, looking around at who might have overheard him. "Don't say such things here. The Ancestor types get their underthings in a bunch if they hear you saying that."

"Ancestor types? You're not one?"

"Duh—apple farmer," she said.

"Oh right, right. Sorry, tired." Zo stuck out his warm dried out hand. "I'm Zo. Brand new grunt in the Boiler Room."

Blondie took his hand in her cool, soft one. "Brynd, Library Docent."

Zo perked up as they grabbed plates from a stack. "Really? I have a friend who wants to apply for one of the student positions with Master Wes. Do you know anything about how to apply and where I could get an application?"

A worker plopped mashed potatoes, green beans, and a piece of salmon on Zo's plate.

Brynd eyed his boiler room clothes. "Everybody and their cat are applying for those positions, what makes your *friend* think they can get one of those slots?"

"They're highly trained with documents and family research. I have no doubt they could do it." That was a total lie, Zo had no idea how good Ryn was at research, but he needed this docent to get the information he wanted.

He sensed Brynd could spot his lie, because she gave him a dubious look as they found an open spot to sit at a long bench table.

"I can get you the application, but the essay will be hard. It needs to heavily reference books on family history research theory. Those sorts of books only reside within the Library, or the libraries of the great Ancestral Houses.

Unless you have access to one of those sorts of book repositories, it's unlikely Master Wes will look past your bibliography."

Zo cracked his knuckles against his leg, thinking. The salmon was surprisingly tender and juicy.

"Can you bring me an application anyway? I'll figure something out."

"Sure," Brynd said, stirring her potatoes with her fork.

Zo gave her a worried look. "It's not difficult to get, is it?"

"I'll have to call in a few favors, but I can manage it."

"Why would you call in favors for a guy you just barely met?"

"Because anyone from the Boiler Room interested in being a researcher deserves a shot to get out of there. That place will kill you!"

Zo laughed, but inside he wished he could cry.

Chapter Nine

The burdens of servitude fall on our backs,
Where freedom existed, bondage came to be,
Where joyfulness flourished, bitterness remained,
Where beauty and grace blossomed, only rot was seen.

— Luc's epic poem as recorded in his Third Journal. Ancestral Liberty, Third Floor Restricted. The Curator has the Key.

A flutter of wings above Ryn momentarily blocked the sun and drew her attention away from the tomato vines she was propping up. Holding her hand to shield her eyes, she watched a bird, heavy laden with papers in its talons, settle onto the path between the squash and the beans. The bird finished her entrance with a flourish as she transformed into the one person Ryn didn't really want to see.

"Hi," Yll said, absently brushing a feather from her clothes. Her eyes followed it as it fluttered to the dirt.

"Hi," Ryn barely managed in response.

Silence stretched between them. A silence Ryn didn't know how to fill, or even if she should. They both shifted uncomfortably.

"What do you want?"

Yll rolled the papers in her hands tighter. "I have a message for you from that Zo guy." Yll held the roll out to her.

Finally! Ryn thought, reaching for the papers. The roll contained a letter from Zo and the application to study with Master Wes. Excitement made her hands tremble. She wanted to run to her room and pour over the documents immediately, but Yll didn't fly away—didn't move at all.

"Thanks," Ryn said reluctantly.

Yll shrugged one shoulder.

The awkward quiet between them continued.

Anxious to find a way to disengage, Ryn finally asked, "Was there something else?"

Yll studied the trees for a long moment, then pinned Ryn with her eyes.

"I want us to be friends again," Yll said.

Ryn stifled a grimace.

"I thought I couldn't come back till I found my ancestry," Ryn bit out.

Yll's face flushed red. "That came out all wrong, I didn't mean to say it that way."

Ryn folded her arms, careful not to crush the papers. "What did you mean then?"

Yll paused, pursing her lips. After a moment she shook herself and crossed to Ryn.

"Look, you're applying to study with Master Wes," Yll nodded to the papers in Ryn's hand, "and I'm applying. If we both get in, we'll need to work together. Together, we can get a Library job."

"You need my help." Ryn's eyes narrowed in realization. "What is it?"

Yll's feet shuffled. "I can't ask my mom for access to materials to write my essay or she'll know I'm applying. Your mom has books we can use to write our essays, and she's not around to know we are using them."

"Why don't you just get your new best friend Prym to let you use her family's library? I'm sure her father has all the books you need."

Yll shook her head. "He's trying to eliminate any competition for Prym and won't let anyone in the village access his collection. Besides, he might tell my mother. Not because they are friendly in any way, just to keep me from competing with his daughter."

Ryn stifled the choking noise rising in her throat. "And these are the type of people you want to be friends with?"

"No...yes...I don't know. They found an empty bottle in my bag at the party. They think I was involved in helping make the party guests sick somehow." Yll eyed her. "You wouldn't know anything about that would you? I left my bag on the table by the punchbowl that night."

Ryn looked away into the woods, trying to keep anything from her face.

Gentle as the brush of wings, Yll laid a hand on Ryn's arm.

"The past is the past, let's work together." Yll's eyes drifted to the tomato bushes. "Please?"

At that moment, head bowed, Yll looked horribly lost. Ryn knew that feeling well. She also knew it was something Yll had been familiar with most of her life. Standing before Ryn was her dearest childhood friend, whom she'd spent many hours as a child playing with—pretending to have magic, sleepovers, and pillow fights...all the things best friends did together. Plus, she had been the one to plant the bottle in Yll's purse. It had been an angry impulse at the time that Ryn now regretted. How could she have even thought to do such a thing to her best friend?

"Alright," Ryn said. "We'll use mother's collection and write our essays together."

Yll whooped. "Yes! Let's get started. We're almost out of time, the deadline is in two days!"

Ryn looked at the papers in her hand. "How did you find Zo to get these papers?"

"I heard he was looking around for a messenger, so I volunteered."

Ryn had to wonder if Zo really knew who Yll was. It didn't matter now. Brushing the dirt and tomato dust from her hands and skirt, she let Yll hustle her into the cottage to find paper, ink, and pens to get started.

***

The next couple of days were a blur of research and writing. Zo's letter had outlined the topic of the paper they were to submit: *The impact of Ancestral family research on society*. Ryn's mother's books didn't address that topic exactly, but there were plenty of works on family research and proper documentation. Her mother's job was to help Clayr collect the correct records to add to the Library's collections, so she kept lots of source material about what was considered the best documentation to establish family lines. At least Ryn and Yll could cite those books. The rest would just have to be guessed at.

Yll told her mother she was spending the night with Ryn. Clayr was so delighted they had made up, she readily agreed. They worked late into the night, only stopping to make the occasional snack. The snap peas fresh from the garden in dressing were a favorite. Jett was out most of the time with some girl he met at the party. She was apparently a long-time friend of Prym's parents, though Ryn had never seen her in the village before now. He came home late and went straight to bed, hardly noticing what Ryn and Yll were up to.

The girls only slept when they finally collapsed in the wee hours of the morning. Jett woke them banging around making breakfast. Trying to sleep with his racket was impossible, so they got up and started work again. They worked all day and into the night again. By the following morning, they both held finished applications and ten-page essays in their ink-stained fingers.

"Done!" Yll exclaimed. Her excitement lifting her droopy eyes.

"Now what do we do?" Ryn asked.

"What do you mean?"

"Zo's letter says we need to present our papers in person to Master Wes at the Library. How do we get there? If we walk there we'll miss the deadline, not to mention everyone will be freaking out, wondering where we've gone."

"Well, mother thinks I'm here with you, so I'm covered."

"Only until Jett is looking for us, probably at your house."

"Right." Yll rubbed her forehead. "Pay for a carriage?"

"Do you have money for that? Because I don't have money for that."

"Ask your brother for money?" Yll offered.

Just then Jett entered the cottage with his girlfriend. In that moment Ryn felt like she was coming fully awake, and realized he'd been out of the house.

"Where have you been?" Ryn asked, emerging from her room.

"None of your business," Jett said, setting out a pan next to a basket full of ingredients.

"You weren't supposed to leave the cottage. I've been trapped here for days, and you've been off who knows where. You're going to get us into trouble."

Jett glared at her. "It's fine. Thalya is from House Viatoro. Travel magic is untraceable. Nobody can track us."

That was exactly what Ryn suspected, and what she was hoping to hear. She approached Thalya standing at the table, preparing to cut onions for Jett.

"Yll and I need to go to the Library. Will you take us?"

Thalya glanced at Jett.

Jett shook his head. "No. Why do you need to go to the Library? We need to stay clear of that place because of..." Jett's eyes drifted to Ryn's ink-stained hands. "You're not thinking of applying to study with Master Wes, are you?"

Ryn's legs felt like liquid, but she lifted her head and said, "yes."

"*Ryn*," his eyes bugged out.

Glancing at Yll and Thalya watching him, he reached around the table, grabbed Ryn's arm, and dragged her into her room. The door caught in a breeze and slammed behind them. Ryn's legs gave out, plopping onto her bed to watch Jett pace.

"I can't...you don't...what a spoiled brat," Jett sputtered.

"Excuse me?" Ryn's heat rose.

Jett turned to face her. "Don't you understand? No, of course you don't understand, all you can think about is being popular in the village, but I was there, I saw mother's sadness, her despair. I heard her crying night after night when the physician told her she could never have another child. I was very little, but the sadness darkened the whole cottage and our family. All she kept saying was 'I want a baby girl, please let me have a baby girl.' And then there you were, and mother's joy was beyond what you could even imagine."

Ryn folded her arms. She'd heard this story before. Not exactly from Jett's perspective, but her mother and father told it many times.

"I know. What does that have to do with anything?"

Jett took her by the shoulders, squeezing them a bit too tight. "Don't you see? Don't you get it? Finding your birth parents will crush mother. Her heart will be broken. She will think she's not good enough for you and that you need to go off and find another mother."

"But that's not true! I love her! I just want—" Ryn's eyes blurred with tears. "I just need...You don't understand what it's like."

Jett pulled out his necklace with its one bead. "Of course I understand. Do you know what it's like to be half Ordinary?"

"At least you have magic! I have nothing, and everyone hates me for it!" Ryn pulled out of his grip. "There's no harm in studying in the Library. If what mother says is true, I probably won't find my family there, but I need to look. I have to be sure. If Ordinary is what I am then so be it, but I'm running out of time. Soon I will be too old, and the beads won't accept me. I have to know for my own peace of mind, otherwise it will haunt me the rest of my life."

Jett fingered his one bead, eyes distant, seeming lost in thought.

He sighed. "Fine. Thalya can take you, and I'll cover for you—for now, but I'm not dealing with the fall out. If by some miracle of the Ancestors you get accepted as a student, you're going to have to explain it to mother when she gets back, and frankly, I don't want to be around when you do, because it is going to be ugly."

Ryn swallowed hard, only managing to nod in agreement. She shoved aside thinking about how her mother would react, first for disobeying and leaving the cottage, and secondly for defying her to study at the

Library. Her stomach did a flip just contemplating it. She would think about it later, right now she had to prepare to meet Master Wes.

***

Yll went home to get fresh clothes while Ryn took a bath, washed her sweaty dirty hair, and changed. She was exhausted, but too nervous to even think about sleeping. Zo's letter said Master Wes would only consider Ancestor descendants as students—no Ordinaries. He recommended Ryn pretend to have Ancestor magic, but how could she do that? She didn't have a necklace or beads...

The thought sent her running into her room to her jewelry box, pulling out the stone bead necklace Jett had made for her. On close examination they didn't look like bone, but at a distance they would probably pass for real. The question now was, of all the beads to choose, what magics should she pretend to have? Her father was from House Dico, so she decided that should be one, easier to do a half-truth—but what should the other be? Pondering, she rolled each bead around in her palm, auditioning each magic. Not fire, or water, or even shapeshifting, nothing someone could ask her to do for them that would catch her in the lie on the spot. Thalya and Jett's voices drifted in from the living room, making her consider their magics. Spirit magic would be hard for someone to ask her to show them, but she didn't want to have the same magic as her brother and possibly lead Master Wes back here—if he was indeed looking for them. Travel magic was something someone could ask her to do, but probably wouldn't, as the dust and dirt kicked up by the swirling breeze of travel magic was something most people didn't enjoy. It was also unlikely Master Wes would ask a novice travel magic student to take him anywhere.

Decision made, she added the travel magic bead to her necklace and tied it around her neck.

She would be Ryn de Dico. Switching her father's magic to her fictitious mother's should hide their family well enough. She'd need to make up something to tell Master Wes about who her parents were.

When Yll arrived, they collected Thalya from Jett's lap and headed outside. Clutching her essay and documents, they let Thalya enfold them in her arms. Two extra people was about the limit of travel magic.

The swirling began at their feet. Dust and fallen leaves assaulted their ankles and legs, growing in intensity as it traveled upward, surrounding them in spinning air until it shot upward, pulling their hair with it.

"Hold on!" Thalya shouted, and then the cottage disappeared.

The spinning air squeezed them together. She closed her eyes as dust pelted her face. The next thing she knew the swirling slowed, and feet she didn't know had left the ground hit hard on cobblestones.

She rubbed dust from her eyes to clear them for the overpowering sight of the towering Library spire. The stone walls, menacing as if wishing to crush her into the dust she brushed from her clothes. And why shouldn't they? She was tiny and insignificant in comparison to its ancient magnificence.

It took sheer strength of will to pull her eyes from the ancient structure and focus on Yll, looking just as small.

"Where do we find Zo?" Ryn asked, trying to push them in the right direction and ignore the looming beast above them.

"This way," Yll said shakily.

The combination of travel magic, plus the Library presence had clearly affected them both.

Ryn turned to Thayla. "Can you wait for us? Or return in a bit? I'm not sure how often you can travel magic."

"The world and time become weird and distorted when you travel too often. I can wait for you. I'll be in the gardens when you're done," Thalya said.

"Great! We'll try not to be long. The shorter time we're gone from the cottage the better," Ryn said, following Yll through the gate to the Library grounds and toward a stone building behind the Library.

At the door to the giant block of a building, they were directed by a guard to the mess hall. There they found Zo deep in conversation with a girl whose white-blond hair made her instantly recognizable as the apple farmer's sister. Zo did not look well. His clothes were sweat-stained and his hair stuck up in weird directions. He was pale and sickly looking.

"Are you alright?" was all Ryn could blurt out as she hurried over to him.

His smile was flat and tight. "It's good to see you, little sis. Are you ready?"

Ryn grinned and held up her papers.

"Perfect. This is Brynd, she's a docent in the Library. She'll take you to the office where Master Wes is conducting interviews."

Brynd's jaw dropped for a minute. Then she pushed Zo on his shoulder. "I thought when you said, 'asking for a friend' you meant you wanted that application for yourself."

Zo grinned, "I told you it was for a friend. Sister to be precise. Brynd, this is Ryn and..." His eyes shifted to Yll, "Hey, didn't I hire you to deliver those documents?"

"Yes. Yll de Muto, glad to meet you." Yll held out her hand to Brynd.

"Great, let's hurry, Master Wes will stop taking applications at the sound of the Library closing bell and the line of applicants keeps growing," she said.

***

Brynd deposited them in front of a squat building next to what she said were the Library dormitories. There were others lined up outside, reading over their essays and muttering to themselves. Butterflies rattled around inside Ryn's stomach as she contemplated giving up and going to find Thalya to take her home. Her words to Jett came forcefully to her mind. She hadn't realized what she was feeling till they came out of her mouth, but it was true. She needed to know for sure if she had magic or not, otherwise the rest of her life would be filled with regret.

They waited outside the small office building as the sun got lower in the sky. She wondered when the closing bell would ring. Would she come this far just to get turned away?

The office door opened, and a young man dressed in a high Ordinary collar left the room dejectedly. A man dressed in a finely embroidered suit, waistcoat, and jacket all in green, appeared in the doorway.

"I thought I made myself clear—no Ordinaries!" he bellowed out to the gathered crowd.

A bunch of the waiting hopefuls slunk away.

"Next!" the man bellowed.

No one moved. Yll nudged Ryn. "That's you."

"What?" Ryn looked dazed watching the previous candidate disappear into the Library gardens.

"The others ahead of you left—it's your turn," Yll whispered.

"Oh!"

Ryn's knees trembled as she entered the office clutching her papers. Master Wes took a seat behind a large desk.

"Sit." He pointed to a chair opposite him.

Ryn tried not to collapse into the seat.

"Name." Master Wes scribbled in a book.

"Ry..." her voice squeaked. Clearing her throat, she tried again. "Ryn de Dico." The lie put terror in her stomach.

Master Wes examined Ryn's open collar. She had borrowed one of Yll's old dresses that was too short for Yll and slightly too long for Ryn, but had an open collar that would show off Ryn's fake beads.

"Application." Master Wes held out his hand.

Trying not to tremble, Ryn put her papers into his hands.

"Those beads are hard to read, what's your father's House?" Master Wes asked as he looked over Ryn's essay.

"Viatoro," Ryn said.

Master Wes' head shot up. "Who was your father?"

Belatedly, Ryn remembered Master Wes was from House Viatoro.

She cleared her throat. "I'm not certain. I never met him. My mother did my ancestry for me. I think she was ashamed to tell me who he was." Ryn was astonished how that story popped into her head and out of her mouth.

Master Wes nodded thoughtfully, his eyes searching her face for...something? Ryn had no idea what.

He collected her papers and placed them into a pile. "Dismissed."

Wait...what? Ryn thought they would at least discuss her essay before... Ryn's hopeful heart sank. She felt tears rising into her eyes, but fought against them so as not to embarrass herself further. She tried to walk straight and not slink out like the previous guy, but she was certain her shoulders betrayed her disappointment. Yll gave her a sympathetic pat as she passed on her way into the office for her turn. In the end Yll seemed to have a similar experience, as she came out looking just as dejected as Ryn felt.

They found Thalya and went home. Only after Ryn lifted the latch and sunk into the chair by the hearth did she think about missing a chance to visit with Zo. Well, it didn't matter now, she was stuck in this cottage forever. The tears flowed then, hard and long until she drifted off to sleep.

***

The sun was sinking low, and the cabin was full of dark shadows when a pounding on the door turned into it bursting open—Zo flew across the room wild-eyed, before he turned to face the men following him.

"I'm sorry, I'm sorry, I'm so sorry," he was whispering.

Groggily, Ryn peaked around Zo to see what looked like two Library guards following Zo through the door. Shooting to her feet, she was instantly fully awake.

"Ryn de Dico?" One of them asked.

Zo glanced back at her briefly before firming his stance in front of her.

Wearily, Ryn nodded.

"We have an order to bring you to the Library." The guard held up a paper. "You will come with us immediately."

Chapter Ten

My family have always been skeptics. Dragon slayers and dragons coming from the stars? Sounds preposterous! But then, where did the magic come from? Mainlander myths talk of a natural magic inherent in the world, but Mainlanders are bereft of anything magical. There had to be something to the story of Praedo and the dragon. I wasn't fully convinced until I stood at the edge of the sheer walled crater at the Origin, put the spyglass to my eye...and saw the sword sticking out of the stone.

— As quoted to Cheryl de Muto in Of Magic, Myth and Lore-Commentary and Anecdotes from the people of Waatch, the Library, and the Surrounding Area. Ancestral Library, First Floor, Lore Room, Shelf 29, Shelfmark 33.

Ryn sniffled as she sat sandwiched between two guards in heavy Library uniforms in the late summer evening. The carriage was hot and heavy laden with the spicy scent of sweat and ripe apples. They bumped along the road in a space that was not designed for six people. Zo sat across from her, looking even more squished between two guards, given he was a lot taller than she was. His face was pale with a sheen of sweat. He raised a shaky hand and wiped at his forehead.

"I didn't want to lead them to you, they gave me no choice," Zo said. "Someone saw me with you earlier, and threatened me if I didn't take them to you."

It made sense. There was no way Clayr would tell them who and where she was. Ryn's eyes locked with Zo's. She could tell he was probably thinking the same thing she was—either they found out who spiked the punch at Prym's Debut party, or she hadn't fooled Master Wes, and she was in deep trouble for impersonating someone with Ancestor blood. Ryn, whose feet didn't quite touch the floor, tried to shift in her seat, but the two guards on each side of her seemed to expand to take up even more space. She was sure her legs would be completely asleep by the time they got to the Library.

Zo opened his mouth, looking like he wanted to apologize again, but turned his eyes instead to the steadily darkening landscape outside. Ryn realized he was probably correct in feeling guilty. Both possibilities of why she was in trouble had been his ideas. She shouldn't have agreed to any of his schemes. Now her mother was away, and no one was here to save her from this awful mess they had created. The thought of her mother finding out twisted her stomach. Either way, she wasn't going to win.

When they finally pulled up to the back door of the Library, Ryn was dizzy from the heat and felt like she was going to pass out, throw up, or both. The breath of fresh air when the door opened helped settle her stomach, but not the pins and needles in her legs. Climbing out of the carriage, Ryn once again felt the weight of the Library pressing down on her. Like it had eyes watching her every step.

The guards led both of them up the stone steps to the Library back door. The fact they were bringing both of them inside, and not just her, meant for sure it was the punch spiking they were in trouble for. Ryn's stomach twisted as the back door was unlocked. The hairs on her arms stood up as she entered the threshold. Her hair became suddenly floaty and clung to her cheeks. A shiver ran down her spine.

They entered a room full of hooks and cubbies. It must be where the workers left their cloaks and personal things when they reported for work. She was amazed at how long and skinny it was, and how it seemed to go on for what seemed like the length of the building. The guards pulled her through a side door.

That was when Ryn's jaw dropped.

The inside of the Library was like nothing she had ever imagined. The library from her dream wasn't even close. The smell of books, old leather, and paper overwhelmed her as she took in the row upon row of free-standing bookshelves. Many of the end caps were carved, most of one Ancestor or another. Some looked like trees, others looked like scenes, carved fruits, or objects. It was hard to tell as they dragged her gaping mouthed self quickly past everything. She desperately wanted to stop and stare at it for hours. When they finally stopped, it was in front of a door with every inch carved to represent the official fruits from each Ancestral House. It honored the Ancestors, plus was symbolic of the fruit each house produced in the way of offspring. The door had the look of ancient wood, but was beautiful and terrifying. The two guards standing at attention on either side of the door opened it for them. As it swung ponderously inward, Ryn's fear settled in her gut. What could a Library Regent do to her? He had no real authority over her, yet her mother had said he could have her family exiled from the village. Would he drag her all the way to the Library to do that? Wouldn't it be easier to just throw her out of her home?

The guard on Ryn's right took her elbow and led her forward into the room. She startled at the sight of the room full of people. Clayr sat behind a desk with a tree carved into the front, or perhaps it was a tree carved to look like a desk. Either way it gave the same effect. There was no doubt the curator's job was all about trees—family trees. Master Wes, surprisingly, stood beside Clayr, with Lar leaning against the bookshelves off to the side. A quick glance around the room revealed no sign of Prym's father, but she did find Prym. Prym was, of course, next to Iden, then Yll, and...was that Thalya, Jett's new girlfriend? They all sat in chairs lined up in front of Clayr's massive tree desk. There was one more empty chair which the guard pressed Ryn into before he retreated to stand by the door. Zo, looking somewhat pale and sweaty, took up a position slightly behind and to the right of her. His arms folded in a stance that conveyed everyone there was wasting his time.

Clayr's eyes were glued to Ryn from the moment she entered the room. Her face was blank in a way Ryn had seen when she was angry with Ryn and Yll for digging up her radishes to make mud villages, but something in her eyes spoke of a heavy sadness. Ryn knew she was in big trouble.

Eyes still locked on Ryn, Clayr's voice came out barely above a whisper.

"Master Wes has requested I gather you all here," Clayr said, with a wave of her hand that looked weak and reluctant.

Master Wes cleared his throat. "Thank you, Madame Curator, for gathering them so quickly. The sooner we get on with this the better."

Ryn's heart beat faster. She looked down the row of chairs at the others gathered. She was certain Master Wes had caught her lie about her ancestry, but what was everyone else doing here? Prym couldn't be in trouble, but she wasn't sure about Iden, or Yll. Ryn knew nothing about Thalya, she wasn't from Sooke, or the surrounding area. Maybe she was in trouble for bringing Ryn to the Library.

Silence settled on the room as everyone waited for Master Wes to pass judgment. Iden held Prym's hand so tight his knuckles were white.

Ryn's heart thumped loud enough she was sure everyone in the room could hear it.

"After reviewing the evidence..." Master Wes started.

Oh no, I'm dead.

"I have chosen the five of you as my students for a term. At the end of which, one of you will be awarded an Assistant Researcher position here at the Library," Master Wes finished.

Clayr frowned.

Lar muttered something. Clayr grabbed his hand.

Ryn shook her head, trying to process what she just heard.

"I object!" Prym shot to her feet. "You specifically stated you would not be taking on any Ordinaries, and this girl is an Ordinary."

Ryn stared at Prym's accusatory finger, sinking into her seat, wishing she could disappear into the floor.

Master Wes turned a withering glare on Prym. "I assure you her paperwork is in order."

Jaw dropping, Ryn's head spun at Master Wes' affirmation of her—a very false affirmation.

"Sit down," Iden hissed, using their still clasped hands to pull Prym back into her seat.

Prym's mother sat forward, whispering harshly to Prym, who kept saying, "but mother," loud enough for the rest of the room to hear.

Clayr's frown and narrowed eyes were directed at Master Wes. It was a look Ryn had seen many times. Usually when she didn't believe a tale Yll and Ryn were telling her.

Master Wes cleared his throat and Prym's corner finally quieted, but Prym sat there red-faced with her arms crossed, glaring at Ryn, who sank a little lower in her chair.

"As part of the learning process you will assist me in my research project," Master Wes said, in a clear attempt at wrestling back control of the room. "Any advances made by you to further my research will put you in a better position to be awarded the Assistant Researcher job. I expect you here every morning when the Library opens, till the sound of the closing bell. You may also be required to sift through materials late into the night. I recommend you get a bed in the dorms, but I do not require it. I will see you all tomorrow morning in my research alcove at first bell. Good evening." And with that Master Wes swept from Clayr's office.

Zo's arms unfolded and his hand came to rest on Ryn's shoulder.

Ryn's mind was struggling to understand what she'd just heard. She...she'd gotten a spot as one of Master Wes' students? And he wasn't questioning her Ancestry?

Someone behind her gave a cry of delight and rushed forward to take Iden and hug him. Ryn turned to see it was his parents. She hadn't seen them when they escorted her in. Jett was lurking in the back—his face a mirror of Clayr's. Prym's mother stood, licking her thumb and wiping something off Prym's face, which Prym swatted away. She took a step to bare down on Ryn, but Iden slipped an arm around her waist and steered her toward where Thalya had joined Iden's parents in conversation.

"You did it," Zo whispered in her ear. "I had no doubts."

Ryn hesitantly smiled up at him, acutely aware of all the frowns and furrowed brows pointed in her direction.

Clayr rapped her knuckles on her desk to restore order to the celebrating room.

"My sincere congratulations to all the winners. Accommodations will be provided for those who need it. Please follow Norm." Clayr pointed to the guard that had led Ryn in. "He will take you to the guard house to sign the necessary paperwork for studying in the Library."

Everyone moved toward the door.

"Ryn, Yll, Lar and Jett, please stay," Clayr's voice raised over the excited chatter.

Prym glared at Ryn and Yll, her mouth a thin line like she was biting back a tirade, but followed Iden, who had a firm grip on her hand, out of the office. Thalya went on tip toes to give Jett a peck on the cheek, then followed the rest. Another guard took Norm's place, shutting the door behind him.

Lar bent forward next to Clayr's ear and the two of them entered a heated, whispered discussion.

Clayr's voice raised to audible, "...I don't know what he's playing at, but I'm certain it's not good."

They both turned their gaze on Ryn. Silence reigned for several pounding heartbeats. They seemed to be waiting for some cue. When it hit, the room erupted into shouting.

"What were you thinking?" Lar started.

"Mother told you..." Jett began. Ryn glared at him for saying that. He knew exactly what she had been up to.

"How am I supposed to protect you..." Lar kept at it.

"You can't stay here..." Jett said.

"This is a disaster." Lar came forward, pounding his frustration into Clayr's desk.

Zo squeezed Ryn's shoulder.

Clayr had her face buried into her hands, rubbing her forehead with her fingers.

"Enough!" Clayr said. "What's done is done. I have no control over Master Wes and who he takes on as students, so there is nothing we can do except try to make the best of this situation."

Despite saying that, Clayr turned to Ryn, eyes boring into her. "Did your mother neglect to tell you to avoid signing up to study with Master Wes?"

"She was explicit they should not leave the cottage," Lar bit out.

Clayr rubbed her forehead again. "Right, right, right. Nothing we can do now." She turned to Lar. "Will your earth magic protect her here at the Library?"

"The Library is built on grounds sacred to ancient wild magic. I cannot touch the soil here," Lar said.

"What's the point?" Jett asked. "They've already found us."

"Seen you, yes." Lar gestured to the fake beads around Ryn's neck. "But Ryn has clearly managed to fool him into thinking she is someone she is not."

Clayr's eyes narrowed. "Yes." Shifting in her seat she added, "Fortunately the guards who brought her here tonight are guards loyal to me. I had no idea who they had gone to collect. I will make sure they don't disclose where they found you."

"You haven't told him who your parents are, have you?" Lar asked.

Ryn shook her head.

"We'll have to come up with a solid pedigree for you. One that will be obscure enough it will throw him off the trail," Clayr said.

"But if Ryn spends hours in the Library with these people, surely they could use magic to divine where she's from," Jett said.

"As long as she's only around them inside the Library. The foundation cancels Ancestor magic. It's not just a rule that no magic can be done in the Library, it's not physically possible to do magic here. We are all Ordinaries inside the Library," Clayr said.

Ryn was taken aback. A place with no magic? In all the years of living so close to Waatch and the Library, she had no idea. The thought of becoming a Library worker became even more appealing.

"So as long as Ryn stays close to the Library, no one could use a wayfinder to discover where she is from," Lar said.

"Yes, but I'm afraid the cancellation of magic doesn't extend as far as the dorms," Clayr added.

"So, she needs to go home every night so I can protect her," Lar said.

Clayr nodded. "That seems wise."

Ryn did some calculations in her head. "That means I'll have to get up before the sun to get here on time."

"And what of the carriage ride?" Zo asked. "Won't they be able to use magic while she's riding to and from?"

Lar's brow crinkled. "I will make certain she's safe."

"Wait, wait." Ryn held up her hands. "What about Master Wes saying we will need to stay late to study?"

"We'll just have to make it work. You should have considered the complications when you applied to be a student." Lar glared at her.

Yll cleared her throat.

Everyone stopped and stared at her.

"What about me?" Yll asked. "Am I in trouble?"

Clayr jumped up from her seat, ran around the desk to pull Yll from her chair, and crushed her to her chest. After a long moment, Clayr released her, holding her upper arms, tears wetting her face.

"I'm concerned about what Master Wes is up to, and this is not what I had in mind for your entrance into the Library, but no my love, you're not in trouble. This is a better move for you to get into the Library without it looking like I got you the job. I wish I had thought of it. Probably would have if I wasn't so worried." With that, Clayr squeezed her again.

Zo yawned loudly.

Clayr stared at him. "Right, you all have an early morning and there's paperwork you need to sign, and oaths you need to take before you leave tonight." Returning her focus to Yll, she continued, "I don't want you staying in the dorms. You're not old enough. You'll ride back and forth with Ryn every day."

"But Mom..." Yll started.

Clayr shook her head. "If you win the Assistant Researcher position, we'll see, but for now I want you at home every night."

Clayr didn't come to the Library every day. Sometimes she worked from home. When Yll was little, Ryn couldn't remember Clayr being gone much, but she had worked for the Library all her life. There was a residence for the Curator on the Library grounds, but Clayr rarely used it. She'd said many times she preferred her home in the village.

Lar took a sheet of paper from Clayr's desk and began writing. "I need to send a message to Ryette. She needs to know what's happened."

Ryn and Jett exchanged panicked looks.

An urgent knock and the guard opened the door far enough to listen to whoever was outside, then he turned to Clayr and Lar. "Someone from the fire brigade is here. Says Lar is urgently needed at a forest fire that just broke out on the south hill."

Lar cursed.

"I'll escort the kids home," Clayr said. "They'll be fine."

"I need to post this letter," Lar held up the note he'd been writing.

"I'll take care of it." Jett held out his hand. "I have mother's contact information."

Lar quickly folded the letter and passed it to Jett on his way out. Watching Jett pocket it, Ryn tried not to sigh out loud in relief.

"I'll go with you," Zo said to his father.

"You cannot," Lar squeezed his arm. "I'll collect Regg on my way."

Ryn didn't understand why Zo couldn't go, and why he impossibly looked two shades paler.

Clayr put her arm around Yll's waist. "Let's go see to that paperwork and get you all home."

Chapter Eleven

The Library Board of Regents was founded in 520 AO as a balance of power to what is now the Curator's position. At that time, the head of the Library was beating his workers and worse, found to be attempting to sell off rare books. But the Board hasn't always been better.

— Myra de Lux. *A Comprehensive History of the Library.* Ancestral Library, First Floor, History section, Shelf 82, Shelfmark 43.

As Zo was herded with the new students across the cobbled drive between the Library and the guard house, he felt a tug on his shirtsleeve. To his side, Ryn was gesturing for him to lag behind with her.

"Are you alright?" she asked.

Zo shrugged. "Sure."

"You look like you're ill," she said.

His eyes shifted to the boiler room across the grounds, causing him to shudder. "It's not good, Ryn. The apprenticeship, it's worse than anything you could imagine." Zo yawned. "And working nights is far more tiring than staying up all night to play games."

She followed his gaze. "Why do they need to heat the Library when it's summer anyway? Isn't it hot enough already?"

Zo shook his head. "The stone walls are thick, cooling the Library too much. The contents of the Library must be kept at a precise constant temperature. The heat also reduces humidity in the air, keeping things from growing mold."

You could keep things from growing mold? That was news to her. "Wait...you work nights? It's nighttime, are you supposed to be at work?"

Zo shook his head, yawning again. "No, the guards got me the night off so I could help them find you." He shook himself trying to stay awake.

When they got to the door of the guardhouse Zo was pretty much asleep on his feet.

"I'm going to bed. Goodnight," With that, he turned to shuffle off to the dorms, not even registering the hurt look on Ryn's face.

He barely remembered finding his bunk and collapsing into it.

***

Sometime in the middle of the night his healing magic bead glowed hot. Zo groaned.

"No," he whispered and rolled over, piling a pillow on his head. He went back to sleep.

***

Someone kicked his bunk. Once, twice, three times...they kept going until Zo finally lifted his head and squinted at them. Morning sunshine was shining through the windows, but most everyone was still in bed. That was Zo's only clue it was still early.

The bed shook again with another kick. "Get up. Boiler Master wants you now."

Zo somewhat recognized one of the other grunts from the Boiler Room standing over him. He threw his arm over his eyes.

"Tell him to go to..."

"He already lives there, mate, but if you would like to go to jail for breach of contract that's up to you," the grunt said, then kicked the bed again as he walked away.

Right. Jail. Right. At the moment spending long hours sleeping in a cool cell sounded wonderful—but only for a few days, not the rest of his life. With that, he forced himself to sit up. Reaching for his pants, he realized he never took them off last night.

Perfect, fewer things to do.

Running his hands through his hair, he considered it combed. He slipped on his shoes that already had a sheen to them from being too close to the heat, then stumbled his way out of the dorm toward the Boiler Room. He'd only been here a few days, but it already felt like an eternity.

The cold dewy morning signaled summer slowly slipping away. It would start raining in earnest soon. Zo imagined the boiler room would become much hotter, and busier. At least he didn't need to worry about being cold this winter. Too often they had camped in the wet chill of winter, with a damp that seeped into your bones and never seemed to leave. Something he was sure his mother had never experienced.

The cute guard stood at the door to the Boiler Room and Zo instantly regretted his grimy disheveled appearance.

"Morning." The cute one smiled as he opened the door for Zo.

"Yeah," Zo's dry throat croaked out.

His steps grew slower. He dreaded the heat of the boilers. The thought of it made him sweat. Opening the inner door to the heat almost knocked him out. He barely held onto the nausea rising in his stomach.

Hal, Master Nix's assistant, was missing from his desk and all the grunts were busy heating the boilers. Zo didn't see Master Nix anywhere. Not knowing what he was supposed to do, he stood there sweating—and fighting to control his stomach, which was empty so it really shouldn't have been a problem.

Finally, one of the boiler controllers walked by.

"Have you seen Master Nix?" Zo asked. "I was told to report to him."

The controller glanced up from his notepad. "I'll let him know you're here."

Then he went on his way, absently making notes as he walked.

Great, Zo thought, *I could have been in bed still asleep instead of sweating in this wretched place.* If this was a prank someone pulled on him, he was going to flip—no, burn—a few tables.

Heavy footsteps and shouting made Zo stand a little taller. A few days and he was already conditioned to this reaction to the Master.

"There you are!" Master Nix said, as if Zo hadn't been there first. "Still sickly I see. Not enough meat on those bones. No matter, I'm going to train you for something that will hopefully be more fitting with your delicate constitution."

Zo's already heat flushed face burned hotter. He was not delicate. He had many times handled the intense heat of a forest fire. There was just something about the soulless, mindless constant heating of metal in this stuffy, enclosed building that his body objected to.

"Normally, Hal would handle this training, but since he's been called away, I have the misfortune of training your sickly hide." Master Nix took a logbook from Hal's desk, and turned toward the tunnels leading away from the boilers.

Zo watched him go, his mind drifting again to how wonderful a cold jail cell sounded.

Master Nix turned back, "Keep up! I'm grumpy enough I have to crawl around in the tunnels today. Don't make it worse. I have a long list of punishment chores I rather enjoy giving new recruits." He flashed Zo a disturbing grin.

Zo cracked his knuckles on the desk, then followed.

It became instantly clear why Master Nix was unhappy Hal was absent for this job. Whereas Hal was a head shorter than Zo, Master Nix was at least two heads taller and a lot bulkier. Stepping into the tunnels was a tight squeeze around the pipes, which were hot. Master Nix seemed to be impervious to the heat, but it was a tight squeeze, even for Zo. Fortunately, Zo was able to slip though without touching anything. Master Nix didn't have to tell him not to touch the pipes, they radiated enough heat to make that clear.

At the end of their travels through the pipeway tunnel, they reached a junction where water magic users were directing the water from the larger pipes into smaller ones that shot off in different directions. The heat decreased significantly.

One of those using water magic to mix the water and direct it through the piping caught Zo's eye. His arms were muscular, as if the process of moving water required physical effort. He flashed Zo a grin causing Zo to blush, turning to hide his face from Master Nix.

Master Nix's gaze locked on him. Zo cracked his knuckles against his thigh, then shook his hand out. Master Nix grunted. Zo focused on the piping above.

"This is the exchange," Master Nix said, "where you'll report your findings." He pointed to another pipe sprouting out of a different wall. "The water masters mix the hot with the cold to send it through the floor coils. Those coils heat or cool the temperature of the Library." He handed Zo the logbook. "Your job will be to take temperature readings in the Library, and return and report."

Zo gazed back down the tunnel. Why did Master Nix bring them all this way if they needed to go back out and into the Library?

"Follow me, magic healer, I'll show you how to take the Library's temperature." Master Nix winked.

He grabbed a long black bag hanging on the wall, then headed off in the direction of the smaller tangled piping.

The moment he followed Nix into the tunnel his hair stood on end, like he had dived into a pool of water and was cut off from air and sound. He couldn't feel his magic, nor did a snap of his fingers bring fire to his hands. He gasped as if he really was drowning without air.

This was the second time he'd felt this way. The first had been when he had entered the Library on his way to Clayr's office for the announcement that Ryn was one of the five students who would study with Master Wes. Somehow today in this enclosed tunnel it hit him harder.

Master Nix looked back at him and chuckled. "We have entered the realm of the Library now. There is no magic here."

Zo shook his hands out, cracking his knuckles on his thighs. Moving his head to crack his neck, he shook off the odd, muted feeling and proceeded forward after the Master.

The tunnel started wide, but quickly became even tighter than the previous tunnel, with the floor rising to make Master Nix hunch over. The piping, now directly over their heads, was fortunately not as hot, because even hunched over, the Boiler Master barely fit through the tunnel.

Zo ducked to follow, and despite Master Nix's size, Zo had to hurry to keep up—almost banging his head on the piping in several spots where they grew larger and hung lower. Master Nix grumbled the whole time about being too old for crawling in the tunnels and how that's what grunts and useless assistants were for—and why, oh why, couldn't they have made the access shafts closer to the junction?

At last, they came to a corner in the tunnel where it headed off in another direction. Master Nix stopped and set the bag down, wiping the sweat from his brow. Opening the bag, he gently removed a long glass cylinder with a curious glass bubble inside filled with a red liquid, and a small round coin hanging from it.

"This is a thermoscope," Master Nix explained. Pointing to a line on the cylinder he said, "If the air in the Library is the right temperature, the top of this glass bubble will just meet this line. If it's too cold the bubble will rise, if it's too hot the bubble will sink."

Master Nix pointed to metal rungs that stuck out from the walls. "Climb the ladder. At each floor of the Library is a small door. Open the door and set the thermoscope on the table on the other side of the door." He handed Zo a small hourglass timer. "Turn the timer and wait. When the timer is done, record if the bubble is where it should be, or—" he pointed to the tiny lines on the cylinder Zo hadn't noticed, "—how many degrees colder or hotter it is." He handed Zo the notebook and a pencil. "After you've done all the floors, come back down and we'll head to the next corner of the Library."

Zo marveled at the delicate glass device. At the moment, the bubble was slightly lower than the middle line where it was supposed to be. He guessed the warm pipes above him added to the heat. He was certainly sweating, but not as much as in the boiler room.

Master Nix returned the thermoscope to its bag and tied it shut, looping the timer into the tie so it hung from the sack.

"Put your arms through here." Master Nix held out two straps for Zo's arms, then adjusted them so the bag was securely on his back. "Climb. At each door there is a seat for you to sit and wait. *Do not drop* or break the thermoscope! They are fragile and difficult to make."

Lastly, Master Nix handed him the logbook.

"Can you put that in the bag?" Zo asked.

Master Nix shook his head. "Nothing in the bag but the scope. Anything banging against it could break it."

"How am I supposed to climb with a logbook in my hands?"

"Figure it out," Master Nix said as he sat with his back to the tunnel wall, legs stretched out, arms folded, he closed his eyes, and almost instantly began to snore.

"Great," Zo muttered. Shoving the logbook into his waistband, he took hold of the rungs and began to climb.

***

The good news was this job was much cooler than the boiler room. The bad news was it was incredibly boring. At least with heating boilers he got to hone and perfect his use of fire magic. Here, he had to sit and wait for the timer with absolutely nothing to do, or anything interesting to look at, except the snippet of the Library he could see from the doorway, but that became old really quickly. One floor had bookshelves near the doorway, and he sat reading the titles. He was tempted to climb out of the shaft and grab a book to read, but the square opening for the thermoscope was barely big enough for him to squeeze through. Plus, he was well aware of how strict the Library was about access. Even though Master Nix hadn't mentioned it, he was pretty sure he was not allowed to enter through that door. Barely big enough to slide the thermoscope through, he was sure if he was supposed to be on the other side, they would have made the opening bigger. Still, the thought was appealing. He didn't see anyone near the doorway, and he could most likely get away with reading while he waited. He wondered if getting caught would land him in jail. Probably.

At the top floor the seat was tiny, causing him to fumble the scope while bracing himself with his knees. He caught the scope just before it fell down the shaft. Sweat poured down the sides of his face. It was much warmer at the top.

After sliding the scope back in its bag, he headed down. His arms and legs were tired from climbing, and his muscles shook. About halfway down the ladder, Zo's foot slipped off the rung. Terror shot through him as he dangled from one hand over the black pit of a hole beneath him. His one sweaty palm tightened on the rung as his body twisted to the side. The bag with the thermoscope banged up against the shaft wall. The sound of tinkling made acid rise in his stomach. He really hoped the scope hadn't broken. The fact that his back wasn't wet was encouraging.

Pain spiked through his shoulder. The slip had pulled hard on his arm, and holding all of his weight with that arm was making his eyes water and sting. Swinging around to get his feet back under him, he stifled a cry of pain. He awkwardly climbed the rest of the way down the ladder barely using the one arm. When he finally got to the bottom, he hung at a weird angle, then dropped to the ground like a sack of grain.

Master Nix was instantly on his feet, grabbing at the bag on Zo's back to keep Zo from crushing it.

"Ahhhh!" Zo cried out when the straps jerked his arm backward.

"What did you do?" Master Nix roared.

"Slipped," Zo bit out.

Master Nix ripped the bag off Zo, then delicately opened it and removed the scope. Both Zo and Master Nix sighed in relief at the sight of the scope still intact and unhurt.

Zo swore, hand going to his shoulder. It felt like it was falling apart.

Master Nix tapped Zo on the collar bone next to his beads. "We'll take you out of the Library boundaries so you can heal that up, then we can head to the next shaft."

Zo leaned back against the wall. The cool wall felt good on his shoulder blade. "I can't."

"What do you mean you can't? You have healing magic!"

"BECAUSE I CAN'T!" Zo's anger was fed by the pain shooting through his arm.

"This is unbelievable. I have a healing magic grunt who can't even use his magic. You know, I only agreed to take you on *because* you had healing magic? I should have realized with you being sickly all the time, but I leave healing magic to the experts. This is going to waste my day, and now I'll have to pull someone in to finish this job. If the temperature is off by even a degree for too long it will be all of our hides!"

The Boiler Master shouldered the thermoscope bag, grabbed Zo by his good arm, and dragged him back down the tunnel in a fury. Zo was certain Master Nix was going to damage his other arm, but there was little he could do. His eyes were watering so bad from the pain that he could barely see. Master Nix yelled to the masters at the junction, then continued to drag Zo down the tunnel. At one point Zo stumbled and fell against a hot pipe, burning his side through his thin shirt.

The rest of the journey was a blur of pain. He was dimly aware of them passing through the boiler room. When Master Nix pulled him outside into the fresh air, Zo gulped it down while the Master called to the guards for a wagon. By the time Zo heard horses and wheels on the cobblestones, he was shaking badly and could barely stand. Someone opened the door to the back of the wagon, and

Master Nix hefted him inside. Then the door slammed shut, and a bolt slid across, locking him inside. It was then he noticed the bars on the window in the door.

Zo's heart pounded and his mind raced.

What?... No.

He didn't screw up that badly, did he? He leaned forward far enough to see out the small window. Master Nix said something to a Library guard, then angrily pointed past the gate. Zo swallowed hard. This morning, he had contemplated how he might find some rest in jail, but he was absolutely not serious about it. The wagon took off at a brisk clip and Zo's injured shoulder smacked against the wall of the carriage. Alone, terrified, and in pain, he watched as they passed through the Library gates on his way to the Waatch jail.

Chapter Twelve

It's never been proven or tested that magic from the father is stronger in the sons, or girls performing better with their mother's magic. I think it's purely an affinity based on tradition. I've seen plenty of boys excel at their mother's magic, and House Ignis girls who can pitch a fireball every bit as well as their fathers.

— Lyv de Dico. "Ancestral Culture and its Effect on Youth." *Journal of Mind Magic Medicine.* Ancestral Library, Periodicals Section, Second Floor, Shelf 100, Box 2.

Ryn stepped out of the carriage, feeling the weight of the Library once again press down on her. In the early morning light, an eagle soared in to rest upon the top of the bell tower. Ryn swallowed hard, hoping this had been the right decision. Jett had burned Lar's note to their mother, so no one was coming to rescue her. From this point on, she was on her own. The idea had sounded thrilling when she decided to do it. Now it seemed like a rash decision that was going to get her into a lot of trouble. There was no way out now but through this path, so she picked up her skirts and headed up the stairs toward the Library front doors.

Yll bounced up beside her like they were little girls headed out to play tag in the woods. Of course, the Library had always been a topic of discussion, because of both their mothers' jobs and the whole village revolving around the Library and what happened inside, but Ryn never knew Yll was so anxious to work here. It was assumed they would both most likely end up working for the Library, probably in the gardens or the kitchen, but it seemed more inevitable and less like a dream job. Yet here they were, fighting to get one open position. What would they do if one of them got the job and the other didn't? Would Yll be bitter? Would Ryn?

At the top of the stairs, the Library front doors loomed over her. Made of wood and polished to a high shine, they were carved with an image of a tree spanning the height and width of both doors. Upon close examination, each branch had an Ancestral family name. A small door seamlessly fitting into the larger doors opened to admit them. When she entered, Ryn felt the hairs on her skin stand up. Her skirts crackled, clinging to her legs, but just as she turned to say something to Yll, she found herself inside the entry, and staring up at a ceiling three stories tall. The ceiling was topped with a dome and covered in a lifelike painting of Praedo slaying the Dragon. The painting was so vibrant and alive for a moment she thought she was seeing an actual dragon flying above them.

With her head tilted backward staring in wonder, she tripped over her hem, stumbling forward. Strong hands caught her around the shoulders and kept her from falling. Ryn's gaze shifted from the ceiling into the face of a smiling guard, barely older than she was, with the kind of open, smooth face that broke many girl's hearts, and instantly made Ryn feel inadequate. His smile was half amused, half pleased with himself. He held onto her longer than was necessary to steady her.

"Hello," the guard said, his grin widening.

"Well done, Fergus," Clayr said, coming in the door behind them.

"Yes, Madame Curator," Fergus said with a bow, releasing Ryn.

Clayr led them across the foyer at a brisk clip. "Bring your credentials to the reception desk, girls."

Ryn found it hard to follow at Clayr's pace. Putting one foot in front of the other, her eyes were drawn everywhere at once. The giant statue of Praedo the Dragon Slayer in the middle of the circular room had his hands stretched to either side of a case containing an ancient looking book. The case seemed to radiate light, but she could detect no source for it.

Against the walls of the rotunda, were statues of each of the original twelve ancestors—those who had been the Dragon Slayer's loyal friends and went with him into battle against the dragon. Each of them held a symbol of their house magic. Ryn stopped across from Ignis. He held a small flame in the palm of his hand. It was surprising how much Lar looked like him, but Zo didn't. Ryn walked the line of ancestors till she found Madame Sano. The Ancestor held a round flat flower in her hand. Ryn had never seen that type of flower before, but she knew it was the symbol for healing. She could see more of Zo's features in this ancestor. He must take more after his mother and her healing side. Examining all the faces in the circle, she didn't see anyone who looked like her, and she didn't feel drawn to any of them. The only feeling that came was one of being out of place.

"Ryn," Clayr hissed, beckoning her over to the desk set at the back of the rotunda.

Hurrying in that direction, Ryn's pace again slowed as her eyes caught hold of the mosaic floor done in vibrant blues and greens that became a giant map of the Ancestral islands. Each island was named and marked with a small home, where she assumed each Great Ancestral Homes stood on that island. It was a captivating work of art. Ryn had a hard time tearing her eyes away.

Clayr cleared her throat and Ryn focused her eyes on getting to the desk before she got distracted by another wondrous thing.

"Give your study permits to the receptionists and they will date them and stamp them," Clayr said.

Ryn pulled her papers from an old satchel she had borrowed from her mother's room to carry her papers neat and orderly. The receptionist took them, and even with Clayr standing right there, she read through them, checked them with a ledger she had in front of her, then signed, dated, and stamped them.

"Thumb." The receptionist held out her hand.

Ryn gave Clayr a quizzical look. Clayr gave a curt nod.

Tentatively, Ryn held out her hand. The receptionist took it, grabbed a pointed tool, and jabbed Ryn's thumb with it. Flinching, she jerked her hand back, but the receptionist held it in a vise-like grip, squeezing her thumb until a large drop of blood formed. The receptionist turned the stamped paper around and pressed Ryn's thumb to a box on the paper. Rocking it back and forth, she got a good bloody thumbprint, then released Ryn.

"You are now bound to the Library as a student until such a time as your studies come to an end," the receptionist said.

Clayr pursed her lips, worry lines appeared all over her face. Yll was sucking her thumb, an image that took Ryn back to when they were very little.

"Come now, let's get you to Master Wes' research alcove." Clayr held out her arms to herd Yll and Ryn like a mother hen.

"I can do that for you, Madame Curator," Fergus' voice came from right next to Ryn, startling her. She hadn't seen him approach.

Clayr looked flustered, her eyes shifting to the sun now shining through the windows above the doors, then to the guard who had already taken Fergus' place there, then back to Ryn and Yll. Clearly, she had someplace she needed to be, but also didn't want to abandon Yll and Ryn.

Fergus' reassuring smile must have won out.

"Alright." Clayr hugged Yll, then Ryn. "If I have a chance, I'll meet you for lunch," she said, disappearing into the Library through a darkened archway.

"My ladies." Fergus bowed with a flourish then offered his arms to the girls.

They had only taken a few steps when Ryn stopped short, pulling Fergus and Yll back. The archway Clayr had disappeared through had writing on it. Written in the Ancient language Praedo brought with him, which he taught to the Ancestors. Knowledge and use of it had been so guarded over the years that most of Ancestor blood no longer understood it, but it was fashionable to use words and phrases, even if its meaning was somewhat lost. Ryn had tutors who had taught her a bit of it, even though she wasn't Ancestor born. The words before her were unfamiliar, yet she somehow understood them:

"When Praedo came to end the strife.
Holding great power he set on the quest,
To conquer the dragon, to vanquish the test.
With twelve companions to fight at his side..."

"What was that?" Fergus asked.

Ryn pointed to the words over the archway.

Fergus gave her a curious look, then gently pulled her into the depths of a building only a few privileged people ever got to see.

"Did you bring a lunch with you?" Fergus asked, interrupting Ryn's awe of the rows upon rows of books just waiting to be researched.

"Hmmmm?" Ryn asked.

"Yes, we brought lunch." Yll patted the side of her bag. "We weren't sure if we would have enough time to go out and get food."

"Good thought. In that case, we will make a quick stop in the cloakroom where you can leave your lunches. No food allowed in the Library," Fergus said.

"Why, because it will attract pests?" Ryn asked.

Yll chuckled.

"Smart, but no," Fergus said. "The Library is built on a site that used to be devoted to the wild magic. From ancient times, animals and insects have been repelled from it. That's why the ancients chose this place to build the Library. It's an added layer of protection. Didn't you feel the static power when you walked through the door?"

The crackling in her hair and on her skirts came back to her mind. "Oh! Yes."

"That's the power that repels pests," Yll said, twirling her finger around. "It also prevents the use of magic within these walls."

Fergus showed them a cubby in the long cloakroom where they could put their things. They didn't have cloaks to hang yet, but that would soon change. Ryn had felt the nip of fall in the air when they left the house before sunrise.

As they walked toward the research alcoves, Fergus regaled them with tales of the Library. He pointed to a blacked pillar and told them about a worker who had dropped a lantern and nearly caught the Library on fire.

"Rumor is they hanged him for it," Fergus whispered dramatically.

"Oh my," Yll said.

Fergus went on—one story after another. All of them about people who had broken Library rules and had been subsequently punished.

"My father caught a researcher attempting to remove materials from the Library." Fergus paused. "That researcher's still in prison."

Fergus turned a bookshelf corner and the walls opened up to a large room with a row of smaller rooms running down the center.

"Here we are," Fergus said. "Master Wes has reserved the first three of these rooms. Must have cost him a lot of coin, those research alcoves aren't cheap to rent."

Fergus paused, a troubled frown briefly crossing his face, then shifted back to his open smile.

"Let me know if I can be of any assistance," Fergus said. "If you ever decide to go out to the restaurant district for lunch, I'll be happy to escort you." Fergus' stomach growled on que.

Yll giggled.

"We'll let you know," Ryn promised.

With that, Fergus bowed again then disappeared into the gloom of the Library.

"He's cute." Yll nudged Ryn.

"Yeah," Ryn replied, but she was focused on the alcoves and the light coming from their arched doorways.

"First bell's gonna ring, we better hurry." Yll grabbed Ryn's hand and pulled her forward.

***

The bell tower sounded surprisingly loud inside the Library, striking first bell and the official start of the Library day. Ryn watched docents in light blue dresses with frilly white smocks, and researchers in severe high necked, black dresses hurrying to their duties past the alcove. Seated around the table with Ryn and Yll were the others who had won a spot to study with Master Wes: Iden, Thalya, and of course, Prym.

Prym was red-faced, and her eyes were full of wrath. Iden had his arm around her shoulders, his hand gently rubbing her arm. If he was trying to calm her, she didn't look calmed.

Master Wes stepped through the doorway just as the bell finished ringing.

"Good, everyone is here, let's get started." He gestured for the docent following him to set the stack of books they carried on the table, then told them to leave and shut the door.

The docent gave him a sidelong look, but did as instructed, closing the door as they left.

Master Wes handed them each a book from the stack.

"This book contains instructions for how to use the Library." Master Wes glanced at Yll. "If you don't already know, that is. I expect you to read it, study it, ask questions of the docents and researchers and be ready to work by tomorrow morning."

Iden choked on that.

"This is an advanced class, de Dico, if you can't handle it, I can bump up the next qualified candidate, it's not too late to do so." Master Wes glared.

Iden held up his hands in surrender.

"Your training will revolve around one very specific research project, which will make the results measurable and quantifiable...the first person who is able to find the information I seek will be the winner of the Library position. This research topic is to be secret. You must not ask for help with the topic directly from any Library worker. You may ask for help with general questions, but nothing about the research. This is to prevent cheating from those who could ask for help in high places." Master Wes' eyes again fell on Yll, much to Ryn's indignation. Prym's father was on the Board of Regents, the governing board of the Library, a position of power higher than Clayr's.

"If I hear of anyone associated with the Library knowing the topic of this research project it will mean automatic expulsion from my tutelage. Is that clear?"

The five of them nodded.

"I need verbal confirmation before we proceed," Master Wes said.

They went around the table, Iden, Prym, Thalya, Yll, and Ryn all agreed to keep the research secret.

"Good." Master Wes pulled a small scroll from inside his coat and placed it on the table.

"This is your research project," Master Wes said.

Prym reached out and unrolled the scroll. They all gathered around to get a better look.

On the scroll was an old-style picture, like it was from an ancient manuscript, of a man riding a horse. He had a lute slung across his back, a piece of paper in one hand, and a pen in the other. He was in the act of writing something.

Yll gasped.

Iden grunted. "The illusive and mythical Luc."

"Are you kidding me?" Thalya said. "There are no records of Luc, despite the legend of him being Praedo's scribe. They don't exist, because he didn't exist. It's just a tall tale told to entertain children."

Yll was pale, her hand pressed to her mouth.

Ryn had heard tales of Luc around the fire in the evening when bedtime stories were told. Her mother had never approved when her father told them of Luc. For some reason she hated that tale, but Ryn had loved it. It was full of adventure and mystery. The thought of how Luc had disappeared from all recorded history would keep her up late into the night. Perhaps that was why her mother hated the telling of it. It never made Ryn ready for bed, but kept her wide-awake, imagining.

"This task is impossible." Prym shoved the picture back toward Master Wes. "There are no records of Luc in the Library or anywhere. Give us a more suitable task. Father would not approve of this nonsense."

"On the contrary," Master Wes said, "I have already received approval from your father to set this task for you all."

Prym's jaw dropped.

"So, you're saying our assignment is to find evidence of the one person, for whom there are no records, in a Library with the most complicated system of shelving in the world, with no help from those who actually know how to use the Library?" Iden asked.

"That is correct." Master Wes stared them each in the eyes. "Scour the Library. Bring any evidence you find of Luc to me." He pointed to the paper in Luc's hands in the picture. "The person who finds me the legendary book of Luc's writings wins for themselves the title of Library Researcher."

Chapter Thirteen

The day I received my bead was a strange day. It felt like I was walking through a dream. Everyone made such a fuss, I thought there would be some huge explosion of magic or something. Instead, they hung the bead around my neck and...that was it. The rest of the day was just a long string of standing around being congratulated by adults. I didn't even get a chance to eat the salmon cream puffs. The explosion happened the next day when my lessons started...

— As quoted to Cheryl de Muto in Of Magic, Myth and Lore- Commentary and Anecdotes *from the people of Waatch, the Library, and the Surrounding Area.* Ancestral Library, First Floor, Lore Room, Shelf 29, Shelfmark 33.

Time floated by in a strange way. Every moment, Zo was struggling to catch his breath and deal with the pain. The jail was not far from the Library, just a few streets over, yet it was taking them forever to get there. It must be how much pain he was in, or how every breath was happening too fast or too slow. He squeezed his eyes shut as he clutched his bad arm to keep it from being jostled in the wagon. His focus became getting from one moment to the next.

When at last the wagon stopped, terror gripped him. This was it. He wondered if they would let him send a message to his dad. Certainly, he could come and bail Zo out of this? But no, his father had said they would put him in jail as well if Zo failed. His mother held a position of high power on the Healing Council on Eileansano, but the thought of calling on that power made him want to put his fist through a wall—with his bad arm.

The bolt slid aside and arms reached in to pull him down out of the wagon. Blinking in the sunlight, Zo's eyes adjusted to the sight of the building the wagon was parked in front of. It was not jail.

It was far worse.

Zo would recognize a Healing House anywhere. They all had the same wood structure meant to look like it was grown instead of built, but the ostentatious pillars and twisty carved entryway was clearly unnatural. What it spoke of was power. The power to restore health...and the power to turn away those who couldn't pay.

He had spent the first ten years of his life growing up around a Healing House. Mostly being patted on the head and sent to a corner to get him out of the way of boys whose patriarchal line was healing magic. He knew they only kept him around because of his mother.

"Easy now." Norm, the guard from the previous night, and the cute Fergus, steadied Zo as he tried to stand on wobbly legs.

"Come, we'll get you to a Healer and get you fixed up quick," Fergus said.

Zo glared up at the Healing House.

Norm and Fergus started to pull him forward.

Zo planted his feet. "No."

"What?" Norm said, still trying to move Zo forward.

"NO," Zo affirmed, digging in his heels.

"But..." Fergus glanced at Norm. "You have healing magic, they can't turn you away, it's not like you're a street urchin. Besides, the Library has an account with the Healing House, they will pay the bill."

Zo's anger flared at the thought of walking through those doors and asking help from Healers. It wouldn't take long to figure out who he was and for word would get back to his mother. The last thing he wanted was his mother involved in his life right now.

"No. I won't set foot in a Healing House," Zo affirmed.

Fergus' jaw dropped a little. Norm sighed, turning to a small building directly across the street from the Healing House.

"Lucky for you, the physician is just across the street," Norm said. "It's usually for those who can't afford the Healers, but..." Norm shrugged.

Norm and Fergus supported Zo to walk slowly across the street to the building that looked more like a home than a place to receive health care.

When they reached the door, Fergus knocked.

"Come!" came a voice from inside.

Fergus opened the door and Norm helped Zo inside.

"What do we have today, boys?" A gray-haired man sat wrapping a woman's arm.

"Boiler Room accident," Norm said.

The man grunted. "Sit him down, I'll be with you in a moment."

Norm eased Zo onto a bench by the door. The place had all kinds of herbs hanging from the ceiling and it smelled of pungent salves. Despite being an all-out assault on the nose, he found it somewhat soothing. The thought of lying down on the bench sounded wonderful and Zo began to slide in that direction. Norm put a hand on his good shoulder to keep him upright.

The gray-haired man tied off the woman's bandage, gave her a jar of something, and sent her off with a promise from her that she would return in a few days. Then he turned to Zo.

"I'm Wilmar, Waatch's resident physician, and who might you be?" he asked.

"Zo."

Wilmar eyed the beads at Zo's neck. "Just Zo?"

"Yes."

"Where's the burn?" Wimar asked.

The pain in Zo's shoulder fed the glare he gave the physician.

Norm chuckled. "Falling accident this time. No burns. Hurt his arm."

"May I?" Wilmar asked, pointing to the arm Zo cradled.

Zo rolled his eyes. Wilmar must have taken that as consent, because his fingers delicately probed Zo's injured shoulder.

"Dislocated," he announced, moving to a shelf to sort through the bottles till he found what must have been the right one. He poured some of it into a mug and added some water, stirring. "Drink this, it will help with the pain and relax the muscles."

Zo sniffed suspiciously at the mug. Then his eyes caught Wilmar's face. He hated healing and all its forms. Even this primitive form without magic made his palm itch to produce flames. He gazed over the mug at the physician. There was something about his face though, and his presence that relaxed Zo into trusting the man. Zo downed the mug's contents, which tasted nasty. It was like a combination of all the herbs Zo had ever smelled in the wild, but never actually wanted to taste.

"Good." Wilmar nodded, turning to Norm and Fergus. "It will be a few minutes before it takes effect. Please stay so you can help me hold him while I restore his shoulder. After that, I'll need him to remain here tonight so we can ice that shoulder and make him comfortable."

Norm nodded. "Sure Wilmar, whatever you need."

"What I need.... What I need is Nix to stop sending me burned, beaten up, heat stroked patients. Tell him to stop abusing his fire workers. Just because it's Library work doesn't mean he can waste them," Wilmar ranted.

Norm chuckled. "You say that every time we bring someone in, and I promise I do tell him. You know he doesn't listen."

Wilmar grunted. "I'm going to start charging him double."

"You know Nix sends injuries to you because the Healers charge too much. He saves the Healing House account for the big accidents," Fergus said.

Zo wondered at the fact that Master Nix had sent him to the Healing House. Was this considered a big accident? Would Zo's stubbornness mean his shoulder wouldn't heal properly? His heart struggled to quicken at that thought, but he found himself getting drowsy instead. He sagged against Norm's hand, making Norm scrabble to keep him from falling.

"It's taking effect. Pull him forward so I can manipulate his arm," Wilmar said.

As Norm held Zo, Wilmar did stuff to Zo's arm he barely registered, then with a quick pop, and cry of extreme pain Zo barely registered he made, it was done. Relief swept through him.

Wilmar sent Fergus to an icehouse out back while the process of wrapping his arm began. After the ice was securely wrapped to Zo's shoulder, Wilmar had Fergus and Norm help move Zo to a bed, then he dismissed them. Removing Zo's shirt the rest of the way, Wilmar found Zo's burned side.

"Liars, there is a burn!" Wilmar grumbled.

Zo wanted to tell him they didn't know about the burn, but his brain wasn't presently operating his mouth.

After treating the burn with another odorous paste, Wilmar finally let him lie down.

"Rest now. We'll add more ice and get you more medicine when you wake." Wilmar's voice was so gentle, Zo relaxed straight into sleep.

***

Drifting in and out of consciousness, Zo was vaguely aware of other patients coming and going. At last, he woke to the sound of a small child crying and found the ice on his shoulder had melted and the burning at his side returned. Wilmar's voice was calm and soothing, but the crying only increased. Curious, Zo struggled to sit up with only one arm, groggily attempting to avoid touching his burnt side. He winced at his failure.

The sight that greeted him when he finally succeeded was a small child in a ragged dress seated on an exam table, her leg clearly at an unnatural angle. Wilmar was slowly and calmly talking to her, but every time his hands came close to her leg, her crying increased till he moved his hand away. Zo stood up dizzily behind Wilmar, turning the girl's focus to him. Her crying lessened. Eyes crossed, he stuck out his tongue, pretending to try to touch the tip of his tongue to the tip of his nose. She didn't laugh but she stopped crying.

"Which came first," Zo asked. "The dragon or the egg?"

The girl gave a slight shrug with her shoulder.

"The egg. The dragon was late because he was draggin'."

She just blinked at him.

"Get it? Draggin' like dragging, you know, tired?"

Oh boy. He must be really desperate if he was resorting to the kind of terrible jokes Regg used to love to tell.

A slight smile appeared on her tear-stained face.

While Zo held her attention, Wilmar went to work, easing her to lie down and examining the injury. Zo found a couple of twigs leftover from herbs on Wilmar's workbench. Using his one good hand he clumsily bent them into funny looking stick people. They made strange characters, but awkwardly on his lap with one good hand and one hand barely free of his shoulder wrappings, he used them to perform a play he had seen traveling puppeteers do many times. The girl giggled weakly as one puppet hit the other over the head. Wilmar prepared a concoction from the same jar he'd used on Zo earlier. Once it was ready, the girl let Zo help her sit up so she could drink the herbs. When she wrinkled her nose at it, Zo made her laugh by holding his nose and blowing out his cheeks. When her cup was empty, they had eased her back to a lying position, the girl let Zo hold her hand.

When she was drowsy enough, Wilmar set her broken leg, clean and quick. The girl cried out, squeezing Zo's hand, tears tracing down her cheeks, but Zo sang to her a lullaby his mother used to sing him to sleep with as a child. He had forgotten all about it. It had popped into his head like it had never left. He wiped away the girl's tears which left dirt streaks across her cheeks. Wilmar wrapped and splinted her leg. When he was done, the girl drifted off to sleep, but Zo didn't let go of her hand.

Wilmar busied himself putting away the supplies he had used and cleaning his workbench. He gave Zo a curious look.

"You're good at this," Wilmar said.

Zo shook his head. "Naw, I just remembered some stuff from my childhood that helped."

"No, I'm serious, you have a healer's touch."

"Don't say that," Zo said.

"Why?"

"I don't want to be a Healer. All they care about is the power they hold over people."

Wilmar brushed some herbs he had crushed into a jar. "I suppose that can be true."

A twinge in his shoulder made Zo wince.

"Sit." Wilmar gestured to the bed Zo had left. "I'll get you more ice."

Zo let go of the girl's hand and returned to his bed while Wilmar took a bag and an ice pick from the wall by the back door and headed out into what looked to be a garden beyond. The muscles surrounding his shoulder and his side flared in pain as he eased himself to sit on the bed, scooting his back against the wall. He wondered how long it would take to heal enough to return to work in the Boiler Room and if Nix would even care. He certainly couldn't climb ladders in this condition. Master Nix hadn't sent him to jail when he got injured, but how long would he let Zo recover was another question. He'd probably put him back on heating boilers, the thought of which made Zo sweaty and queasy.

"Here we go." Wilmar came back in with a bag full of ice and some herbs from the garden. "We'll get you some more pain reliever, then get you all iced up for the night."

Wimar made him drink more of the nasty stuff, which was harder to do when not motivated by extreme pain. Once he'd choked it down, Wilmar removed the wet clothes and rewrapped ice to his shoulder and side. While he worked, he talked to Zo. Using his soothing voice, he told him all about how he discovered he loved helping people heal, but he was an Ordinary with no healing magic. He had apprenticed himself to the former Waatch physician and taken his place when he retired.

"Physicians wear out quickly," Wilmar chuckled. "We are on call day and night, and we can't heal ourselves like Healers can."

The medicine, with the sound of Wilmar's voice, plus the gentle ways his hands moved to wrap Zo's hurts, put him into a state of relaxation he couldn't recall experiencing in a long time.

"Let me teach you some breathing techniques that will help you manage the pain...among other things," Wilmar said.

Zo stiffened. "The Healers meditate to find calm so they can heal."

Wilmar waved his hands as if to dispel Zo's rise in anger. "Not meditation, just breathing."

Wilmar began to walk Zo through a basic box breath. He vaguely recalled Madame Sano trying to teach it to him during one of his first healing lessons. The memory put fuel on the anger simmering just below Zo's surface. Wilmar gave him a cross look, obviously sensing Zo was not focusing. Taking a deep breath Zo shoved the memory aside and focused on following Wilmar's voice. When Wilmar let him return his breathing to normal, Zo felt himself sinking into sleep. Wilmar helped settle him down into the bed.

"Sleep now," he said, pulling the curtain around the bed, blocking out his work lights.

Zo drifted off into a deep, dreamless sleep.

***

In the middle of the night Zo woke to crying again. He fumbled with the curtains and struggled to sit up. Wilmar's treatment room was dark. Zo stumbled his way in the half light, guided by sound, to the side of the little girl. He found a hand to hold, while her other hand clutched at his bandages. Gingerly, he sat on her bed to wrap his one good arm around her so he could hold her. Her crying settled to hiccups by the time Wilmar made his way into the room, dressed in a nightshirt and holding a lantern aloft.

"You saved me again." Wilmar yawned. "I'll get you both some more medicine that'll get you through the rest of the night."

Zo swallowed hard at the thought of drinking the nasty stuff again, but the relief it brought was appealing. If he could just use his healing magic, he wouldn't have to endure any of this. He could be healed and on his way by now. He started to reach inside for his healing magic, but the touch of it made his anger rise, causing the magic to slip away. The girl hiccupped and hugged his arm like some kind of stuffed toy.

Wilmar brought the medicine, and when the girl shook her head at it, Zo sighed and drank his first. Watching his example, she tentatively took her cup and drank it, her face wrinkling in distaste.

"I know how you feel," Zo said.

When she released the cup she grabbed onto Zo's arm again, holding it like she never planned to let him go. Wilmar went to a wooden box, rummaging around until he returned with a stuffed, knitted cat. The girl squealed in delight and Wilmar replaced Zo's arm with the stuffed cat. As she settled down to sleep, Zo reluctantly returned to his bunk.

Wilmar got him some more ice, settled him down, then gave him a wistfully sad half smile before taking his lantern with him back to bed.

Despite the medicine in his system, Zo didn't drift off to sleep right away. Everything about Wilmar and his place felt so right to him, but even the slightest touch of his healing magic made him burn with anger. The dichotomy of those two things made Zo toss and turn, trying to get comfortable, till the drug finally got the best of him and the darkness of sleep took him at last.

Chapter Fourteen

The two powers of the Board of Regents and the Curator's office have clashed through the centuries. That's why the Library system is so antiquated. Neither side could agree long enough to make changes. Clayr has been the only Curator in generations to make any kind of change. Allowing Ordinaries to work in the Library was a bold move. The Board attempted to stop her, but apparently there's no Library law that says a worker has to be of Ancestor descent.

— Myra de Lux. *A Comprehensive History of the Library*. Ancestral Library, First Floor, History section, Shelf 82, Shelfmark 43.

The morning had dawned way too early for Ryn. It was getting dark earlier. At the height of summer, by the time she rolled out of bed the sun had been up long enough to make her feel as if she had slept in. She hated winter. It was dark when she got up and dark before dinner. She hated the dark. Yawning, she watched the trees roll by from the carriage. It had been cold last night, and the recent rain made it dark earlier, causing a few of the leaves up at the top of the trees to turn yellow. Fall was definitely on its way. Getting up early would get harder and harder.

Yll was dozing in her seat when they reached the Library, barely stirring when the carriage came to a jerky stop. She was still yawning when they entered the alcove and went straight to work studying the instruction books Master Wes gave them to learn about Library research. Prym sat hunched over the book, hands shielding her from everyone else like she was embarrassed to be seen with the rest of them. Ryn noticed she rarely turned the pages. Yll was pacing and mumbling to herself while she read, like she was trying to memorize the book or something. Thalya sat thumbing through her copy like she was speed reading.

Ryn tried to absorb everything as quickly as she could. At one point she leaned back to stretch—and realized Iden was missing.

"Where's Iden?" Ryn asked.

"Shhhhh," was Thalya's response.

Prym looked up. "That new guy in the village—the one you like to hang out with—had an accident yesterday in the Boiler Room. Iden went to check on him." Prym sneered.

"What?" Ryn said, shooting to her feet. "I need to go find him."

Thalya pulled on Ryn's skirt. "Sit down. We're not going anywhere. We can't leave the Library till they ring for mealtime."

Ryn shook her off and joined Yll in pacing. Zo was hurt? How hurt? Lar was gone, and where was Regg? Oh yeah, he went with Lar. There was nobody around but her, and she hadn't even known. Nobody had told her. Looking down at her book on the table, her mind scattered. Grabbing the book, she left the alcove. She needed to walk, and think, and calm down. She reached the line where the alcove great room became bookshelves and paused. It was time to put what she'd read so far into practice.

First things first, she needed to know where to find the reference books. According to the research book, reference books contained the directions for finding the sources she would need. The big question was—where were the reference books kept? The only way to find out seemed to be to ask. Master Wes said they could get help with the use of the Library, just not help with their specific research. The thing was, she didn't know where to find someone to help her. There was no one about this early. The students had all gotten to the Library as soon as it opened, but before first bell. She did know one place she could find someone, which was at the reception desk in the grand foyer. It was also a place she actually knew how to get to, so it was the best choice to start.

When she got to the reception desk, she was surprised to find the blond apple farmer's sister who had been eating lunch with Zo when Ryn had come to apply to be a student. Had she been there when Ryn got there that morning? Ryn couldn't remember.

"Hello," the girl smiled at Ryn.

"Hello...I'm sorry, I've forgotten your name," Ryn said.

"Brynd," the girl smiled. "How can I help you?"

"I saw you with Zo a while back. Do you know what happened? If he's alright?" Ryn asked.

"Oh yeah, he got hurt in the Boiler Room yesterday and Master Nix sent him to the Healers," Brynd said.

"I heard that. Where is he now? How's he doing?"

Brynd shrugged. "He hasn't come back."

That wasn't very helpful, but she couldn't do anything about it at the moment. Time to focus on what she had brought her to the reception desk.

Ryn held up the book on doing research. "I want to try to put what I'm learning into practice. Where do I find the reference books mentioned in here?"

"Oh! Certainly, we have been instructed to help Master Wes' students with whatever they need." Brynd turned to the other person at the reception desk and told them she'd be back shortly, then guided Ryn toward the interior of the Library. As Ryn turned to follow her, she noticed Fergus once again standing guard at the front door. She knew he hadn't been there when she had arrived earlier that morning. He gave her a suppressed smile, like he was fighting a grin, but playing the serious guard. He winked at her. She returned with a tentative smile and slow wave of her fingers then hurried after Brynd.

Brynd showed her to a large room adjacent to the research alcoves with rows upon rows of floor to ceiling shelves. Books in all sorts of odd shapes, sizes, and colors packed the shelves. Ryn was completely overwhelmed.

Snapping shut the jaw she hadn't realized had dropped, Ryn asked, "Where do I start?"

Brynd gave a soft laugh. "What are you trying to find?"

Ryn couldn't tell her about Master Wes' research topic, so Ryn chose to begin with her own quest to find her birth family. She had to find that book her father had shown her, but how to start?

"Well, maybe as practice I should find my parent's records," Ryn said. "That should be easy enough, right?"

Brynd eyed the beads Ryn had around her neck. Ryn's hand went to them self-consciously.

"That's a great idea. Which of your two Ancestral Houses would you like to start with?" Brynd asked.

Ryn thought furiously. Looking up the Houses of the beads she wore wouldn't find her the records she was looking for, but to tell Brynd that might reveal that she didn't actually belong to either of those houses.

Ryn cleared her throat. "Um, actually I'd like to start with some land records. Could I see the deed for my family's home?"

That seemed like a safe place to start anyway. She didn't have to show Brynd the record once she found it, and maybe finding records for her parents would lead to clues about the orphanage she came from.

"Sure! Reference books for land records are this way."

Brynd led Ryn through the maze of shelving to a wall of books.

"Reference books are in order by place starting with Waatch and ending with the furthest island." Brynd showed her one end where the Waatch records started.

Ryn was staring down the wall of books toward the end. "What's the furthest island?" she asked absently.

"Exile, of course," Brynd said.

Ryn gave her a startled look. "How do you have records from Exile? It's Exile—nobody returns from there."

"We have our ways." Brynd's smile had a mischievous hint to it.

Ryn scanned the shelves for Sooke, finally finding the reference book at the very end of the books for the Waatch area, which seemed appropriate since the village was literally on the outskirts of Waatch. Pulling the book from the shelf, she set it on a small table nearby.

"What names and dates are we looking for?" Brynd asked.

"My father's name is Moult," Ryn said, reluctant to mention her mother's name since she had been so secretive lately. Ryn also wasn't sure whose name their land would be in. "I don't know the date. Sometime before I was born?"

"Alright, so let's go back twenty years, then move forward looking for Moult."

Brynd flipped through the pages till they found references to land records twenty years previous. Ryn scanned the pages for her father's name, as Brynd turned them.

"There!" Ryn pointed to a reference for a Moult de Dico.

Brynd ran her finger across the records to the Library directions. "Second floor, Document section, Shelf thirty-two, Box twelve."

"Let's go!" Ryn said.

***

On the second floor they entered a section that was surrounded by a half wall, topped with stained glass panels, each depicting the most heroic act of each Ancestor during the great battle with the dragon. The scenes were elaborately crafted with a mosaic of small colored pieces of glass, which somehow seemed to glow from within, giving off multicolored light which illuminated the hall.

"Here we go." Brynd pulled a box off the shelf.

Brynd lifted the loose documents from the box, then carefully went through each page. About halfway through the stack she found the right page, the document was dated two years before Ryn was born, around the time Jett would have been a baby. A Moult de Dico bought a piece of land north of the boundaries of Sooke to Crystal creek.

"That's it!" Ryn said.

Brynd eyed Ryn's beads again, but didn't say anything. Ryn was aware her bead order suggested her mother was House Dico.

"Curious," Ryn said. "It doesn't mention my mother at all."

"Should it?" Brynd asked.

"I thought so." Ryn closed the land record box. "Maybe I should look at marriage records."

"Marriage reference books are two shelves over from where we found the land records." Brynd pointed back the way they'd come. "I need to get back to my post. Let me know if you get stuck and I'll try to get released to come and help you."

"Thanks!" Ryn said, somewhat relieved Brynd wouldn't be looking at marriage records with her, and seeing her mother's name. "And if you get any news about Zo, please let me know."

Brynd reached out and put a hand on Ryn's arm. "Of course. As soon as I hear anything I'll come find you."

Ryn nodded, and her and Brynd parted ways.

***

Ryn easily found the marriage record reference books, but no reference to her parent's marriage. In fact, the marriage reference book for Sooke was missing for the dates relevant to when her parents would have married. Frustrated, Ryn walked up and down the aisle trying to find it. How could it be missing? She found herself wandering down other reference book aisles hoping she could find the book somewhere, maybe out of place. She reached a dead-end corner of the room and decided to turn back to try to find help, when angry words and the sound of someone crying came from close by.

Quietly, she followed the sound till she rounded a corner and saw Prym's father, his stance tense in front of a barred and locked reference section. Ryn ducked back around the corner before he could see her.

"This is the most restricted part of the references," Prym's father said.

Ryn peaked around the bookshelf to get a better look.

"If there's any reference to Luc it will be in there," he said. "Unfortunately, it's so restricted it must be locked at all times." Ryn watched him turn a key in the lock.

A sniffle brought her attention to the inside of the barred section and a mess of blond hair that looked up from the floor.

It was Prym.

"I'll let you out as soon as you find a reference to Luc." Prym's father spun the keys his Regent status must grant him around his finger, catching them in his palm.

"Daddy, please." Prym stood and reached for him through the bars.

"Sorry, my love. This will give you a head start. You need to beat the rest of those idiots to the prize. It's in there somewhere. As a member of the Board, I can't be seen helping you and the section must be locked." He put his hand through the bars and wiped her tears from her cheek. "I'll be back to check on you at the closing bell." He withdrew his hand and started to walk away. "Best find what you need for Master Wes before then. I'm not letting you out till you do." He spun the keys again. "And students found in locked restricted sections without permission are punished."

He turned his back and walked away.

"Daddy don't leave me." She reached out for him through the bars. "Please, please, don't leave me here."

Chapter Fifteen

There's no such thing as "Haunted Children." No one would willingly give up their bead, and no one would take it from them. It would be of no use, no one would use a bead taken from someone else. It only works when bestowed upon a child by the Ancestral House they are born to.

— As quoted to Cheryl de Muto in Of Magic, Myth and Lore-Commentary and Anecdotes from the people of Waatch, the Library, and the Surrounding Area. Ancestral Library, First Floor, Lore Room, Shelf 29, Shelfmark 33.

Zo woke, damp from the melted ice, a little groggy, but feeling much better. It was still dark and the bed curtain was drawn, but the sound of the physician puttering at his workbench kept Zo from falling back to sleep. Giving up, he rolled over, opening the curtains to the bright morning sunlight streaming in through the eastern window.

"Good morning." Wilmar was entirely too cheerful for this early.

Zo grunted.

Wilmar dropped what he was doing and came to Zo's side, fingers probing his shoulder.

"Still hurting?" Wilmar asked, examining Zo's burn.

"That still hurts, but the shoulder's feeling much better." Zo tried to lift it as Wilmar unwrapped it, but he only got so far before a twinge of pain shot through his shoulder.

"I wouldn't get so excited. You should keep it wrapped for the next several days. Come see me after and we'll give you some exercises to help it heal."

Zo grunted again.

"What?" Wilmar asked.

"Master Nix was teaching me to do temperature readings in the Library. Now I'll have to go back to boiling water," Zo said.

"You know there's a really *easy* solution to this problem," Wilmar said.

"No." Zo didn't shout it, but wanted to.

Wilmar sighed and pulled up a chair. "Would it help to talk about it?"

"I don't see how it would."

Wilmar sat quietly waiting. He was probably wanting Zo to elaborate, but despite how comfortable Zo felt in Wilmar's presence, he'd just met the man, and he wasn't about to discuss his family life with a stranger.

After long minutes Zo stubbornly let stretch between them, Wilmar nodded like he understood, and stood.

"We'll get that shoulder re-wrapped and send you on your way then." He eyed Zo. "You need to come back in two days though, so we can start with those exercises. If we don't get it moving again, it will freeze up and you won't be able to use it properly."

A flutter of fear twisted Zo's stomach. He couldn't heal himself, and he refused to let anyone else heal him. He'd just have to rely on natural healing. Everyone else did it, and he could too. The little girl didn't have healing magic to heal, only Wilmar's skill.

Zo realized he hadn't heard the girl since he woke. Standing awkwardly, he looked over the workbench to the little bed she had been on...it was empty.

His eyes searched the room, but she was gone.

"Where'd the little girl go?" Zo asked. "She didn't look like she had a home or family."

It was Wilmar's turn to grunt. "She doesn't. Her handler came and got her early this morning. They hire her out for work. At the moment, she works scrubbing floors in some magic home."

"Is that how she broke her leg?" Zo asked.

"Someone kicked her because she was in the way," Wilmar said.

"But...she can't scrub floors with a broken leg. Can't you keep her here? Until she's healed?"

A deep sadness passed over Wilmar's face. "If only I could, but she's not mine to keep. This is the healer's job—to see what is broken, but only be able to fix the physical ailment. It's why retirement's looking really good."

At Wilmar's urging, Zo sat back on the bed. While Wilmar took new bandages and wrapped Zo's shoulder, Zo's thoughts were on the little girl, and how she had smiled at him through her tears when he made silly faces. He wanted to run out of Wilmar's and go looking for her, but then what? It's not like he was anywhere near prepared to take care of a little girl. It was all so unfair. Zo caught Wilmar's eyes and he could see the helpless frustration mirrored there, but tempered with years of experience.

Just as Wilmar was tying off the bandages, the door burst open.

Iden stood in the doorway, breathing hard like he'd been running.

Zo was shocked speechless.

Iden leaned back, shutting the door, as he took two long, deep breaths, closing his eyes. Then he sprang across the exam room to hover behind Wilmar.

"Are you alright?" Iden asked.

Zo pointed with his chin to Wilmar. "I apparently have to give up climbing around inside the bowels of the Library for a while, but I should recover."

"I heard they took you to the Healing House. They only take the worst cases to the Healing House. I was afraid something terrible had happened."

"What's with the worst cases going to the Healing House? Why did they take me there?" He turned to Wilmar. "Was it really that bad?"

Wilmar eyed the beads at Zo's neck, whipping his hands on a cloth. "A dislocated shoulder isn't dangerous, though once it's been dislocated it could happen again. I suspect their care had to do with your Ancestry—and perhaps a parent?"

"Why would they even know that? My father doesn't talk about my mother."

"I don't know." Wilmar stood and took a couple packets off his workbench, handing them to Zo. "These will help with healing and the pain." He followed it with paper notes. "These are the instructions. Make sure you are back here in two days—got that?"

Zo stared at the packets of medicine in his hand. He knew one of them was probably the really terrible tasting one. He contemplated yet again the road his anger over his healing magic had led him down. It only made him angrier with the situation.

"I'll be sure he gets here," Iden said, reaching down to help Zo stand.

Zo looked up at him in amazement. They had just met. How did Iden know he was here? And wasn't he supposed to be studying in the Library with Master Wes?

Zo let Wilmar and Iden help him put his shirt on one arm then draped the other around his wrapped shoulder and arm. Slipping his feet into his shoes, Iden held the door for him.

"Don't forget!" Wilmar called.

"Right," Zo said, heading out into the street, confronted once again by the sight of the Waatch Healing House directly across from Wilmar's. It was smaller than the Sano Healing House, but it still evoked memories. In his memory he saw himself on the House Sano porch, running from one of the Healing Masters chasing him with a slipper held high, because Zo had interrupted meditation time by setting the hem of his robe on fire. *Oh well.*

"Hey—you alright?" Iden asked.

Zo started. He hadn't realized he'd stopped in place while the memory played out in his head.

"Yeah... No—I'm starving. I don't remember the last time I ate," Zo said.

"Well, let's fix that." Iden smiled.

As they turned the corner, Zo wobbled on the uneven surface of the cobblestone street. Iden slipped his arm around Zo's waist. Zo shrank from the touch. They weren't that far from the Healing House—what if someone saw? Zo focused on the faces of the people passing them in the street, waiting for someone to be appalled, but no one even glanced their way. In fact, a few more streets down he saw two men who were clearly a couple, not just close friends or brothers. No one paid any attention to them. Zo knew Ordinary mainlanders didn't have the same strict rules about passing on bloodlines, but he never had an occasion to really test that indifference out. Several more blocks and Zo began to relax. Tentatively, he slipped his arm across Iden's shoulders so Iden could support him better. Not one head turned on the streets. He was pretty sure if he was on Eileansano someone would have cried foul by now. Zo leaned closer into Iden's side as they weaved their way through morning foot traffic, almost invisible to everyone headed about their business for the day.

For his part, Iden must have felt the tension easing, because he asked, "So, what happened?"

"Slipped on a ladder rung, flailed about trying not to break the delicate instrument strapped to my back, must have pulled my shoulder out," Zo said. "How about you? How did you know? And aren't you supposed to be in Master Wes' class?"

"Ah, here we are," Iden said, guiding Zo to a door, which when opened, released the most delicious smells.

Zo's stomach went nuts growling.

Iden chuckled. "Best breakfast place in town," he said.

A hostess guided them to a table in the corner.

"The usual," Iden said. "Two of them."

"Make that three," Zo said.

That elicited a hearty laugh from Iden.

Once the hostess left Zo tried again.

"You didn't answer my questions."

Iden's blue eyes danced with amusement in the light of the candles on the tables and the nearby window. "It's the talk of the Library—how Nix broke another grunt."

Groaning, Zo buried his face in his good hand.

"And as for Master Wes' class," Iden shrugged one shoulder, "I *know* how to find materials in the Library, I don't need to spend all day memorizing a stupid book on the subject."

Zo eyed him. He was pretty sure Iden was downplaying the reality of the situation.

The hostess interrupted Zo's next question by bringing them three plates of the most amazing fried cake made from tiny pasta and cheese topped with an egg, smoked salmon, and gravy. And there was bacon on the side—bacon! Zo dove into it before his stomach could further protest its recent treatment. The food was amazing, but by the time he hit the second plate he started to slow down, and noticed Iden slowly eating and smiling as he watched Zo enjoy the food.

"So," Zo began, pointing with his fork at Iden's promise necklace. "What's with Prym?"

Iden took a sip of his mint tea. "You have to play the game."

"And where does playing the game get you? Married to that spoiled brat?" Zo crunched on another piece of bacon.

"That's the beauty of it. She's so caught up in herself she won't care what I do. Bonus: I make the parents happy and I get to keep all the inheritance. The Library has a nice pension plan. My parent's pension will go to me, provided I work for the Library myself. I'll be set for the rest of my life," Iden said, taking another sip of his mint tea.

Zo eyed him skeptically. "If that's what you want in life."

"What I want, and what I'm going to get are completely different things."

Unattainable wants. Despite the walk here through the streets of Waatch giving him hope he might be able to get the things he wanted in life, Zo felt it all slipping away just as quickly as it had started. The thought of working in the Library Boiler Room for the rest of his life made him panic inside. That was not the life with fire magic he had envisioned. Traveling around starting fires for people *was* a pretty lonely life, and he liked Waatch, but being surrounded by Ancestor descendants in the Library meant he would need to continue to hide who he was and his attractions. His mother's power as a member of the Healing Council was long reaching. So far, they had managed to avoid it, but if she knew where he was, she could drag him home and arrange a marriage like Iden's. No matter how he sliced it, his life would likely end up as Iden's—a slave to someone else's ideal.

The door to the eatery banged open and Regg came running through the door, breathing hard. As soon as Zo recognized his smoke-smudged and fire-singed brother, he shot to his feet, fear spiking through, him sending his heart racing.

"Regg!" Zo called out to him.

At the sound of his name Regg's eyes found Zo, relief flooding his face as he raced across the room, stumbling over chairs and people till he grabbed Zo in a tight hug. Now Zo was truly terrified.

Fear gripped Zo at the thought of the answer, but he had to ask, "Regg, what happened? Is Dad alright?"

Regg looked to Iden, then back to Zo, eyes lingering on his wrapped shoulder. "I've been looking for you. Are *you* alright?"

Chapter Sixteen

But what was the cause of so much commotion?
What turned all my odes into burial hymns?
What tinted the lights of the day with black shadows?
The old vicious dragon and his conquest thirst.

— Luc's epic poem as recorded in his Third Journal. Ancestral Liberty,
Third Floor Restricted. The Curator has the Key.

Ryn hid behind the bookcase, heart pounding in her chest. What should she do? Prym's father had always intimidated Ryn. Before they turned eight, she had spent a few afternoons playing with the rest of the village children at Prym's house. Prym's father was strict and let Ryn know she wouldn't be tolerated. If she got caught defying him now, it could be disastrous—especially if Master Wes found out. Besides, Prym deserved everything she got. She was a nasty, unkind person who belittled everyone around her.

The sound of quiet sniffling drifted down the aisle. Guilt, and the knowledge that Ryn really wouldn't cold-heartedly leave her there, made her want to growl with frustration. Turning the corner, she stalked *toward* the caged, restricted part of the reference section.

Prym was still huddled on the floor, staring at the books on the shelf, tears running down her cheeks. The moment she noticed Ryn coming was obvious, because she quickly wiped her eyes and stood, pulling books like she knew what she was doing.

"Hi," Ryn said. "Looks like you have a problem."

Prym held her head up. "No problem, I'm just doing research."

"Oh." Ryn pulled on the barred door, which didn't budge. "So, you want to be locked inside there? Alright." Ryn turned to go.

"Wait!" Prym rushed to the bars. "I don't know how, but if there is a way, I would like to get out."

Ryn suppressed a smile. "I thought so. I've made friends with a Docent. I'll go see if I can get some help."

Prym paled. "Um. I'm going to be in trouble for being in here."

"We'll see," Ryn said.

Now Ryn did grin as she wandered back toward the foyer reception desk. An opportunity like this didn't come along very often, but Ryn did feel somewhat guilty for the aftermath of the punchbowl incident. She hadn't realized what the true effect would be. She tried to place herself in Prym's shoes, and how she would feel if someone did something like that to her. Though to be real, she would never have a party with so many guests—she didn't have that many friends, and her family certainly didn't have the kind of influence that would compel such great attendance.

Rounding a corner, she almost ran into Yll and the lantern she held up.

Hand pressed to her heart, Yll said, "You scared the Ancestors out of me!"

"Why aren't you in the study alcove?" Ryn tried to recover from their near collision.

"You were gone so long, I thought I should come looking for you." She leaned in closer to whisper, "There are rumors of students getting lost in the Library and never being found."

"That's just silly," Ryn said, but she looked down the darkened aisle and shivered.

Yll glanced both ways checking for who knew what. "Let's get back."

"Can't, I need to find this docent I met. It seems Prym has gotten herself into a predicament she needs help with," Ryn said.

Yll frowned. "She still hates me. She still thinks I helped you spike the punch bowl even though I told her I don't know where the vial in my bag came from."

"I'm not a fan either, but I can't leave her where she is."

***

They found Brynd in the grand foyer, and Ryn pulled her aside, whispering their predicament in her ear.

"Really?" Brynd said. "Wow, that man has a reputation, but I didn't think he'd do something like that to his own daughter. Let me get a set of keys."

When they turned the corner on the aisle ending with the restricted reference section, Brynd gasped. She rushed forward, shuffling through the keys in her hand. When she reached the door, she tried three keys before she found the one that fit. Prym was staring at the books she'd pulled from the shelf, but hadn't opened. When she saw them coming, she stood at the door impatiently tapping her foot. Yll reached a tentative hand out to Prym, but she just scoffed at it. As soon as Brynd unlocked the door, Prym rushed out—and Ryn slipped in behind her.

"What are you doing?" Prym asked.

"Your father seems to think our research begins here, so there must be something important to look at. While we have the door open, might as well have a look." Ryn began browsing the titles of the reference books. "What kinds of references are stored in this section?"

"Ancient history mostly. Things from the Origin down to the forming of the great Ancestral Houses," Brynd said, moving to join Ryn.

Ryn noticed what looked like endcaps for bookcases, but they were all smashed together, there was no way in between them.

"What is this?" Ryn waved at the bookcases.

"Oh!" Brynd said, "It's compressed shelving. The Library looks vast, but a thousand years of materials does fill it."

Brynd stepped up to a wheel like one used to steer a ship, but with only four handles. She began turning the wheel and the first two bookcases separated, revealing books shelved on both sides that before were enclosed between the two.

Yll's jaw dropped.

"What?" Ryn asked. "You didn't know about this?"

Yll shook her head.

Ryn entered the new opening and scanned the books. There were many about each Ancestor, and a few on the dragon, but nothing that looked promising in their quest for Luc. A trail of thought tugged at her to look deeper. Stepping out of the opening, she took the wheel. It was harder to turn than Brynd made it look. Turning it, the next bookcase moved to compress against the first one, creating an opening between the second and third.

Ryn scanned the shelves. Amongst the Ancestor books she found a couple on Praedo, the Dragon Slayer. She pulled those off the shelves and handed them to Yll, who read the titles and immediately started flipping through them.

"Perhaps if I knew what you were looking for, I could help?" Brynd said.

Yll shook her head. "Can't tell you." She glanced at Ryn. "Master Wes wants us to figure out the Library on our own without help."

Ryn blanched at that, but wheeled to the next shelves.

"Well that's dumb. How can you learn to be a Library researcher if you don't get help from those who know it?" Brynd said.

"We don't need your help," Prym sniffed, trying to look haughty, but her tear-stained face ruined the effect.

Ryn shook her head as she scanned the next set of shelves. There were even more books on Praedo, but Ryn didn't feel right. When she rolled open the next section, a bell sounded.

Ryn's head shot up. "Is it lunchtime?" she asked.

Brynd shook her head. "Why do you ask?"

"What's the bell for?" Ryn asked.

Brynd frowned. "Bell? What bell?"

"Never mind." Ryn scanned the shelves. The whole section was filled with reference books leading to sources on Praedo. It would take them days, maybe a fortnight, or a whole moon to go through them all in the hopes of finding a reference to Luc. Ryn's heart sank.

Joining her, Yll gasped. "We'll never find what we're looking for in all this."

"Well, all we can do is one at a time." Ryn reached for the furthest book, on the bottom shelf at the back of the bookcase. Best to work their way outward instead of inward, but her hand grabbed a book three books in from it.

Something about the leather on the cover felt warm and inviting, but there was nothing special about it. Still, it captivated her so much she walked it to the table and sat down to read. Ryn scanned the entries. All were references to books about Praedo's journeys and quest to destroy the dragon, each book covering a different aspect of his trials, but no mention of Luc and his writings.

"Wow, that's interesting," Yll said from over Ryn's shoulder.

"What's interesting?" Brynd asked.

"None of your business, little docent," Prym said, moving to block Brynd's view of the book.

"If it was going to be anywhere, this seems like the place it would be," Ryn said, flipping through the pages a little faster.

"Wait," Yll said just as Ryn's fingers came to a halt on their own.

There—a book by Praedo's scribe. It didn't mention Luc specifically, but it was a solid lead, definitely a place to start.

Prym snatched the book off the table and bolted from the restricted section.

"Hey, you can't take that!" Brynd called after her.

Prym broke into a jog.

"What does she think she's doing?" Ryn asked.

"Taking the credit!" Yll said, starting after Prym.

Ryn and Brynd looked at each other, then hurried after them. Ryn struggled not to run, being right next to a Library worker and not wanting to get into trouble on her first day.

By the time they caught up to Prym at the research alcoves, an out of breath Prym was showing the book and its entry to Master Wes, who was praising her for her insight and ingenuity.

Ryn swallowed hard to keep from yelling. Yll on the other hand, had less control.

"But *we* found it!" she blurted out.

Master Wes looked up from the book at Yll and smiled. "Ah, good. The competition has begun." He held up the book. "Full marks to Miss Prym for bringing it to me first. You'll just have to be faster next time."

He set the book on a table and began to scribble down directions. He handed each of them a piece of paper.

"First person to bring me this book gets the next points. Good luck."

Thalya, Prym, and Yll took the papers and left, but Ryn hung back. Something told her there was more.

The way Master Wes was eyeing Brynd made both of them shrink.

Brynd put a hand on Ryn's arm. "I need to get back to my post."

Ryn nodded her thanks.

"Not interested in winning?" Master Wes asked her once they were alone.

Ryn tried to think of a way to explain that her short legs would never beat the others to the bookshelf, but before she could say anything a researcher appeared, bringing Master Wes a note.

Scanning it, he folded it and put it in his pocket. "I am needed elsewhere. Whoever is in possession of that book when I return will be the winner of this round." Then he walked away.

Winner of this round? Ryn thought. *He never said anything about winning rounds, just finding Luc's writings. Ugh.* How else would he change this contest before they were done?

Ryn waited till he disappeared into the gloom of the Library before she opened the reference book. There was something else in it. She could feel it. Flipping pages, she scanned for anything that could lead her to Luc's writings.

Almost at the back of the book she found it.

On the Legend of Luc, Praedo's Scribe

She almost couldn't believe it. A direct reference to Luc. Looking at the directions made her heart sink though.

Third floor, section twelve, case thirty, shelf mark ten.

That was the third-floor restricted section. Only Library workers were allowed on that floor. To obtain it she would have to tell a researcher what book she wanted, and that meant giving away their research topic through the book title. If a Library worker knew, word would get back to Master Wes and Ryn's chance at the researcher position would be over. How could she get the book without anyone knowing?

The lunch bell rang as Brynd hurried up to her, completely out of breath.

"Zo's back!" she managed to get out.

Ryn closed the book, hiding it on a shelf for later use, and dashed after Brynd.

Chapter Seventeen

I think it's disgusting that Praedo had them make beads out of his bones. Why would anyone want to walk around with someone's bones around their neck? Yet we hang them around our kids' necks, and they wear them with pride. It's a good thing it disappears into your skin when the lessons are over. Too bad it burns a scar in the process.

— As quoted to Cheryl de Muto in Of Magic, Myth and Lore-Commentary and Anecdotes from the people of Waatch, the Library, and the Surrounding Area. Ancestral Library, First Floor, Lore Room, Shelf 29, Shelfmark 33.

Regg let go of Zo and locked eyes with his brother. "Dad's fine. They didn't need me anymore, so they sent me home. I just got back and heard you were hurt. When I couldn't find you at the Healing House, I was worried something bad had happened because of how you're always being dumb."

Iden chuckled.

Zo breathed a sigh of relief. "Don't scare me like that."

"Looks like I was right, and you didn't let them heal you," Regg said, pointing to Zo's bandaged arm. "Mom's going to hear about it anyway, you know that, right?"

"How did you find me?" Zo asked. "We didn't tell anyone where we were."

"We ate here with Mom and Dad when we got our family lines certified at the Library. Don't you remember?" Regg asked.

Zo looked around. This place did seem familiar. Why didn't he notice it before?

"That still doesn't explain how you found me here," Zo said.

Regg shrugged. "I caught a glimpse of you on the street. I ran to catch up, but it's hard to not get run over in the morning rush."

"You hungry?" Iden asked.

Regg turned on Iden. Zo's first thought was wondering what Regg was going to say to their father about this scene, but then he remembered Regg had a thing for Prym—and Iden was promised to her.

"Yes," Regg finally said.

Iden waved to the server, who scrambled back into the kitchen.

"Sit, little brother," Zo said as he uprighted his chair and dug into the rest of his breakfast.

"I'm as tall as you now," Regg said.

"But not as old," Zo said, pointing at Regg with his fork.

Regg faced Iden, shoulders squaring. "Why don't you let her go?"

Iden sipped his tea. "Politics."

Regg's face darkened.

Iden set down his teacup. "Let go of those thoughts you're having. Prym will chew you up and spit you out, and that's just for starters. Your family is not connected enough for the daughter of a Library Regent."

The server placed a plate in front of Reg,g who glanced between Iden and Zo, grumbling under his breath something Zo didn't catch. He was sure it was unflattering. Regg dug into his food, like a man who'd been living on fire camp rations for days.

"How goes the fire?" Zo asked.

"Mostly out. Dad will be back soon. He won't be happy when he hears you were sent to the Healing House," Regg said between bites.

"Physician, not the Healing House," Zo said. "I won't set foot in a Healing House."

Regg swallowed. "Even worse."

Zo and Regg finished eating at the same time.

"Time to go," Iden said. "Thanks to your wonderful brother here," his hand waved at Regg, "I am reminded of my significant other who's unfortunately wondering where I am by now." Iden stood, pulling out coins and setting them on the table.

Zo pointed to the promise necklace. "Doesn't that thing give her an idea about where you are?"

"Which is precisely why I need to get back before I never hear the end of it."

***

As they walked the streets of Waatch, Regg rested his hand on Zo's shoulder and pulled him a few steps behind Iden. Zo eyed his hand suspiciously, but before he could wiggle out of his brother's grip Regg began speaking in a hushed voice.

"What are you doing? He's promised to a Regent's daughter. Are you trying to get yourself killed? You work for the Library." Regg fingered Zo's bandaged arm. "Accidents can be arranged."

"*Oh well.*"

Zo made to shrug Regg off, but the muscles in his arms had gone slack. The aching in his shoulder decreased. Despite how frustrated he was, the tension left him. Regg squeezed his neck, causing his muscles to radiate pain up his neck and down his arm.

"Since when do you care?" Zo said. "I thought you were eager to see me boiled in the Boiler Room for what you assume I did at that stupid party."

"I am. I was, but you're walking on dangerous ground here," Regg whispered. "And you're still my brother."

Iden turned to face them and winked. "I think I'm worth the risk."

A strangled noise of frustration was Regg's response.

***

Once they hit the Library grounds, they immediately ran into Fergus coming out of the Guard House. Zo assured him he was feeling better, and Fergus reminded him to check in with Master Nix. Fergus then informed Iden that indeed

Prym had had an exciting morning already, and that she forcefully suggested he bring Iden to her immediately.

"Her eyes did that weird thing girl's eyes do when they're about to burn the place down around you," Fergus said, his face twisting into something Zo had never seen a girl do.

Iden took a very long, deep breath then let it out slowly. "It's a good day to be alive." He smiled, and embraced Zo in a way that made Zo search the surrounding area to see who was watching.

"Later." Iden waved to them as he walked off, escorted by Fergus.

"That's trouble right there," Regg said as they watched Iden and Fergus mount the steps to the Library.

"Everything is trouble, and I'm suddenly very tired," Zo said.

***

Master Nix surprised Zo with an exuberant hug and a look of utter relief on his face. Zo was again baffled by why he was making such a fuss over an injury that wasn't life threatening. Master Nix then surprised him by telling him to take as much time off as he needed to heal. Zo felt like he needed to hold his jaw with one hand to keep it from scraping the floor.

Master Nix eyed Regg. "You should join us, I could use another person on the fires since it's so disagreeable with your brother here."

Regg gave a nervous laugh. "I'm good. The fire marshal asked me to apprentice with him as soon as I finish a few more lessons on control."

"That's unfortunate, as your brother here is very talented, I'm guessing it runs in the family," Master Nix said, then squeezed Zo's arm and whispered into his ear, "I told Iden where to find you, I hope that was alright."

Along with holding his jaw closed, Zo's eyes felt like they would bug out of his head. Master Nix said he was talented? Where was all this coming from? Wasn't this the guy who had tried to kill him with grueling heat and horrible shifts in the Boiler Room for the past several days? Zo supposed Master Nix must know who Iden was because of Iden's parents, but that last bit seemed too intimate.

Regg laughed nervously, dragging Zo away from the heat of the Boiler Room and out into the cool breeze of the sunlit morning, rapidly turning into afternoon. The lunch bell rang out from the bell tower.

"What, you don't want to be a grunt in the Boiler Room?" Zo asked. "It's a prestigious position."

"No, no. I'm good," Regg said.

"Watch out, Dad seems to think it's a great way to support a family. Library workers are well paid," Zo said.

"I'm thinking of something else." Regg eyes started off down the path toward the Library. "I'm thinking of becoming a Library researcher."

Zo followed his eyes to see Yll, Ryn, and Brynd rushing toward them.

Zo's eyes narrowed. "I see."

The girls stopped in front of them, looking for all the world like they wanted to give them some highly embarrassing display of affection. Zo was a little sad they held back. Yll brushed her fingers at the soot covering Regg's clothes.

"Are you alright?" Yll asked Regg at the same time Ryn asked it of Zo.

The girls glanced at each other and giggled, apparently sharing some joke between them.

"I'm starved," Regg said. "Don't they have some sort of mess hall here?"

"You just ate breakfast," Zo said.

Regg waved him off. "I can always go for more food." He grinned at Yll and let her and Brynd lead him off toward the mess.

"You didn't answer the question," Ryn said.

"I'll be alright," he said.

Actually, his shoulder felt a lot better than it had before. His eyes narrowed at Regg's retreating back, but he hadn't felt his brother's healing. Regg had a distinctive way of healing. Was there a lesson on healing subtly? Zo wouldn't know.

He turned his focus to Ryn. She looked pale and was fiddling with her fake bead necklace. It was a tick he should tell Ryn not to do. Ancestor descendants believed skin contact with the beads was important for bringing the lessons. Zo didn't find that to be true. As a kid, he had wrapped his healing bead in various materials in an attempt to keep Madam Sano out of his head, but that shrew always came anyway. That fueled his anger, and in the end, kept her away.

"Something bothering you, little sis?" he asked.

She gave him a hard, appraising look. "You work for the Library."

"What gave that away—my beat up and bandaged body?" Zo laughed.

Ryn stared up at him.

"Yes. Well, if you count boiling water to heat the Library, working for the Library."

"I'm not supposed to tell anyone who works for the Library," she said.

Zo shrugged, then bit his lip to keep from uttering a long string of curses as his shoulder radiated stabbing pain. Maybe Regg hadn't healed him after all.

The pain must have been all over his face, because Ryn took a step forward, reaching out in concern. Zo wiped away the involuntary tears that had sprung to his eyes. Ryn must have interpreted them differently.

She looked around. There was no one nearby, but she stepped closer.

"We're looking for the writings of Luc," she whispered.

"Who?" he asked.

"Luc," she looked around again, lowering her voice even more. "Praedo's scribe."

Zo vaguely recalled something about a scribe, but couldn't remember much about him.

"And?"

Ryn rolled her eyes. "Legend has it he kept some of Praedo's beads of bone and hid them somewhere. It's believed he wrote in his chronicles of Praedo where he hid them. Master Wes wants us to find that book. It's our test for obtaining the promised Library job."

Zo searched his memory: it was starting to sound familiar. "I thought that was just myth and legend."

"Maybe, but if I want to work in the Library I need to find that book, or as close as I can come to it. I found a reference to him this morning, but Prym stole it from me and took all the credit. After everyone left, I snuck a look at the reference book again and found a promising source. The problem is it's on the third floor. Off-limits to anyone who's not a researcher, and we aren't allowed to ask for help. If we do, Master Wes will expel us from his class. I have the directions to find the book, but I can't access it, and can't ask anyone to help me. I'm stuck."

Zo let a smile spread across his face. "I can get you onto the third floor."

Ryn looked startled. "How?"

"Meet me at the dorms tomorrow night," he said. "Come prepared for some sneaking around."

***

The next day, Zo showed up for work without his shoulder bandages, begging Master Nix to finish training him how to be a temperature taker. Master Nix was reluctant, but Zo promised he felt good enough. Hal still hadn't returned, so Zo found himself in the underbelly of the Library with Master Nix again. He was much more careful this time. Mostly out of necessity. His shoulder felt better, but if he over-extended, it let him know about it. He brought his own notebook this time to take careful notes about where each shaft was and what parts of the Library each opening seemed to access. Master Nix hovered over him like a worried mother hen, but the temperature taking job got done for the day, and Zo had collected all the information he needed.

Then he double-checked with Fergus. Zo was right, Fergus was scheduled to stand guard at the Boiler Room that night. Everything was in place to help Ryn with her quest.

Chapter Eighteen

What will bring joy back to the chants?
Who will deliver from the iron yoke?
What will scourge the draconic lord?
The strong arm of Praedo, his power and sword.

— Luc's epic poem as recorded in his Third Journal. Ancestral Liberty, Third Floor Restricted. The Curator has the Key.

The next day, rain drizzled on Ryn and Yll the whole way to the Library, making it appear even more brooding than usual. The skylights in the research alcove were dark, plunging the room into a gloom that was palpable. Yesterday, Thalya had been the first to return with the book on Praedo's scribe. It turned out to be a more recent work, written only a few decades ago, chronicling the history of the myth of Luc, but not his actual book. Ryn suspected that might be the case, because she had a stronger lead on a better book. She really hoped Zo knew what he was doing and could get her onto the third floor.

She fidgeted as her fellow students returned from the restricted reference section with many of the source books Ryn had pulled the day before. Master Wes officially obtained permission for them to temporarily remove the books from their caged section, with a stipulation that a docent remain with the materials at all times. Since Brynd had been with them yesterday, she was chosen to keep watch over the materials. That was not what was causing Ryn's anxiety. Surreptitiously, she kept her eye on the reference book she had set on the alcove shelf yesterday, hoping no one would notice it and decide to search it further. If someone else found the reference to the book on the third floor, her chances of getting to it first would drop considerably, even though realistically she wasn't sure how any one of them could get to those materials without Library help. One of them would give the directions to

Master Wes and let him gain access, but if Ryn could get to it herself, and assess the value of it before she gave it to him, that would be something. Prym and Thalya had lost points with Master Wes when the book they found yesterday turned out to be a bust, so Ryn didn't want to overreach. If Ryn could check it and bring it to him first, that would put her leaps ahead of the others.

Yll found a reference to a book about a "Luc the bard." She offered it up to Prym in an annoyingly sycophantic way that piqued Ryn's doubts about her loyalties. Prym dragged Iden away from the poetry book he was reading, forcing him to accompany her into the dark Library in search of the book. He didn't protest. He was treading lightly since her tirade yesterday in front of the Library staff. He had shown up right after Thalya beat her to the book. Despite her being a Regent's daughter, all the staff had sympathized with Iden, given he had gone to check on Zo. It seemed Library workers were incredibly loyal to their own, even someone new.

Once Prym was gone, Thalya found something of interest and shuffled out into the dark, leaving Yll and Ryn alone with Brynd watching over.

"Are you trying to appease Prym and be her friend again?" Ryn asked.

Yll looked up from the reference book she was flipping through, hesitating just a beat too long. "Just trying to keep her from breathing down our necks, I'm sure that lead isn't going anywhere."

But Yll's face was red, her voice sheepish. Ryn was not sure what to believe.

Yll pointed to something on the page. "There. *Stories of Old: Legendary Myths and Where to Find Them.*"

"I'm pretty sure that will just be another book on the stories surrounding..." Ryn looked over at Brynd. She would probably figure out what they were looking for, but it was best if Ryn didn't say it directly. "Certain people."

Yll shrugged a shoulder. "Could still be useful, you never know."

"Alright, I'll come with you," Ryn said, grabbing a lantern from the table to light the darkened Library.

"I'll stay with the books," Brynd said, happily propping her feet up on a chair, and grabbing the poetry book Iden had left. "Find a docent to help if you get stuck."

"As if we could ask for help," Yll muttered under her breath, as they escaped the alcove.

The directions lead them to the northeast corner of the first floor. Passing an open door, Ryn was startled by the fact that it was well lit with no books. Curious, Ryn stepped through the doorway into the room.

"Where are you going?" Yll asked, following Ryn.

"What is this place?" Ryn approached glass cases with objects lying on plush fabric.

"This is the objects room. The Library doesn't just keep books and documents, it also collects historical objects, though far fewer. Objects take up more space than books, and as we saw with the compressed bookcases, the Library doesn't have all the space in the world," Yll said.

Ryn gasped and stepped into a pool of light falling upon a glass box, light glinting off a steel blade and a jewel encrusted hilt.

"Is this...?" Ryn started.

"The sword that slew the dragon?"

Ryn nodded.

"No, it's just a replica, but a very old replica dating back to shortly after the Origin." Yll's fingers hovered over the glass. "It's so old some people believe it is the actual sword, but the history books say the original sword..."

"Is at the Origin 'driven into stone deep in the crater the death of the dragon left, walled in by the jagged cliffs.' I know, I did actually read my history book," Ryn said.

Yll giggled. "I think you borrowed mine to read."

Then she sobered, face tilted up to stare into the face of Praedo, whose painting hung above the sword. Yll pressed her fingers to her forehead before she stepped back from the sword in an almost bow.

Ryn gazed up at the painting. Bathed in the light from above, Praedo seemed to glow. His face was young and appealing, with kind, soft green eyes framed by long wavy brown hair. Ryn wondered if the painting had been done when he was alive, or later, from descriptions of what he looked like. Certainly, if the painting was a couple thousand years old, it wouldn't be in this good of condition. But Ryn knew only what an art tutor had taught her about painting, and that hadn't been much. Mostly because she showed no aptitude for drawing and painting.

"We should go," Yll said. "We still have a book to find."

"Right," Ryn agreed, but had a hard time tearing herself away from the object's room. Books were wonderful, but there was something about being in the presence of the actual bag one of Praedo's companions had carried—shriveled with age, but solid and real—that books couldn't convey.

Ryn's foot traced the symbol of Praedo's sword embedded in the floor, silently promising to return soon, while Yll stood tapping her foot at the door to the objects room.

Yll held her lantern high, and they plunged back into the Library.

In this corner of the Library, the aisles were quiet and dark. The books stood on shelves like sentinels to the testament of time, and the power of information.

"What was that?" Yll turned, shining her light down a bookshelf row.

The lantern revealed nothing but a dark tunnel of books.

"What was what?" Ryn asked.

Yll rubbed her eyes. "Too many early mornings in a row. I'm starting to see things."

A nervous fear settled into her stomach. "Let's find this east room the directions talk about."

They both hurried off, nerves making them almost break into a run.

The room appeared down another aisle and around a corner. It had a small window in it, but between the cloudy weather and the enormous tree growing outside, the room was still deep in shadow.

"What shelf was it?" Ryn asked, a shiver running up her spine.

Yll consulted the paper she had written the directions on. "North wall, second shelf from the top, shelfmark thirty."

The second shelf was close to the ceiling. Next to the window was a small study table with chairs. Pulling a chair over to the north wall, Ryn roughly guessed where thirty books across was and set the chair there. Looking up at the shelf, Ryn wasn't sure the chair would give her enough height to reach the shelf.

"Move over shorty, I'll get it," Yll said, nudging Ryn out of the way so she could climb up.

"Watch who you're calling shorty," Ryn said, helping Yll up onto the chair.

Yll giggled. "It's so weird to be younger than you but taller."

"You outgrew me years ago," Ryn said.

"I know, but it's still weird."

Yll counted down thirty books from the end, and pulled the heavy volume from the shelf, nearly falling from the weight. Ryn pushed her back upright to keep her from tumbling off the chair. Yll opened the cover of the book to look at the title page.

"This is it!" Yll said, handing the book to Ryn before climbing down.

Ryn took the heavy tomb over to the table and began turning through the pages. There were drawings of different creatures and beings, some Ryn had heard of, some she had not.

"What's a water sprite?" Ryn asked.

"They're supposed to live in lakes and streams," Yll said. "Like the sprite of Crystal Lake."

Ryn gave Yll an incredulous look. "There's no water sprite in Crystal Lake."

"Haven't you ever seen a waterspout out on the lake?"

"Yes, but that's caused by the wind, not some mythical creature," Ryn said.

"I don't know, I've seen them on perfectly calm days. Usually when someone is being naughty by the water." Yll giggled.

"You're funny." But Ryn kept flipping the pages, drawn ever deeper into these supposed mythical creatures. The background and stories about these beings were captivating. Ryn stopped on a page with a full illustration of a large wolf. She'd never seen a wolf before, but she had thought she'd heard one once.

"Do you think they're real?" Ryn asked, staring into the eyes of the wolf, it seemed so wise.

Yll waved her hand. "Who knows. I have seen some weird stuff around Crystal Lake, but there's probably some mundane explanation behind it."

Ryn turned the page and read about the wolf. "'Said to be the offspring of the dragon and local maidens, the wolf devours its mother upon birth—'"

"Gross."

"'—and lives only to hunt, and do the will of the dragon,'" Ryn finished.

"Now how can it do the will of the dragon if the dragon is dead?" Yll said. "Clearly these things can't exist since the dragon's been dead for nearly two millennia."

"I don't know, says here they live unnaturally long lives."

A breeze blew across the book flipping the pages back to the water sprite.

Startled, Ryn looked around for the source of the breeze. "Is that window open?" she asked.

Yll moved to examine the window. "No, doesn't look like it opens, which would make sense, we wouldn't want anything to upset the delicate temperature balance of the Library."

Ryn's eyes shifted to her, then back.

"Seems like any window letting the sunlight in would do that," Ryn said.

"Oh, you haven't seen the study hall or the Researcher's work hall yet. They have huge windows in them," Yll said.

"Great, we need to visit those more often. The dark is getting oppressive."

Ryn moved away from the book in search of what could have caused the breeze. On the west wall, air gently brushed her skin, but it wasn't coming from the doorway. In the corner where the west wall met the north wall, she thought she found the spot, then it abruptly stopped. Oddly, there was a book there, laid on top of the others. Despite the Library being full to busting at the seams, Ryn had never seen a book carelessly set that way. Pulling it off the shelf she opened it—and gasped.

"What?" Yll looked up from the Myths and Legends book.

"The reference book for marriage records in the villages and areas surrounding Waatch. I was looking for this book yesterday, but it was missing from the shelf in the reference section where it was supposed to be," Ryn said, her feet absently carrying her to the table.

Flipping through the pages, she slowed as she got to the years around when she thought her parents had married.

"There!" Ryn pointed. "Ryette and Moult, Sooke."

"That's odd," Yll said, looking over Ryn's shoulder.

"What?"

Yll pointed to the directions to the document. "The marriage record is on the third floor."

"What does that mean?" Ryn asked.

"Only records for people of great importance, like Library Regents, members of the Healing Council, and Matriarchs and Patriarchs, are kept on the third floor."

Ryn examined the entry more closely. "These are the right names, the right place. Why would my parents' record be kept on the third floor? My mother's an Ordinary, and my father has no standing in his Houses."

Yll shrugged. "Maybe I'm wrong, but I listen to my mother talk about the Library a lot. She says the third floor is highly restricted for a reason—powerful information is kept there."

Ryn was bewildered. Why would the reference book containing her parents' marriage be left far from where it was supposed to be shelved, and why would the record of their marriage be kept in the most secure part of the Library? Her little practice research on her parents had taken a bizarre turn. Now she was curious about not only her birth parents, but what strange things were going on *with* her parents.

Ryn took the paper on which Yll had written the directions to the Myths book, and pulled a pencil from her pocket to write down the directions to the marriage record. With a little luck she would be on the third floor tonight. She could look up the record herself, and get to the bottom of this mystery.

"Did you find anything about Luc in that book?" Ryn asked.

Yll shook her head.

"Return it and let's get back. This is a dead end. Hopefully no one else has come up with a better lead," Ryn said, carefully tucking the paper into her pocket.

Something felt off, and she was determined to find out what.

Chapter Nineteen

A creature living in the tunnels under the Library? Never seen it, but I wouldn't be surprised. The Library has a mind of its own.

— As quoted to Cheryl de Muto in *Of Magic, Myth and Lore- Commentary and Anecdotes from the people of Waatch, the Library, and the Surrounding Area.* Ancestral Library, First Floor, Lore Room, Shelf 29, Shelfmark 33.

Zo tiptoed quietly out of the dorm room on his way to meet up with Ryn. His more reasonable day shift was too crowded with workers. Infiltrating forbidden sections of the Library required being in the Library underground while most slept. He hoped sneaking out of the dorm would give him deniability, but he had made up errands and explanations just in case someone questioned him. Once outside, he breathed in the scent of the changing seasons. The smell of drying leaves and harvest swirled on a breeze that made the tree branches sound like the crashing of the ocean waves. Dressed in light Boiler Room clothes, the crisp fall air blew right through him, making him shiver. Ryn hid in the shadows behind the thick trunk of a massive ancient oak tree. She was wearing the trousers Zo had given her, too long for her, but rolled up. Her long brown hair was stuffed beneath a messenger boy cap.

"You ready?" Zo asked.

A breeze sent a leaf tumbling by, and Ryn shuttered, arms wrapped around herself.

"Yeah," she said.

"I've arranged to get us past the guard at the door, so just keep your head down, and follow me," Zo said.

He led her through the garden and across the courtyard to the Boiler Room door. Zo had timed this entry for the changing from second shift to third shift. Second shift Boiler Room workers were leaving as third shift arrived. Zo inserted himself into the flow of workers with Ryn, who was

178 The Slayer's Magic

annoyingly right on his heels, almost stepping on his shoes. They passed Fergus at the door, who gave Zo a knowing nod and let them through. Zo had told Fergus Ryn wanted to see the underbelly of the Library as part of her training to learn how the Library worked. Library workers, who weren't researchers, took great pride in their jobs in the care of the Library. They were thrilled when someone displayed interest in how it all worked. Most outsiders never gave much thought to how the Library was maintained, or its methods for preserving records for hundreds, if not thousands, of years. To most people, it somehow just happened. Unfortunately, any official tour was out of the question. Despite the pride in their work, the Library's workings were strictly monitored. Fergus was risking trouble by letting Zo take Ryn into the tunnels.

Once inside the Boiler Room, Zo ushered Ryn down the tunnel leading toward the underbelly of the Library.

"Don't touch the pipes, they're hot," Zo warned, still feeling the heat from his burned side.

Ryn moved further away from the pipes, hugging the tunnel wall. When they got to the junction where those with water magic mixed the hot and cool water, and directed it through the pipes, Zo went to the cabinet where the thermoscope was kept. Handing it to Ryn like she was his assistant, he headed for the tunnels directly under the Library. Just before reaching that magic line where he would enter the influence of the Library's no magic zone, both his beads started to glow, calling him to his magic lessons.

Zo swore. "No, no," he growled, "NO!"

His shout drew the attention of the water magic workers. Ryn pulled her cap down further over her eyes and pulled Zo down the tunnel. As soon as he hit that invisible wall, it shut his magic down and the beads stopped glowing.

"Well, that's convenient," he said.

"What are you doing?" Ryn whispered.

Zo fingered his beads. "Magic lesson was coming. My beads were glowing. Looks like since the Library does not allow magic, it just got me out of a lesson. Actually, two lessons—wonder what that old bat of a Healer wants from me now?"

"Great, can we just keep going before someone gets suspicious of us and decides we don't belong here?" Ryn's whisper was harsh and clipped.

"Right, right, right." All things Zo would have to think about later—like when they left.

At the moment, he needed to focus on getting them safely to the third floor. Later he would worry about hurrying someplace safe for his lessons. If he was really lucky, he could shut Madame Sano out again.

Taking the thermoscope from Ryn, he gently laid it on the ground by the wall. The last thing he needed was to break it and need to explain why he was here unauthorized.

"Follow me." Zo waved Ryn forward deeper into the underground. Ryn walked uncomfortably close. Zo was about to snap at her, when he felt the Library's attention shift. Like it knew they intended to violate its secrets.

Ryn stumbled over a loose piece of masonry, and he caught her by the arm. She was trembling.

His impatience with her melted away. "Hey, we're alright."

"Do you feel it?" Ryn's wide eyes gazed upward into the underbelly of the Library.

"Yeah. Let's hurry." He picked up their pace.

They hurried down the tunnel as fast as they could. Zo had to stoop, but Ryn barely bent her head. By the time they reached the bend signaling the turn down the eastern wall, Zo felt like something was following them. He paused there to listen, but the tunnels were as silent as they always were. When the ladder came into sight, Ryn reached up, but couldn't touch the bottom rung. Zo lifted her up, pushing her ahead of him. His shoulder protested.

"We're climbing up a ladder?" Ryn asked.

Zo's eyes were on the tunnel back the way they'd come.

"We'll there's no stairs. What did you expect from secret access?" He jumped onto the lowest rung as soon as she was far enough above him.

"I don't know," she grumbled, "Secret stairway access?"

"Climb higher!" Zo fought to keep the panic from his voice. The hairs on his arms were slowly rising.

There was something dark coming down the tunnel that the lantern light didn't quite reach. Ryn pulled herself up, but the rungs were a bit too far apart for her to easily climb. Zo scrambled up after her, lifting his legs into the shaft and above the tunnel ceiling line just as something dark and cold passed beneath. Holding his breath, he waited for the thing to climb up after them, but it seemed to move on, continuing on its way.

Zo let out a ragged breath.

Ryn stopped, the lantern light showing the concern on her face.

"Are you alright?" she asked. "Is your shoulder hurting?"

Zo looked up at her incredulously. Had she not felt the thing behind them? He shook himself. Maybe the dark was playing with his mind.

"It'll be fine. I'll just use it to hold the lantern. Keep going. We're both going to be slow at climbing and if we don't keep moving, we won't make it out before morning."

Ryn climbed higher. Zo was behind her struggling to climb with one good arm and a lantern, while keeping an eye on the blackness below them. He felt something waiting down there. Something that knew they shouldn't be here.

"There's a door here," Ryn's voice came from above.

"That's the first floor, keep going," Zo said, turning to focus on keeping up with her.

"Ugh."

"Just think, I get to do this every day. It's my new job," Zo said.

"Well, you're going to have really huge arm muscles from it," she said.

That was a bright thought. Zo grinned to himself.

Somewhere between floors two and three Ryn slipped. Zo shoved his good shoulder under her foot to prevent her from jerking her arm out of its socket like he had.

Grunting from the shock of her heel digging into the spot where his shoulder met his neck, he winced.

"Sorry! Sorry!" She called down to him, getting her feet back under her on the rungs.

Zo gritted his teeth against the new hurt. "Just keep going."

She scrambled the rest of the way up the ladder, pulling herself up to sit next to the access door for the third floor.

He inhaled deep breath to gather strength and push away his various pains, then pulled himself the rest of the way up.

"Now what do we do?" Ryn asked.

Zo shielded the lantern light so they could barely see.

"Lift the latch. Open the door just enough to see if there is any light on the other side," Zo said, hanging on the ladder with Ryn on the seat.

She lifted the latch, peeking out through the crack.

"Looks pitch black out there," she reported.

Zo sighed with relief. "Open the hatch slowly, then crawl through. Careful of the table on the other side."

The door swung open silently. It was designed so the silence of the Library would not be disturbed by Library maintenance.

Ryn crawled through onto the table, then hopped down, taking the lantern from Zo as he squeezed himself through the hatchway. Sometimes there were advantages to being tall. Sometimes there were not. Pushing through headfirst, his hips got stuck. Ryn set down the lantern to help pull him out, and they ended up in a tangle of hands and arms.

"You had to go through headfirst?" she whispered.

"It seemed like the better choice to pull myself out," he bit back, much too loud and harshly.

"Shhhh." Ryn let him steady himself on the table then helped get his belt through the opening, which was caught on the doorframe.

He finally slid free into a heap on the floor, his shoulder protesting how he landed on it. He saw stars before he collected himself and stood up.

"Don't shut the door all the way," he said to Ryn as she was closing it. "We need to be able to find it again, and when the door is shut it's completely hidden."

Once they were set, Ryn took up the lantern and headed out into the Library. They wandered around as Ryn tried to figure out where they were exactly. She kept consulting a paper in her hand and the shelves around her. There were many of the compressed shelves Ryn said were opened by turn of a wheel. Zo was fascinated by this and tried to spin one, but she pulled him away deeper onto the third floor. Zo thought she must have got her bearings when she seemed to recognize something, hurrying off down a row of shelving.

She stopped short and groaned.

"What?" Zo whispered.

"Locked section. We need keys."

Zo swore.

"Of course we do. If it's as important a book as I think it is, of course it's under lock and key," Ryn knocked her fist against her head.

"Where do we find keys?" Zo asked.

"At the Assistant Researcher's desk?" Ryn answered. "There's a desk where you put in your request for the materials. I'm assuming they have the means to access those materials."

The time they'd already taken pressed on his mind. If they didn't get out before first shift arrived, they would be caught for sure.

"Let's find this desk," he said, fighting back his impatience.

Ryn looked up at him and shrank. Clearly, he wasn't keeping his frustration from his voice.

"Right," she said, hurrying off back down the way they had come.

She led him through the twisting and turning of rows and rows of shelving that first went one way and then another. When at last it opened up into a wider aisle, they could see light up ahead on the ceiling.

"Somebody must be at the desk," Ryn whispered.

"Great. Douse the light and let's get closer," he said.

They crept forward to peek around the corner. A Library guard, Zo couldn't tell which one from the back, sat in a chair with his feet up on the desk. Arms folded, head down, he was emitting a quiet snore. A quick inspection revealed a key ring hanging on the wall behind the sleeping guard.

Zo gestured for Ryn to wait as he snuck forward on the balls of his feet, lifted the keys from their hook, then gripped them tight so they wouldn't clack against each other. He was almost back to where Ryn waited for him, when the guard choked on his snore and started coughing. Zo scrambled around the corner.

Grabbing Ryn by the arm, he hurried them away from the reception desk. He didn't say anything, hardly dared to breathe until they were once again standing in front of the locked section.

"Keys," Ryn whispered, the hand she held out shook.

"I got this."

It took a few tries, but he finally found the right key.

The sound of steps and intermittent light shining on the ceiling told them the guard was on the move.

"Hurry," Zo said as Ryn rushed inside scanning for the right book.

She counted books and pulled one off the shelf.

"This is it, let's go," she said.

Zo didn't have to be told twice. As soon as she was clear of the caged section, he closed the door and locked it. One of the keys banged against the lock. Zo and Ryn froze.

Footsteps pounded in their direction. Ryn went pale.

They left the keys in the lock and fled through the shelving. Turned around as he was in the dark, nothing looked familiar. Footsteps grew louder and the lantern light got closer. Zo thought he recognized the aisle leading to the hatch, but Ryn cut down a different turn. His panic spiked when he saw lantern light shone down the aisle they just left. He wanted to grab Ryn to ask her what in all the name of the Ancestors he didn't worship did she think she was doing, but the quieter he was the better.

Ryn stopped short, pulling a box forward. Flipping through the pages, she grabbed one then put the rest back into the box on the shelf. She tore off around the corner toward where he hoped the hatch was hiding.

Relief flooded him when the slight crack of the hatch came in sight. Ryn held it open while Zo shot through feet first, scrambling for the ladder. Ryn handed him the book, the paper, and the lantern before climbing though and pulling the door shut just as they heard footsteps run right to the door. Trying to breathe as silently as he could, they watched as lantern light seeped through a crack in the hatch door. The door rattled, but Ryn had fortunately latched it. Zo pointed down the ladder and Ryn nodded.

Ryn took the lantern while Zo carried the book, the document now tucked inside its pages. Going down was even slower, with both of them having one hand occupied. He wanted to warn Ryn to be careful, but the third-floor hatch door above them rattled again and he didn't dare make any more noise than climbing already did.

When they got to the bottom of the ladder Zo stared into the darkness below, but he didn't sense the cold, black shadow he felt before. He hoped it had been his overactive imagination. Scrambling the rest of the way down, he set the book aside so he could take the lantern from Ryn and help her safely to the ground.

Ryn's eyes got wide in the lantern light. "Do you feel that?" she whispered.

The hairs on the back of his neck raised.

Thrusting the lantern at her, he scooped up the book. "Run!" he said.

They ran as fast as they could with her shorter stride and his needing to duck down the tunnel. He felt icy claws scratching at his back.

"Faster!" he urged Ryn on.

She was breathing hard as she stumbled on the same piece of masonry she had before, almost falling on her face, but reaching out to the side, she grabbed a pipe to steady herself.

"Ow!" she jerked her hand back.

"Keep going!" Zo practically scooped her up, hurtling along as she got her feet under her and ran with him.

As they neared the junction, Zo replaced the lantern on the wall, pulled the thermoscope bag strap over his shoulder, and ran for that line—the one where the Library boundary ended. He hoped whatever was chasing them would stop there.

He was right, the cold dark presence was gone, but as soon as he passed that line and felt his magic return, everything went dark as Master Ignis and Madam Sano stood glowing in front of him, arms crossed, both of them looking displeased.

His magic lesson had started, and he no longer had complete control of his mind or his body.

Chapter Twenty

I've been asked why they don't have some sort of shelter for kids around town for when they have a magic lesson. Being catatonic in the middle of the street wouldn't be safe. Truth is, they do have such things in the villages on the islands, but town folk won't allow them in Waatch. Who knows why. I suppose it doesn't matter much since Ancestor types keep their children close in Waatch, and don't let them wander the streets.

— As quoted to Cheryl de Muto in *Of Magic, Myth and Lore-Commentary and Anecdotes from the people of Waatch, the Library, and the Surrounding Area.* Ancestral Library, First Floor, Lore Room, Shelf 29, Shelfmark 33.

Ryn ran for her life. Something cold, dark and creepy chased them through the underbelly of the Library. She wondered if the information she carried was the cause. Zo pulled her along until they burst into the place where all the pipes split off into different directions. Once they left the tunnel, Zo slumped forward. Ryn shoved herself up into his side to keep him from falling. She didn't understand what had happened to him. One minute he was running flat out, and the next she was holding him up. Since he had been behind her, she immediately thought whatever was chasing them had caught him. Her hand probed his back for injuries, while her eyes searched him up and down for the problem. When she looked into his eyes, she found them glazed over, like he was seeing, but not seeing her. Both of his beads glowed bright enough to illuminate the space between them.

"What the... I thought they gave you time to get to a safe place before this happened," she said, but either he couldn't hear her, or he couldn't respond.

Some of the water workers had watched them run out of the tunnel and were staring at her.

"Just a magic lesson," Ryn called to them. "It didn't give us enough time to get out of the tunnel."

The workers gave her skeptical looks, but went back to work.

Setting the book and the thermoscope bag down, she debated what to do. If he started doing a fire lesson here in the tunnels, that would be all kinds of bad. She needed help, and there was only one person nearby she could possibly call on.

"Stay here," she told Zo, even though he clearly couldn't hear her. "I'll be back with help...I hope," she added under her breath. She left Zo and the book and ran through the tunnel for the Boiler Room.

She burst out the door to find Fergus standing guard next to it. She heaved great gulps of air and bent over while she struggled to talk.

"Help," she spit out between breaths.

Fergus was immediately by her side.

"What's wrong?" Fergus asked. "What happened?"

"Zo..." Ryn gasped, "he...he started his magic lesson...couldn't get him out," Ryn spat.

"Show me," Fergus said.

Despite being completely out of breath, Ryn turned to run back the way she'd come.

Fergus put his arm out and slowed her down. She was in a complete panic, but he made her walk at a sedate pace. She was imagining all kinds of horrible things happening, like—Zo setting fire to the tunnel, which would consume the book and document they'd liberated. She tried to walk faster, but Fergus took her hand, holding her firm to his pace. She remembered then she had taken a Library book from the restricted section, was halfway to removing it from the Library, and was bringing a Library guard to the exact spot she had left it. She remembered Fergus' story about how his father caught someone taking Library materials and got sent to jail. Her anxiety grew with her need to help Zo, keep him from burning the place down (wouldn't Regg love to know he'd been right about that, even if he had been teasing), and sneak the book out so she could have time to read it. She wasn't looking to remove it from the Library. She would happily sit and read it in the research alcove—if only there was a way directly there from here. She stared into the darkened tunnel ahead of them and shivered. She could still feel the eyes of whatever it was that had chased them on her, even though they hadn't reached the junction yet.

She shivered again and Fergus squeezed her hand. "Don't worry, everything will be fine."

Fine for him, Ryn thought.

When they arrived where Ryn had left Zo everything was in chaos. The water workers were scrambling to put out the flames curling around Zo's hands. He was clearly old enough to have advanced lessons, and nobody knew what kind of fire magic he would throw in the confined space. Someone rushed up with a damp cloth and Fergus held Zo's hands while the worker wrapped the cloth around them.

"Thanks, we'll take it from here," Fergus said to the workers.

Ryn scooped up the book, trying to keep it out of Fergus' sight while Fergus bent to carry Zo over his shoulder.

A grunt escaped from Fergus as he stood with Zo slung over his shoulder. "Watch I don't bang his head on something, and he doesn't set my clothes on fire."

Ryn held the knot tying Zo's hands together terrified at any moment he would make them burst into flame. So focused on her task, Ryn barely noticed them making their way through the heat of the Boiler Room, into the cool night air outside. Fergus made his way across the courtyard, then set Zo down and unwound his hands.

Ryn let out a squeak as Zo immediately let out a stream of fire in front of him.

"Go Ryn," Fergus said. "We're going to be in trouble, but if you get out now, I can cover so no one knows you were here."

"But..." Ryn started.

"Hurry." Fergus was sweating, eyes on the trees. Behind them was the guard house.

Ryn gave one last look into Zo's distant eyes. Once again, something she needed had put him into trouble. She turned and fled as guilt clawed up through her stomach.

She ran around the Library toward the southeast corner of the grounds. There was a small cottage there for the Curator when she worked late and couldn't make it all the way home. Clayr rarely used it. In Clayr's eyes it wasn't big enough to house her and Yll permanently. She preferred to leave Waatch and the pressures of the Library behind every night, and travel home to the village. Tonight, Ryn had told Yll she was going somewhere with Zo, and then study late so Yll suggested they stay in the cottage for the night. It meant cramming themselves onto the narrow extra bed in the loft, and losing sleep from trying not to fall out of the bed, but Ryn agreed. Now she was grateful she didn't have to flee far.

Pausing at the tree where she met Zo, she slipped her discarded skirt over Zo's old trousers then made a beeline for the cottage. The windows in the Library bell tower seemed to glare down at her menacingly. She had that feeling again of unseen eyes watching her, seeming to know everything. That feeling had been in the underbelly of the Library, and now it returned. Winding her way through the gardens via lamplight, she tried not to look guilty as she passed a guard making his rounds.

The cottage windows were all lit up, drawing Ryn in, warm and inviting. She hurried up to the door and knocked their secret knock. Yll opened almost immediately.

"Where've you been?" Yll asked.

"Long story. It ended up taking longer than I thought." The door slammed shut behind her.

All of her fears from the evening bubbled up as Ryn latched the door.

"What's up?" Yll raised an eyebrow.

Ryn looked around the cottage. "Where's your mother?"

"Went to dinner with the Collections Manager," Yll said.

"Good." Ryn took the book she was clutching to her chest and slowly lowered it onto the small cottage table.

"What's that?" Yll moved to get a better look.

"Hopefully my ticket to being a researcher, having permanent access to the Library, and finding my birth parents."

Yll flipped open the cover to the title page.

"*On the Legend of Luc, Praedo's Scribe*," Yll read, she looked at Ryn. "Where...how...?"

"From the third floor," Ryn whispered.

Yll paled to white in the lantern light. "You have a third-floor restricted section book *outside the Library*?"

Ryn twisted her hands together to keep them from shaking. "Yes," she could barely force the word out.

Yll immediately started closing all the curtains. When she pulled the last one, she turned on Ryn.

"Have you lost your mind? Do you know what they do to you if you remove materials from the Library?" Yll's voice pitched to a shrill.

"Yes..." Ryn squeaked, cleared her throat. "No..." Ryn placed her hand on the book. "Maybe. I don't know, but hear me out. I found a reference to this book. I knew if I asked the Researchers to pull it, it would reveal what we are searching for, and Master Wes would be upset."

"So just have Master Wes pull it!" Yll's exasperation was showing in her waving arms.

"Yes, but what if it's another dead end like the last one? Master Wes would be irritated that he had to get special permission to be on the third floor pulling materials for nothing. I had to be sure it was something. Did you see how he roasted Prym for the first find? I didn't intend to leave with it, but things got hurried."

"How did you even...never mind." Yll put up her hand in front of her. "I don't want to know. If I know, they might find me guilty with you. If it's from the third floor, it has to be worth it."

Ryn sat at the table in front of the book, while Yll pulled the other chair around so she could read along.

Ryn began to flip the pages. The book was old, at least a couple centuries. It was a book about Luc, but this author seemed to have much more intimate details about his life. The author claimed his source was Luc's journals. *Plural* journals, which sent shockwaves down Ryn's spine. Ryn kept flipping pages. The author referenced all of them being kept in the Library.

"Did that book just say there's multiple journals?" Yll asked.

Ryn nodded, continuing to skim through the book.

It was divided into chapters about Luc's life. Ryn was looking for reference to the Dragon Slayer's beads. At one point the author took a chapter long aside to discuss Luc's epic poem. He claimed the poem was bound in a book by itself, and was short, but the author teased it contained all of Luc's secrets without mentioning which ones specifically.

"But what other secret could it possibly be?" Yll asked. "This is the proof we've been looking for that Luc's writings are real and they are for sure somewhere in the Library!"

"Yes, Master Wes was right—but where?" Ryn flipped to the back of the book to the place source materials were referenced.

All of Luc's journals gave the same direction for finding it—the curator holds the key.

"So mother knows where it is? Maybe we should just ask her," Yll said.

"NO! If we ask her, we will alert her to what we are researching, and Master Wes will expel us. There has to be another way..."

Yll startled at the sound of keys jangling and sliding into the door lock.

Ryn slammed the book closed and fled up the steep steps that led to the loft. Shoving the book under the bed, she took a deep breath to still her heart as she heard Clayr greet Yll with a kiss and inquired after Ryn. Ryn slowly walked down the stairs as if she was sleepy and had been preparing for bed.

When Clayr saw Ryn, she breathed out a sigh of relief. "Ryn, thank goodness. There was a series of disturbances in the Library tonight the guards are sorting out. It appears Lar's son might be involved in it. I was worried you might have gotten mixed up in it too."

"She's been here all evening with me, mother," Yll said.

Ryn shot her a look of grateful appreciation.

"Well, it's late," Clayr said, removing her shawl. "You two have an early morning, we should head to bed and get some rest."

"Yes, mama," Yll said, giving her mother a hug.

"You two go on up and I'll come tuck you in," Clayr said.

"We're not babies anymore, ma," Yll said.

"I know, but let a mother enjoy having you with me under one roof for just a little while longer," Clayr said.

Ryn and Yll trudged up the steep steps, and proceeded to dress for bed. Ryn was careful to slide the trousers off with her skirt and bundle them together. She had on an undershirt and bloomers instead of a shift because of the trousers. Yll just stripped off her dress, leaving only her shift. They crawled into bed and squished together.

"Not like when we were little and fit perfectly on one bed," Ryn giggled.

"Those were the days," Clayr said as she reached the top of the stairs. "Goodnight," Clayr said, kissing each of them on the head. "Sleep tight, don't let the bed bugs bite."

Yll giggled.

"Nite," Ryn said.

Clayr blew out the lantern and headed downstairs. Ryn had plans to get up and look at the marriage document tucked into the back of the book about Luc, but as she waited for Clayr to turn out the lights and go to bed, she fell fast asleep.

***

Ryn was dreaming about her father and the house on the cliff again.

All he said to her was, "You're close."

She woke with a start, finding she occupied the entire bed herself, which was so comfortable after a night of sleeping on the edge she gave a sigh of relief, and then realized Yll was gone. Climbing out of bed, she looked down into the cottage below from the loft. Clayr was also gone.

Perfect, Ryn thought as she scrambled under the bed to get out the book so she could examine the document alone. She had a feeling she didn't want Yll to see that document till Ryn had a chance to look at it. She lifted the bed skirt to find...no book.

"What?" Ryn said.

She pulled up the skirt so she could see better, then lit the lantern and looked again, but it was gone. Ryn reeled. She searched the bed, she searched the dresser drawers, she searched the shelves and the small cabinet that served as a closet—Nothing.

Ryn started to panic. She refused to believe her best friend had taken the book. Someone must have snuck in and took it. Who else would know it was here? No one. Maybe Yll just put it somewhere safe. That was it. She was protecting Ryn.

Ryn's stomach twisted.

The bells in the Library tower rang out their morning song. Ryn blew out the lantern and got dressed, putting the discarded trousers in a drawer. She had to get to the mess hall. Hopefully she could find Yll and figure out what happened.

***

A quick scan of the mess hall revealed no Yll, no Zo, and no one Ryn knew, so she grabbed a muffin and headed to the Library. She took a bite of the muffin, but her stomach was so tied in knots she barely managed to swallow it. The doorway to the Library tingled with its usual intensity, but on the other side there was no Fergus waiting. Ryn swallowed hard. She had hoped to find him here to confirm everything was alright from last night. She left her muffin in the cloak room and headed for the alcove. As she approached, the sound of betrayal came with Master Wes' voice.

"*On the Legend of Luc, Praedo's Scribe*. Prym, you are brilliant, where did you find this?" Master Wes said.

Ryn stepped into the alcove just as Prym responded.

"Oh, I found the reference for it in one of those reference books." She gestured to the pile on the table. "It was tough to track down, but I managed it." Prym put her hand to her head like she had toiled all day in the hot summer sun.

Ryn felt her face flush with anger. She searched the alcove to find Yll shrinking into the corner. *How*, Ryn thought, *how could she?* Ryn couldn't believe it. Couldn't believe Yll had taken the book and given it to Prym. All the air seemed to be sucked out of Ryn's lungs. She was gasping, unable to process what just happened.

Master Wes searched the book and came to the same conclusion Ryn had the night before—there was a book of Luc's epic poem, it was in the Library, and somehow Clayr held the key to it.

"Excellent! Excellent progress! Full marks to you Prym, but this next part will be a challenge. We will all work on finding this key the Curator has. I will give the researcher position to the person who finds it and bring it to me first. If I find it before you, the deal is off. So, get moving on it!" Master Wes flipped through the end of the book and Ryn's parent's wedding certificate slipped out.

"What's this?" Master Wes put it to the light to examine it, his forehead creasing in concentration. "Where did you find this?" he asked Prym.

Prym shrugged. "I didn't know it was in there," she said, glaring at Yll.

"Well, I don't know how you did it, but this is the other piece of information I have been sent to gather. Funny they should be in the same place."

"May I see it?" Ryn asked.

Master Wes' eyes narrowed at Ryn, but he handed her the certificate.

Ryn had to read it over a few times to process what it said.

Moult de Dico married to Ryette de Viatoro, in Sooke, 1610.

"You're a Viatoro from this area. You wouldn't happen to know where I could find this woman, do you? She is the Matriarch-in-waiting. Her mother, the Matriarch of House Viatoro, very much wants to speak to her." Master Wes hovered over Ryn.

Ryn couldn't process it. Couldn't believe what she was seeing and hearing. Her mother had travel magic? And not only that, she was the heir to the Ancestral House seat? Her mother, the one person Ryn thought was just like her, wasn't Ordinary at all. Her blood raced, her breath was shallow, she couldn't see well. She handed the certificate back to Master Wes and fled.

Chapter Twenty-One

The earth moved and rocked asunder.
The dragon fell and crashed in the deep,
Where the waters devoured and his corpse sleeps.
Injured our hero fell to the ground...

— Excerpt from Luc's Poem as recorded in *On the Legend of Luc,*
Praedo's Scribe. Ancestral Library, Third Floor Restricted Section.

Zo stared in disbelief at Master Ignis and Madame Sano. Both ghostly figures stood in front of him, arms crossed, expressions of contempt on their faces. He was dimly aware of Ryn next to him, supporting him.

Zo swore.

"Zo de Ignis, son of Lar, son of Fyri de Sano, that is not a respectful attitude toward your elders," Madame Sano said.

"Get your wrinkly, old, Ancestor ass out of my head," Zo spat at her.

Master Ignis held out a handful of flames. "That's definitely not respectful. Should I make him sweat?"

Madame Sano put her hand on his. "Hush Ignis, I can handle the child, I've had worse."

"How are you even here, you old bat? I thought I was plenty angry enough to keep you away," Zo said.

"Apparently your hard edge is slipping. You must be softening toward learning healing or I couldn't be here, but by all means, stay angry, I really don't want to have to teach you. Disrespectful child."

Madame Sano drew herself up to tower over Zo. "But do understand you have nearly aged out of the opportunity to learn healing. Just a warning since you've put yourself in a position to burn yourself to a crisp here in the underground." Madame Sano's smile was venomous. "Tootles." She waved her fingers goodbye, then evaporated.

Zo swore again as he stared down Master Ignis. His father's close resemblance to Master Ignis always unnerved him. Lar could be his son, not his many generations descendant.

"Shall we begin? It's time to work up a good firestream," Master Ignis said.

Zo eyed the water magic workers in his peripheral vision. Ryn was gone, thank goodness.

"People will get hurt," Zo said.

"That's why you should have heeded the beads," Master Ignis said.

"I was in the Library where there's no magic, I should have had time to get out."

Master Ignis shook his head. "Time started when the beads started to glow, and keep running, inside the magic blocking Library or not. It's been hours, plenty of time to get yourself to a safe place. You're out of time, we must begin. Once initiated I cannot stop it."

Zo swallowed hard as fire sprang to life around his hands. The compulsion to obey was too strong after having followed Master Ignis' lessons for years.

Relief flooded him when his hands were doused, and Fergus carried him out. Master Ignis seemed irritated by the interruption, but relieved the risk of injury to others was removed. As soon as Fergus set him down, the lesson began in earnest. He was barely aware of what was going on around him till the lesson came to a close. It finished as Master Ignis faded away and Master Nix replaced him.

Oh boy, Zo thought.

"Zo of Ignis, what in the name of the all the Ancestors do you think you are doing?" Master Nix was redder than he ever was in the blazing Boiler Room.

Zo glanced at Fergus standing next to him.

"I found you alone in the middle of the Junction having a fire lesson," Fergus gave him a look that would seem stern and pointed to Master Nix, but his words told Zo Fergus had managed to get Ryn away.

Zo covered a sigh of relief, then turned to face Master Nix. "My side itched and I couldn't sleep, so I thought I'd explore what it was like to take the Library's temperature at night. My beads started to glow for a lesson, but the Library blocked it. I didn't know the time to get out was still running, Master Ignis explained that to me too late." Zo bowed his head, hoping it made him look penitent.

Master Nix stared at Zo for a long time without saying anything. Perhaps he was trying to decide whether to believe him or not. Zo was grateful his lesson had made him sweaty, because his forehead was dripping sweat into his eyes.

At last Master Nix grunted. "The guards reported a disturbance, possibly an intruder on the third floor. You didn't happen to see anything, did you?" Master Nix's eyes narrowed at him.

"No, but I did feel this weird chill that seemed to follow me. Is that normal?" Zo asked.

Master Nix chuckled. "That's the protector of the Library. Don't mess with it, and don't go wandering through the tunnels at night, or you might not come back next time."

Master Nix grinned in a way that made Zo unsure if he was teasing him or being serious.

"Come with me." Master Nix put an arm around Zo, careful of his injured shoulder. "Your punishment is, I'm sending you for your check up with Wilmar."

Zo groaned. All he wanted at the moment was some decent sleep, but the sun was already rising, and Master Nix was making it clear he had no choice but to do what he was told.

When they got to the west gate of the Library grounds a carriage stood waiting—with Zo's father standing next to it.

"Can this night get any worse?" Zo murmured to himself.

When Lar saw them coming, he rushed to Zo and enfolded him in the kind of hug he hadn't given Zo since he was little. He wrapped his arms around his father, shocked by how good it actually felt, hurting his shoulder in the process. He didn't care. Unlike Regg, his father was cleaned up from his firefighting, but his hair still smelled of smoke.

Lar broke from the embrace and examined Zo. "Are you alright? They said you were in some trouble and that I should wait."

"No trouble, they just needed to wait for my fire lesson to end so I could explain what happened," Zo said.

Fergus opened the carriage door for them, and Master Nix made sure Zo was hustled toward it.

"I've alerted Wilmar. Let's not keep the physician waiting. He'll take that out of my hide too." Master Nix rolled his eyes.

Lar nodded and moved to help Zo up. Zo swatted away his hand.

"I'm not a kid, dad," Zo said.

Lar's face deflated at the chastisement. "I know."

Zo climbed into the carriage using his good arm to pull himself up. His father was followed by Fergus.

Great, Zo thought.

As soon as the door shut, and the carriage took off, his father started:

"What happened? How did you get hurt? Why are we going to see the physician? You should have healed by now. And what's this I hear about you spending time again with..." his father glanced at Fergus like he was afraid of what Fergus would overhear. "I thought *they* lived in the village...and I thought I told you to find a nice Library worker."

"*He is* a nice Library worker," Zo said firmly. "Or he will be."

His father covered his face with his hands. The only sound was that of the carriage rattling its way along the cobblestone road.

When Lar removed his hands from his face his eyes were hard as flint. "You understand that as a descendent of the Ancestors there are certain obligations to pass on what you've inherited?"

Zo sat stoney faced.

His father got more agitated. "Did you know I've been promising your mother for years that I've raised you to be a powerful healer and a credit to House Sano? She has threatened countless times to take you away, but I've managed to convince her you were learning better with me. If she finds out you can't even heal yourself, and that you're..." Lar glanced at Fergus again. "...struggling to find a girl, she will descend upon us lightning fast and take you to Eileansano."

"I won't go back. I'm of age and she can't force me," Zo said vehemently. "And I thought I was under contract to the Library."

"She has the power to override that contract. She can and she will—your mother is a powerful woman."

Zo gazed out the window at the passing houses. The curtains in the windows reminded him of that day. The day he had set the front hall's curtains on fire:

His mother was waiting for him with his student Healer's robe in the hall when he returned from a morning of adventuring in the hedge maze. She was angry before he even spoke.

"I'm not going," he told her.

"Yes, you are." She reached for his arm.

His fire bead began to glow, intense and bright. He held it up by the cord.

"No, I'm not. I gotta get outside." He pushed passed his mother.

"You come right back here when you're done. I've arranged for you to meditate with the Headmaster. He has a new technique to calm you down enough to let the Healing lessons in."

Zo thought about the last time he had to meditate with the Head Healing Master. It was incredibly boring. So boring, Zo had lit a fire in his hands and had played with the flames till the Headmaster caught him and sent him to clean fish in the kitchen. Sometimes he still caught a whiff of fish on his robes.

"No!" Zo yelled at his mother. Fire leapt to his fingertips. As he turned around, the flames caught the curtains on fire.

His father smothered the flames, and Zo had been locked out of the house for the rest of the day. From then on, his mother always looked at the burnt wood on the walls whenever she wanted to prove her point about fire and healing.

The carriage came to a halt outside Wilmar's shop. Lar and Fergus followed Zo inside, watching as Wilmar examined Zo's shoulder, but Wilmar seemed to pick up Zo's agitation at their audience.

"If you two wouldn't mind taking a walk for a while," Wilmar said to them. "I need to work with Zo. It'll take a bit."

"We can wait," Lar said.

Wilmar stepped in front of Zo and folded his arms. "I think you're needed elsewhere for a while," Wilmar said pointedly.

Reluctantly, they stood and let Wilmar shoo them out the door of his exam room and onto the street.

Then Wilmar returned his focus to Zo. Examining his burned side and testing his shoulder.

"Well, these are remarkably healed for just a few days. Are you sure you haven't used your healing magic on them?" Wilmar said.

"I'm sure it wasn't me," Zo bit out.

Wilmar held his gaze for a long time, Zo didn't look away. Wouldn't back down.

"What's your favorite place?" Wilmar asked.

"We move around a lot, I don't have a favorite place."

"Alright, favorite type of place then."

Zo looked off to the north, toward the bay, "I like to be by the water."

"Great, close your eyes and think about the water lapping gently on the shore. Can you see it?"

"Healers meditate so they can clear their minds in order to heal," Zo said, crossing his arms. His shoulder wasn't happy about it.

"Humor me," Wilmar said. "Us Ordinary physicians need to learn to be calm in a crisis. If we lose our composure and become like the sick or injured person's worried family member, we become as useless."

"Who says I want to be a physician?" Zo countered.

"So disagreeable, I can see why you and your Ancestor teacher have issues." Wilmar took Zo's good shoulder. "Whether you like it or not, you are a gifted young man. Please try."

Zo sighed. He really didn't want to do anything that resembled healing magic, but Wilmar's kindness seemed to seep into him whenever he was in the man's presence, so he did as he was told.

"Good, now let's breathe with the waves—long breath in and exhale all the way out."

He worked with Zo's breathing, reminding him to relax certain parts of his body as they went. By the end Zo was completely relaxed and Wilmar fell silent.

As Zo focused on how he felt, his mind drifted, He began to think about his body as a whole, and eventually his mind began roaming around inside, like when he used to heal himself. He found the burned and damaged tissue in his side and his magic so easily flowed into it...

And then his mind relived that night:

His parents were having a vicious fight. It had escalated from the arguing they'd been doing for moons. For a while now, his mother had actively strived to paint fire magic as bad, and Master Ignis as evil. She taught Zo every off-colored myth and rumor she could find about the fire Ancestor's life, anything that would drive a wedge between Zo and his fire master. That night as his parents screamed at each other, his door opened. Zo pretended to sleep as his mother came to hover over him, her shaking hands grasping the beads around his neck.

"You cannot take his fire bead," his father said from the doorway. "Do you want to destroy his spirit?"

To his relief, Zo's mother let go of his beads, but turned on his father. "How do you know? There's no written evidence of the effects of taking someone's bead from them. I've seen research that says it's possible before the child finishes their lessons." She turned back toward Zo, her fingers gently tracing the side of his face. "If he only has Healing magic it can be his focus. He will stop being distracted. I know he can be a great Healer, he just needs to stop learning fire."

Zo's father crossed the room and took his mother by the arms. "Have you lost your senses completely, Fyri? I've seen a Haunted Child in the woods when I was a kid. They were wild with vacant eyes. Do you want our son to be broken like that? It won't make Healing his focus, it will damage him forever!"

Zo's mother let out a deep-throated growl, fists at her side. Then she stormed out and slammed the door.

Zo opened his eyes fully and held his father's gaze for a long time, both of them saying nothing. Eventually his father sighed, pressing the palms of his hands to his eyes. Zo watched in silence till his father straightened, pulled the covers back up around Zo, then quietly left.

The next morning Lar packed up the boys in a wagon. Regg sat in the back playing with a wooden horse. Their father loaded things around Regg, who was seemingly oblivious, but his play was much subdued compared to normal. Zo turned from the wagon to stare at the door to the house he had known his whole nine years of life. It was his world. She was his world. He waited, hoping, silently praying to the Ancestors that she would come out the door, rush down the steps, scoop him up, and tell him that she loved him more than anything else in the world. That she didn't care if he did fire magic, and that she loved him for who he was—but the door remained shut tight.

His father called for him to come get in the wagon. Zo let go of his hope and hardened his heart against the *feelings threatening to overwhelm him. Tearing his eyes away, he obeyed his father and climbed into the wagon next to Regg. As his father drove them away, Zo took his last look at that house and swore he'd never see it again...*

The image burned anger through Zo. His mind popped back to the present with such a rush he got an instant headache. He shot to his feet as flames came curling around his hands.

Wilmar, who had been close to Zo, meditating along with him, scrambled backward to keep from getting burned.

Zo was breathing hard, like he was drowning, gasping for breath.

"Whoa, whoa, whoa—It's alright," Wilmar said. "We're safe here."

Zo shook his hands out and tried to get control of his breathing. Sitting down hard, he put his head in his hands. Wilmar stood over him anxious, but saying nothing.

"I need to go," Zo stood. "I need to burn something down."

Wilmar didn't stop him, but Zo caught a sad, pitying look on his face, which made him even angrier. He left Wilmar, slamming the door behind him. He strode down the street, his eyes avoiding all contact with the Healing House, though he felt its presence loom over him. The streets were bustling with normal Waatch activity, but Zo ignored it and let his legs carry him in long angry strides. The flow of people on the street veered around him, but occasionally he bumped into someone who wasn't paying attention. He kept going without acknowledging the collision. He was too afraid to open his mouth to say anything. If he did all the anger would bubble out onto the innocent bystander, so he just kept going. As he drew closer to the Library district, and its various shops that catered to Library and researcher needs, he happened to catch a glimpse of a little girl on crutches. His heart beat fast, hopeful it might be the same little girl he'd helped Wimar with the other day. He slowed to get a better look at her face, but she turned a corner and disappeared.

Zo took a deep breath, bending over to put his hands on his knees as painful thoughts and feelings washed through him. His heart warred within itself, threatening to tear him apart—the want to help and save, and the hatred and need to burn it all down.

There had to be a way to live with both halves of his heart. He had to find a way.

Chapter Twenty-Two

But alas! My verses turned into a lament,
Under the bright flashes of the traveling star,
Who would have thought that a radiant sky,
Omen would be of such pain and despair?

— Luc's epic poem as recorded in his Third Journal. Ancestral Liberty,
Third Floor Restricted. The Curator has the Key.

Like a tunnel collapsing on itself, the shelves of books and Library walls closed in on Ryn. If she stopped, her brain tried to process that her mother, the woman who raised her, was not the person she thought she was. Now everyone had magic—everyone but her. And how had Ryn never seen her mother do magic. Where were her beadscars? At the conclusion of a person's lessons their beads burned, leaving a mark forever, yet Ryn had never seen them on her mother. There was a burn mark on her chest from a fall into a fire as a kid, but it wasn't in the same place as beadscars would be—or was it?

Ryn didn't want to think about it. She wandered aimlessly. She was seeing, yet not seeing, the Library around her, but in her mind, it whispered to her. It told her to turn left here, and right there, and to wind her way through those shelves. The more she listened, the more she fell into a dreamlike state. When she came to herself, she was standing in front of a door. At least it looked like a door. It had a doorframe, but it had no handle and no latch. On the door was carved a tree, every branch and every leaf so detailed Ryn could almost see them shaking and shimmering in the breeze. She reached out her hand to feel if it was real.

The voice in her head said, *yes, come inside.*

"Ryn!"

Ryn sprang back, startled by Clayr's voice.

"Your mother is on her way back." Clayr was breathing heavily, like she'd been running in the Library. "We need to get you home before she gets there. She'll be a worried mess if she gets home before you."

Ryn turned slowly to face Clayr, as if she was just waking. At first, she couldn't process what Clayr was saying.

"Come," Clayr enfolded Ryn in a hug. "Let's get you to a carriage. If you leave immediately, you'll hopefully get there in time."

Ryn let Clayr pull her along, still somewhat dazed. The closer she got to the Library exit, the more she came to herself—and realized she burned with anger toward the daughter of the woman guiding her through the Library. At that thought, Ryn tried to push away, but Clayr pulled her tighter. In the process, something hard and metal jingled, pressing against Ryn's hip. The Curator's keys! They were here, right next to Ryn. All she had to do was slip her hand into Clayr's pocket and she would have them, but then what? What did they open, and how would they help her find Luc's book?

Fergus wasn't at the back door of the Library, as Clayr swept her out and down the stairs. Ryn realized Fergus' presence had come to mean everything was right with the world of the Library. Now everything was wrong.

As Clayr shut Ryn into the carriage, numbness settled over Ryn. She barely perceived Clayr giving the driver directions to take Ryn home. Waatch slipped away outside the window with Ryn barely registering it. As they climbed the hill away from town toward the village, the leaves on the trees took on more colors. Yellows, oranges and reds—some trees still partly green, but turning rapidly. It smelled of fall—of shorter, colder nights, and damp, wet everything. Summer was fading as the sun trekked lower on the horizon across the sky. Ryn normally loved this time of year. Fall signaled her birthday was coming, but was it really her birthday? How did her parents know when her birthday was? The thought of Ryn's parents made her want to crawl out of her skin, or jump out of the carriage and run away into the woods, but then what? Where would she go? How would she live? She had no answers to those questions, so she let the carriage bring her closer and closer to her home, and the life that was a lie.

When the carriage pulled to a stop outside the cottage, Ryn could hear her mother and Jett yelling at each other inside. The carriage driver opened the door for her, but she didn't want to get out. She almost told him to turn around and take her back to the place she would probably never be allowed to return to now, but she knew that would only make things worse. Taking a deep breath, she stepped out into the cool autumn sunlight and shuffled toward the door.

As she lifted the latch, the door flew open and Ryn found herself engulfed in a crushing hug.

"Oh Ryn, I've been so worried about you," her mother's voice was breaking like she was trying to hold back a torrent of tears.

Ryn let herself absorb the comfort and safety of her mother's hug for a moment—but when she thought of telling her mother not to worry, she couldn't say the words. She couldn't say she was alright, because she wasn't.

Her mother pulled her into the cottage and shut the door. The little girl who trembled in fear of being in trouble took over Ryn, and she watched as the driver, her only chance of escape, drove away.

Her mother's lips pursed white. "You both promised me. *Promised* me right here that you would stay by the cottage, yet I'm not even gone for a full moon and I find this:"

Her mother held up a Waatch newspaper which announced the lucky students who would get to study with Master Wes.

Ryn shook off that little girl. She forced her fear of rejection away, and stood a little taller.

"Ryn de Dico from Sooke. That can't be me, *I* don't have magic..." Ryn couldn't help letting the sarcasm slip out. Her stomach quelled at saying the next part, but Ryn's rising anger let it slip out between her teeth. "But *someone* we know does."

Ryn's mother got very still and pale. Jett folded his arms and looked back and forth between Ryn and Ryette.

"What are you talking about, Ryn?" Jett asked.

Ryn swallowed a huge, hard lump. "I found Mom and Dad's marriage certificate."

Ryette swore. Ryn flinched.

"That's under lock and key in the restricted section," Ryette said.

"Restricted section, yes, lock and key—not so much," Ryn said.

Jett's face was still looking bewildered. "Why would your marriage certificate be under lock and key?"

Ryn's mother stood pale and expressionless, like a statue about to crack.

"Don't say it, Ryn," her mother begged.

"Say it." Jett's focus was completely on their mother.

"Mother is from House Viator," Ryn said.

Jett's jaw dropped.

"Not only that, but she's the Matriarch-in-Waiting. She's the Matriarch's daughter—next in line to lead House Viatoro." Ryn turned to Jett. "You are the Matriarch's grandson."

Jett's mouth was moving, but nothing was coming out.

"I can explain..." Ryn's mother began, but Jett seemed to be gasping for air....

And then he exploded. "I have a second magic—*and you never told me?* I'm a few short moons away from aging out of being able to take the lessons and learn the magic, *and you were just going to let it pass? I'm going to be half Ordinary forever, and you were just going to allow that?*"

Ryette rushed to try and soothe him like she always had. "It's complicated. They are trying to use me and you, to manipulate us into something horrible, a dangerous experiment, that some conniving, power hungry, descendent convinced my mother would work. All it's done is break people's minds. I refuse to let that happen to you. I was protecting you!"

"Protecting me? *Protecting me*? I almost lost the chance for my own travel magic, and you were just protecting me?" Jett put his hands in his hair. "I'm dating someone from my own House!"

"You're what?" Ryette shouted.

"What a disaster! You have..."

Jett's tirade became ugly. The things he spat at their mother were unkind at best, cruel at worst and unlike anything Ryn had ever heard anyone in her family say to each other. Throwing her hands over her ears like a little girl, she raced to the door and out of the cottage. Tears were streaming down her face, and she could barely see. Somehow, halfway across the yard she ran straight into Thalya.

"What's wrong, Ryn?" Thalya asked.

"Take me to the Library please. I need to get away—*far* away," Ryn said.

Thalya glanced at the cottage and the fighting that could be heard perfectly in the yard. "Sure. Sounds like a bad time to visit Jett anyway."

***

They landed by the east gate just outside the Library grounds.

"Why don't you take me to the front door?" Ryn asked.

"You know how the Library foundation blocks magic?"

"Yeah?"

"That barrier extends all the way to the walls for Travel magic" Thalya said.

"Oh! Uh, thanks."

Ryn entered the gate, without giving Thalya a second glance. She wandered the path in a fog, surprised when she actually found herself at the steps to the Library front door. The steps seemed long, and her legs heavy. The portal tingle raced down her spine as she passed through the front door. She stopped short at the sight of Fergus guarding the door.

"Oh my goodness, are you alright?" Ryn asked him. "How's Zo?"

Fergus smiled his relaxed smile that was so very un-Library guard like. "He's fine." His eyes narrowed at her. "You don't look fine. What's the matter?"

Ryn took several deep breaths to keep tears from flooding her eyes. Glancing around, she realized they were making a scene in front of workers. Fortunately, the end of lunch bells saved her.

"I have to go, I'll tell you later," Ryn said.

"You better," he said.

Ryn felt his eyes watch her go.

Once inside the Library proper, her steps slowed. She didn't want to return to the alcove. She couldn't face Yll and her betrayal, but she didn't want to leave the Library. Outside was the world she didn't fit into. The one person in her life, the only one left who knew what it was like to be Ordinary—wasn't Ordinary at all.

Ryn squared her shoulders. It was time she found out who she really was. Maybe her parents were Matriarch and Patriarch of two rival Houses like Viator and Pentral. The thought reminded her Ryette was house Viator. There was no way Ryn was house Viator, or her mother would have known that. Anger fueled her march to the reference section where she tore through books in search of directions to every orphanage record she could find.

It turned out the orphanage records were all together on the second floor, which made it quite convenient.

Ryn sat in the upstairs reading room with piles of orphanage records on the table in front of her. It was lovely that the reading room had a ceiling high window that let in lots of light, warm on the cool fall day. No books were stored here, but there were tables for reading and studying materials in the sunny light of the windows. Ryn flipped through page after page, searching for a little girl dropped off at an orphanage almost sixteen years ago. She found a few entries that were possibilities, but they didn't feel right. They were either in remote parts of the mainland or somewhere on the islands. She just couldn't picture her father picking up a baby girl at an orphanage on an Ancestral Island.

It was tedious, but it was good work that was keeping her mind from contemplating how messed up her life just became. As she reached for another book to browse, the silence of the reading room was broken by a voice.

"There you are!"

Ryn looked up to find Master Wes striding toward her. She clamped her teeth together hard to keep her jaw from dropping.

"I've been looking everywhere for you," Master Wes said. "I'm expecting you're searching for the answer to the mystery of the Curator's Key, correct?"

He picked up one of the books on her table and frowned.

"No...I..." Ryn lowered her eyes. "It seems Prym has everything in hand, I'm sure she'll find it."

"Except she doesn't, and she won't," Master Wes said, sitting on the edge of her table, eyes boring into her. "You're the one who's found everything so far."

This time Ryn's jaw did drop.

"How...how do you know?" she asked.

"I'm not as blind as you think I am. A good researcher knows his sources," Master Wes smiled. "I have eyes around the Library." He stared directly into her eyes. "I know it was you giving the Library guard a merry chase upstairs last night."

Ryn swallowed hard.

"Now, given that you went to all the trouble to retrieve the book, and are currently at the top of my list for winning the researcher position, I'd say it's time we found Luc's book." Master Wes leaned in, making Ryn sweat. "We're so close after all."

Ryn wasn't sure about how close they were. Knowing the book was somewhere in the Library was like knowing it is *somewhere* in the world. It was still like looking for a needle in a haystack, it could take years to unravel the mystery of the Curator's Key and find the book.

Ryn shrugged one shoulder. "I suppose."

Master Wes pulled out a book she hadn't noticed he was carrying. It was titled *Hidden passages and Lost Items in the Library*.

"That doesn't look like a Library book," Ryn said.

"It's not, it's a fanciful book printed mostly for visitors to Waatch in order to stir their imaginations about the Library, but I found something very interesting inside."

Master Wes flipped to a chapter on the Curator's office. According to the book there were all kinds of hiding places inside the Curator's office. Especially *in* the desk, which was built at least a couple hundred years ago, possibly longer.

Master Wes closed the book and pressed it into Ryn's hands. He looked around the reading room, but there was no one else there.

"You have access to the Madame Curator's private quarters. Get her keys. Find the book. I'm counting on you."

Ryn swallowed. "Yll and I aren't presently on good terms."

A flash of annoyance passed over Master Wes' face. "Your petty squabbles are unimportant. What's important is getting that book. Do it and the researcher position is yours. It doesn't matter what it takes."

Master Wes leaned in so that he loomed over her. "And do it tonight. You've stirred up too much attention with your little foray onto the third floor last night. I need this business concluded now. Another discovery is demanding my attention, and I am being called home. If you want that Library position, it's now or never."

Ryn nodded, afraid to trust her voice. Master Wes scared her more than she dared admit.

Master Wes leaned back. "Good. Meet me tonight in my research alcove with the book and you will be rewarded."

Ryn's head reeled, thinking how she could possibly accomplish what Maser Wes demanded, but she bowed her head when she said, "Yes."

***

Ryn spent the rest of the afternoon pouring over the book Master Wes had given her, with the addition of some others she found in the Library. Despite being somewhat sensationalized, the visitor guidebook was mostly accurate, at least according to the other sources she found. The most surprising part was that the tunnels and shafts Zo had led her through were not the only secret passages in the Library. She made notes on ones she wanted to find in the margins of the book, then reshelved the others in hopes of covering her tracks. Normally Docents reshelved books pulled by students and researchers. This ensured they got returned to the right place based on the reference book's directions. It was a notoriously tedious process Ryn had heard docents complain about.

***

At the sound of the closing bell, Ryn left the Library. A chill wind blew leaves, swirling about her feet. She needed to wait till Clayr left the Library for the day. Ryn hoped they would stay in the Curator's Cottage on the Library grounds tonight, otherwise she'd have to find a way to follow them to Sooke. She hadn't seen Thalya since she brought Ryn back, and Ryn didn't have any money to hire a carriage.

Ryn's stomach growled, reminding her she hadn't eaten anything all day, so she headed to the mess hall. The workers there let her have a warm bowl of vegetable soup and a roll. It was all Ryn thought her churning stomach could handle. She couldn't believe she was going to steal Clayr's keys, and worse—break into her office with them. There was still no sign of Zo, so Ryn found a table as far away from everyone else as she could, and forced herself to eat.

"Well, well, well, little miss Ordinary."

Ryn looked up from her soup to find Prym and her admirers—including Yll and Regg—who had his arm around Yll's shoulders.

"I wanted to thank you personally for doing all the work so I can be a Library Researcher. It was so helpful of you," Prym said.

Yll bowed her head and shifted, looking uncomfortable.

Ryn had to bite her tongue hard to keep from spilling that Master Wes was onto Prym.

"So glad I could help," Ryn bit out. "I, unlike some people, can't stand the sight of other people in distress."

Yll's head sank further.

Prym loomed over her. "Listen you little worthless scrap of dirt. This is just a downpayment on what you owe me for ruining my party. I will see you pay for it. Daddy is particularly fond of throwing people in jail for small offenses."

"Even his own daughter," Ryn said.

Prym flipped Ryn's bowl upside down, spilling it all over the table and Ryn.

"I'm not through with you," Prym said, then she and her entourage turned and left, Yll and Regg following them.

Anger burned in Ryn. She was going to find Luc's book, and she was going to leave that snotty brat in whatever cage Prym's father decided to throw her in for not winning the Library position.

Ryn got up and begged a rag from a mess hall worker. As she was wiping soup off her skirt, she saw Regg pick up a couple of apples and attempt to juggle them for Yll—it went badly with the apples rolling across the floor. Yll laughed.

Ryn lost control.

She found herself standing in front of Yll yelling from her gut. It was the loudest Ryn had ever been.

Yll's eyes got wide.

"How *could* you?" Ryn shouted. "Who are you? I thought you were my friend. No—I thought you were my sister! Now suddenly you have magic and I'm not good enough?" Ryn gestured toward Regg and the rest of Prym's friends. "These people who have tortured us for years for being Ordinary are now more important? So important you would betray the one person who's been there for you all your life?"

Ryn's nostrils flared.

Yll snapped her jaw shut. Her face twisted into a sneer.

"Do you expect me to *avoid* the community now that I have magic? A community you yourself are *dying* to be a part of?" Yll thrust a finger at Ryn's chest. "Why are we here? Huh? Why are we in Master Wes' class? Because you want to find your Ancestors so you can do magic! Don't be a *hypocrite*, Ryn. You want this as much as I do, but you would begrudge my place as an Ancestor descendant."

Ryn's face burned hot. "So, you would throw yourself in with *that* horrible person?" Ryn's hand flicked in the direction Prym had gone. "Now that you have magic you have to be just like them?"

Yll's mouth was flat, her lips pressed.

"*Fine*! Go! Be with them. I don't need you!" Ryn shouted.

Ryn stalked off, trying to ignore the fact that every eye in the mess hall was on her. She dodged a person frozen in place at the end of a table watching her, and bumped into a worker carrying a tray of dirty dishes. The tray and dishes crashed to the floor, broken pieces scattering everywhere. Ryn ran out the door.

As soon as she was outside, she burst into tears. She had never fought with Yll like that. Sure, they had argued over where to go or what to do, but they had never yelled at each other. Not like this. Ryn wandered the Library grounds, barely able to see the pathway through her tears. She clutched at her stomach, wracked with sobs. A Library guard, she couldn't see who it was through her tears, only the uniform, asked her if she was alright. She turned and fled. She just wanted to be alone. Her world was crumbling. Her mother had lied to her and now her best friend cared more about her magic than she did about Ryn. And Ryn had hurt them in return. Everyone was going to abandon her, and she would be left alone.

Well, she would show them. She would find Luc's book and she would prove to she was the best researcher. Nothing could stop her now.

Ryn waited in the bushes outside the Curator's cottage for the lights to go out. She was in luck. Clayr and Yll had decided to sleep in the cottage again tonight. It was taking forever for them to go to bed, though. Regg had stayed until late. Ryn had watched him wipe tears from Yll's cheeks, then kiss her on the doorstep, before he said goodbye and left. The light from the cottage had backlit them in a dramatic way Ryn couldn't help but feel envious of. Ryn had never been kissed herself, and she was pretty sure that was Yll's first kiss. Unless Yll had kissed someone before and hadn't told Ryn. Who knew anymore? Ryn sat in the bushes, cold and alone. It hurt Ryn's heart even more to think about a time when she would have laid in bed with Yll tonight giggling like sisters about the kiss. Ryn twisted the fake beads at her neck, nearly snapping the cord they hung on.

Finally, the lights went out, and Ryn waited in the dark. How long would it take them to fall deep enough asleep Ryn wouldn't get caught?

When Ryn's nerves made it so she couldn't wait any longer, she crept toward the cottage's back window. She recalled from earlier in the day it wasn't latched and was open a crack. Gently she slid the window open, hoping it wouldn't make a sound going up. She pulled herself up and scrambled through the window, banging her shins on a chair she clamped down on her teeth hard, so she didn't cry out. Tears sparked in her eyes, and she wiped them away, limping toward Clayr's bedroom. All was dark, and the door was open a crack. Ryn pushed on it. The hinges creaked a little, causing Ryn to freeze. Clayr murmured something, but her breathing returned to the regular rhythm of sleep.

Deeply wishing she had taken Clayr's keys from her pocket earlier in the day, Ryn crept forward. Light from the lamp posts outside shone into the room. On the side table next to Clayr's bed was an extinguished lantern, a stack of books—and the keyring of the Curator's keys.

Ryn had spent the evening thinking about how to lift the keys without them jangling and making a noise. She had watched Zo do it the other night on the third floor, so she used both hands to quietly squeeze the keys together, then lift them off the table.

Clayr rolled over in her sleep and her arm almost hit Ryn. Heart thumping in panic, Ryn crept back slowly out the way she had come.

She slid out the window, blood thundering in her ears, then closed it behind her. She couldn't believe she had the keys in her hand. They were hard, and cold, and buzzing with energy.

Now to get back into the Library, past the guards. There was only one way she knew how to do that. At the edge of the Curator's Cottage lawn, she paused. Once she left there was no going back from this choice. Her fingers closed tight on the keys as her anger rose again. They all deserved what they got.

She ran for the Library dormitory, hoping Zo was in bed where he should be.

Chapter Twenty-Three

The process of Magic lessons is not well documented. It seems each student's lessons are personal and tailored to each individual based on their relationship with their Ancestor. How a piece of the Ancestor's bone draws their spirit to the learner is still a mystery. There's talk of forming a research committee on the topic, but really there's no interest in putting the money into it. The system works—that's all that matters.

— Lyv de Dico. "Ancestral Culture and its Effect on Youth." *Journal of Mind Magic Medicine.* Ancestral Library Periodicals Section, Second Floor, Shelf 100, Box 2.

Zo's feet chafed in his sand-filled shoes, but he didn't mind. It had been a nice evening out with Iden—dinner at a fun noodle place and a walk on the beach. A chill autumn breeze had kicked up on their walk back through Waatch, but the coolness made his skin tingle with the anticipation of the turn of the season. As they approached the Library grounds, Zo's arm slid off Iden's shoulders.

"If you could do something besides marry Prym and work in the Library, what would you do?" he asked.

Iden was quiet, the only sound was their shoes on the cobblestones.

"There's this small community on Oydico that is trying to live life using only mind magic to communicate. They are close knit, because of how intimately you need to know someone to communicate directly to someone's mind, but every once in a while, they open to the addition of someone new. I want that. They live simply and they strive for absolute harmony to preserve the ease of mind communication. I want to explore that intimate life, in tune with everything around me."

Zo's heart sank. He could see no part for himself in that dream.

"Sounds amazing," he said, forcing enthusiasm into his voice.

"Yeah," Iden sighed. "But that'll never happen. My life's planned for me."

Zo's footsteps slowed as they approached his dorm. He didn't want the night to end. Master Nix had given him the night off, but he had to work again the next day. He hoped his recovering shoulder wouldn't mean he had to work heating boilers again.

"Well..." Zo said,

"Well..." Iden's eyes locked on his.

"Zo!"

Glancing to the side, Zo saw Ryn rushing up to him, clutching a book and a keyring.

She ran straight into him, throwing her arms around him.

"I'm so sorry I left you. Fergus made me go." She pulled back and looked him over. "Are you alright? Did they hurt you? I was so worried they would do something awful."

"Naw, I told Master Nix I was just curious about the tunnels at night..."

Now that she was up close, he could see something was off. The hem of her dress was muddy, there were twigs in her hair, and her eyes were red, sunken, and dark. She looked like she'd been dragged through the forest by her hair.

"Are you alright?" he asked her.

She looked nervously at the Library. "I need your help."

"Anything," he said.

"I need to get back into the Library via the tunnels."

"Anything but that." Zo shook his head. "We made it out by the skin of our teeth without punishment last time. Master Nix won't buy my excuses a second time."

Ryn clutched the book to her chest. The keys in her hand jangled as she shifted.

Iden's eyes got bright in the Library garden night. "Did you get the Curator's keys?" he asked.

Ryn shifted to hide the keys behind the book. "Maybe," she said.

"The solution is simple," Iden said. "Just use those keys to open the Library door."

"Oh!" Ryn's eyes perked up. "Right! Why didn't I think of that?"

Zo laughed. "Because I taught you too much sneaking around."

"I've got to go." She turned back toward the Library.

"Wait!" Zo grabbed her arm. "You haven't told me what's going on."

Ryn's eyes brimmed with tears. "Yll betrayed me, and gave the book we retrieved to Prym. My parent's marriage certificate revealed my mother is not who she says she is, and I need to bring Luc's book to Master Wes tonight, or I will lose my chance at the researcher position." Her voice broke at the last, head dipping down.

"I'm coming with you," Zo said.

Ryn shook her head. "No, you're right. We got lucky you didn't get into trouble for our last escapade into the Library. I don't want you getting into trouble for me."

Zo gave her a lopsided grin. "Trouble is my middle name."

"No." Ryn's mouth formed a firm line.

"You're right, nobody has a middle name," he joked, casting about desperately for a solution she would accept. "Take Iden then, he knows the Library pretty well."

Iden held up his hands. "Only because my parents made me study maps of it growing up." He chuckled. "But seriously, I'll go with you if you want."

Ryn's eyes narrowed suspiciously. Zo could see what was going through her mind—Iden was promised to Prym.

"Please," Zo said. "I think the parents are right, I don't trust Master Wes. You need someone to have your back."

"I've had too many people sticking knives into my back lately. Yll went straight to Prym to give her the book on Luc."

So, it *was* a trust issue.

Zo's sigh sounded uneasy even to himself. "Alright, but be careful."

Ryn nodded, then turned and fled back the way she'd come. Zo watched her go till she turned the corner of the Library, headed for the back door. As soon as she was out of his sight, he had an overwhelming sense of dread.

"I'm going after her," Zo said.

"I'll go with you," Iden shifted.

Zo shifted his focus back to Iden. "No. You stay here and keep watch. Try to distract anyone looking for us."

Iden shrugged. "I'll try."

Zo squeezed Iden's arm then ran after Ryn. At the corner of the Library he slowed, lest someone leaving the guardhouse notice him running up the steps. Sticking to the shadows between lamp posts, he mounted the stairs to the back door. As he drew closer, he found the door open a crack. There was no sign of Ryn. She must have gone into the Library. Hopefully she was the one who didn't close the door all the way, and not someone following her.

He reached out to push the door open.

An arm grabbed him from behind as a cold sharp edge pressed to his throat.

"Don't move," a voice whispered in his ear.

Zo raised his hands in surrender.

"Move away from the door."

Zo backed away. The knife dropped and a hand spun him around.

A sigh of relief escaped Zo. "Fergus, man, you scared the life out of me."

"What in all the name of the Ancestors do you think you are doing?" Fergus said. "I just prevented you and Ryn from getting roasted, literally, and here you are sneaking into the Library? What are you trying to do to me? Get me terminated?"

"No...it wasn't me. I mean, I was just worried...She needs help." His normal capacity to talk himself out of situations seemed to have escaped him with the knife at his throat.

"She....?" Fergus raised an eyebrow, then the lines of his face hardened. "Where's Ryn?"

Zo winced when his eyes involuntarily darted to the door.

Fergus groaned. "Not again."

"She was determined to get this thing for Master Wes. I offered to go with her, but she refused. After she left, something felt terribly wrong. I needed to come after her. I didn't mean to cause trouble."

Fergus dragged his hand down over his face. "I saw her earlier and she didn't look good. Any idea what's going on?"

Zo was quiet. He knew Ryn didn't want Library folks to know about what they were researching. He wasn't sure what he could tell Fergus without getting her in trouble.

"Right. Well, I'm going to assume since the last disturbance was on the third floor, that is where she's headed tonight. I'm sorry, but this time I can't cover for her. This is my job and I have to report intruders. If I look the other way it will cost me the job my family has held for generations, *and* possibly earn me some jail time. This time it's not just running around the basement, this time it's breaking and entering the Library. I'm sorry."

"We have to do something." Zo's voice rose in anger, spurred by worry.

"Find her parents. If they have some influence with the Library they may be able to mitigate her punishment," Fergus' eyes shone hard and cold in the dark, then he pushed past Zo and into the Library.

Zo swore, then tore down the steps not knowing where to run for help. He needed to find his father. He had no idea where Ryette was, and his father was the closest thing to a parent for Ryn right now. Plus, Ryette had put his father in charge of watching over Ryn while she was gone. Zo wasn't sure where to find his father though. If he was all the way at their cabin in Sooke it would take Zo hours to get there, get his father, and get back. Clayr was also someone who was watching over Ryn, but she was also the Curator of the

Library—and Ryn had her keys. Unsure of which path to take, he ran for where he had left Iden.

He found Iden leaning against the tree talking with Regg, of all people.

Zo ran up to them, out of breath.

"What happened?" Iden asked.

Zo shook his head. "Where's Dad?" he asked his brother.

"With Ryette. She came back. Jett and Ryn argued with her, and they both left. Ryette went looking for Jett and couldn't find him, and now she's here looking for Ryn."

"I need dad," Zo said.

"At the mess hall maybe? I told him I'd seen Ryn there earlier."

"Great." Zo took off toward the mess.

"Wait," Regg said, running up alongside him. "What's going on?"

"Ryn's in trouble. Big trouble." Zo ran faster.

Chapter Twenty-Four

The village of Sooke is one of the only places on the mainland where everyone living there is of Ancestor descent. It's an Ancestor island of its own in the middle of the mainland. The difference is there's no concentration of one magic. It's every variety of those who've been working in the Library for generations.

— Myra de Lux. *A Comprehensive History of the Library*. Ancestral Library, First Floor, History section, Shelf 82, Shelfmark 43.

Entering the Library through the back door turned out to be easy. Ryn had watched Clayr open the door more than once. There were only two keys on the keyring of the correct size for the back door. Once inside, she held the latch down till the door quietly shut. A lantern sat on a nearby table, illuminating the entrance and the cloak room. Finding no guards or workers nearby, Ryn lifted the lantern and took it with her.

At night, the Library was in complete darkness. During the day there were scattered windows, and the occasional lantern to give light, but at night, all was still and black. Ryn's nerves took over her imagination. She could only see as far in front of her as the lantern light showed, which purposefully wasn't far. The darkness just beyond the light came alive, like its own creature. She felt it all around. It was ahead of her and behind her. Everywhere she moved it was just beyond the light.

The incredible brightness in the midst of blackness added to her unease—she was visible to anyone who might still roam the Library. It was like a bright beacon screaming "here I am, I'm not supposed to be here—come and take me away!" Seeing beyond the light was impossible. The light was giving her away, yet the thought of dousing the light and moving in the dark terrified her. The light was comforting and frightening at the same time.

The shelving and hallways appeared different in the dark, but after only a few mistaken turns Ryn was able to make her way to Clayr's office. She recognized the door from when she had been brought there for the announcement of her acceptance as a student with Master Wes.

Something creaked nearby. Ryn scanned the area, but saw nothing beyond her light. Hand shaking, she fumbled for the second large key, inserted it into the lock and turned. The bolt slid aside. Lifting the latch, she scurried into the office like something was right on her tail.

She thought she would feel relief once she closed the door behind her, but Clayr's office at night was even more intimidating than during the day. Noticing the curtains open she quickly moved to close them, lest someone walking the Library grounds see her in Clayr's office. Once closed in, she had an ominous feeling of being trapped. An overwhelming urge to flee the Library and disappear into the night pulled at her. She could give up everything here and just go home. But go home to what? An Ordinary life with a household full of magic...a community full of magic? Who was she without knowing who she was? Nothing. At least working at the Library, she would be something. Library researchers were respected. Plus, she would have a lifetime to figure out where she really came from.

Setting the lantern in the middle of Clayr's desk, Ryn opened the Library guidebook to the Curator's Office page and began to search for each of the supposed hidden spaces. Most of them were either fanciful reading or Ryn couldn't figure out how they worked. The supposed hole in the wall behind a loose brick in the corner didn't exist. In fact, the brick wasn't even loose. The painting of Waatch before the Library was built, depicting an enormous tree rooted in its foundation, did indeed have a cupboard behind it, but there was no keyhole and no visible way to open it, so Ryn moved on to the next hiding place. A certain book in the bookcase was actually a box. One of the keys on the key ring fit the lock, but inside was an odd-looking pendant, clear, like a glass bubble, with something red and liquid inside. She locked the box again and returned it to the shelf. Ryn moved to the desk. Unlocking the right bottom drawer, she opened it. Feeling around at the side of the drawer, she depressed the latch that opened a hidden compartment. Inside was a promise necklace and a bunch of journals. Flipping through them, Ryn could see they were all Clayr's journals. She couldn't understand why Clayr would have them hidden in a secret compartment, but she didn't have time to read through them to see if Luc's book was mentioned. Just as she was snapping the false drawer back into place, she heard someone knock at the door. Closing the drawer, she scrambled under the desk. The door creaked open.

"Madame Curator?" a feminine voice asked.

Footsteps crossed the wood floor to stand right beside where Ryn was curled up under the desk, trying not to breathe.

Ryn could hear the shuffling of papers on the desktop above her.

"Must be working late," the voice murmured to themselves. "I hope you don't mind me leaving you more work." The person yawned. "Because I'm headed home."

Then the footsteps retreated, and the door closed.

Ryn breathed a sigh of relief even though her blood thundered in her ears. She needed to get out of here, but she still hadn't found Luc's book.

Crawling out from under the desk, Ryn's knee depressed part of the wood floor and it clicked open. This was not something mentioned in the guidebook. Scrambling out from under the desk, Ryn took the lantern to shine the light into the opening. There was a lid with a lock underneath the hinged wood floor piece. One of the small keys on the keyring fit the lock. Trembling with hope, excitement, and nervousness, Ryn turned the lock and pulled the door open. Inside was a small book. Reverently Ryn pulled it out, taking it, and the lantern, and setting them both on the desk.

"This is it," Ryn whispered, then regretted how loud her voice sounded in the silent dark.

Opening the book, she found it wasn't Luc's book at all, but a small reference book. She barely registered the other titles as she scanned for Luc's name. Several pages in she found it—Luc's journals. One of them with a reference to his epic poem. She groaned as she slid her finger over the directions.

"Third floor, southeast corner, forbidden antiquities room," Ryn read.

There was also a direction reference to a book titled *Of Meteors and Showers*.

Marching footsteps sounded outside the door. Ryn grabbed the book and dived under the desk, returning it to its box and shutting the trap door. Sweat trickled down Ryn's back, but the door didn't open. The footsteps retreated away from the door. Ryn scrambled out, pushed Clayr's chair back in, took the lantern, and fled the office.

She had escaped possible detection there, but how was she going to get onto the third floor again without being seen? The staircase was wide, expansive—and exposed.

Then it hit her.

She dove in a spot where a bookshelf made a jog around a corner forming a little niche, flipping through the guidebook till she found what she was looking for: *secret staircase to the upper floors*.

According to the guidebook, it was located behind a bookcase between the alcoves and the Researcher's room. She followed the hall south from Clayr's office till she found a bookcase in the middle of the wall. It was somewhat out of place, and yet every possible surface of wall space in the Library seemed to contain a bookcase, so it wasn't very noticeable. The guidebook said to pull on the book titled *Sneaky, Clever Dragons*.

Ryn scanned and scanned the bookshelf, but could not find it. She was just about to give up and search for another bookcase when she heard footfalls on the flagstone floors. Panicked, she turned to flee, and caught a glimpse of a small book with gold lettering on the binding. She pulled on the book. It didn't come free of the shelf, but tipped. Ryn heard a click and the bookshelf swung inward. She hurried inside, shutting the bookcase just as the sound of booted feet passed.

She sagged against the door, the weight of how out of her depth she was settling into her heart. She couldn't believe she was sneaking around the Library at night without permission. She forced away thoughts about what would happen to her if someone caught her, if she let her mind go there, she wouldn't be able to move from this spot, and she had to move. The best thing to do was to just get it over with.

Mounting the stairs, she continued up two flights past a door she assumed went to the second floor. Then up two more flights to what must be the third floor. Oddly, the stairs continued upward, but as far as Ryn knew there were only three floors to the Library. She figured they must lead to the bell tower or something.

She dimmed the lantern before pulling on the door handle to what she hoped was the third floor. She peeked out.

If the ground floor of the Library was dark and quiet at night, the third floor was oppressively so. The weight of the knowledge from all the books and documents shelved here pressed down on her. She was an insignificant bug compared to the history preserved here. She took a deep breath. When she had been here with Zo it hadn't felt quite so overwhelming.

Gulping, she pushed forward through the thick air. Momentum seemed to make it easier, probably why she hadn't felt this bad when she was with Zo—he was always in motion.

With the lantern low by her side, she wove her way through the shelving. None of it looked familiar from when she had been here a couple nights ago. She just kept heading right, which she guessed was west, and forward, which should be south. She finally found what she hoped was a corner. She couldn't be certain because it wasn't two walls coming together at a corner, but the two walls formed a box, like there was a room behind it, but it was, of course, covered in shelving and books.

Ryn scanned the shelves. There had been no shelfmark in the reference book. Sweat prickled her scalp as she searched. She grumbled under her breath about how Zo wasn't doing his job, because it was entirely too hot in here. Of course it was nerves, but it made her smile to blame him. Finally finding the book on meteors, she tried tipping it, but it wouldn't budge. She pulled and pulled—still nothing. Frustrated, she tried to yank it off the shelf—and the spine came away in her hand.

She tried to swear like Zo did, but nothing came out.

As she scrambled to put the book back together, she noticed a keyhole in the fake bookbinding. One of the keys on her keyring fit. The bookcase slid aside, revealing a room that smelled like old people—if all they had in their home was books and wooden boxes, that is. Despite smelling ancient, there was one of those strange, compressed shelves taking up the bulk of the room, but these shelves didn't compact all the way. Each of the books or boxes was chained to the shelf.

"Oh good grief," Ryn whispered, then covered her mouth and looked back at the dark opening to the Library.

She stood still, but didn't hear anything. All was still deadly quiet.

She released her breath and started scanning shelves. There were no directions beyond it was somewhere in this room. She wasn't even sure what she was looking for. She cranked the wheel and moved one shelf to the side. The sound of chains rattling as the shelf moved got her heart racing. A chill breath of air blew past her like icy fingers up her spine. The lantern flickered. Ryn shivered, but kept turning. She didn't want to dwell on what could possibly cause a burst of airflow in the still, dark Library. Just like when she found her parent's marriage record, she needed to keep going. At last, she rolled the other shelves out of the way, after making a huge racket.

And there it was. Somehow Ryn knew it was what she was looking for. It was on the bottom shelf, and it wasn't a book, but a box.

The lid was emblazoned with the Slayer's Sword: Praedo's symbol exactly as depicted on the object's room floor. She knew this had to be it. Kneeling beside the box, she tried all the keys in the lock holding the box chained to the shelf. None of them fit.

This couldn't be the end. She had come so far, and she was certain she held Luc's book in her hands, but she had no way of removing the box from the shelf, and no way to open it. She shook the box in frustration, chain jangling. Her heart raced as she again looked out into the absolute darkness of the third floor.

Setting the box back onto the shelf, she reached out and placed her hand on top of the box, her palm feeling the carving of the sword under it. Something sharp pricked her hand. She tried to pull it away, but it wouldn't come free. She felt something wet between her palm and the box, then her hand unstuck. She pulled it away to find it bloody. Her blood, smeared on the box lid, began to flow across it, entering the channels of the carving and filling it with red. A light glowed from the sword.

The box popped open.

Ryn rubbed her eyes and looked again. It was late at night now, and she had been up since early morning. Lifting the lid, she looked inside. In the box was a book fitting perfectly to the sides of it. She had to turn the box upside down to get it out, but once it fell into her hand, it felt so right. Like a glove made for her hand. Excitement raced through her, but now she almost didn't dare open it. What if it wasn't what she was looking for?

Taking a deep breath she opened the book—

In shadows deep, where ancient echoes sing,
Shores were cursed by the serpent's wing.

Where the beastly dragon ruled the land,
The most majestic mountains stand.
Citizens cowered afraid for their life,
When Praedo came to end the strife.

Ryn felt instantly connected to it. Like it was a part of her. She clutched it to her chest. She didn't want to give it up. She didn't care if she didn't get the Library position. She held in her hands the book that was the foundation to everything she was. She wasn't going to give it to Master Wes. She was going to sneak it out of the Library and take it home. It was hers and she was keeping it.

A whispered voice came like a shout in the dead silence. "You're in violation of Library law. Put your hands up and back slowly away from the shelves."

Chapter Twenty-Five

Sweet melodic accents dying in the ash,
Great agrestal anthems profaned in the flames,
Fire in the forest, trees becoming blaze,
And a solemn requiem left in the night air.

— Luc's epic poem as recorded in his Third Journal. Ancestral Liberty, Third Floor Restricted. The Curator has the Key.

Zo felt a storm coming. He raced across the Library grounds while every leaf and branch thrashed in the wind. The Library seemed to be in turmoil.

So focused on finding his dad, he crashed into Master Nix coming around the corner of the mess hall. The bucket of clams Master Nix was munching on almost went flying.

"Whoa! Slow down there!" Nix said.

Zo hands on his knees breathing hard. "Have you seen my dad?" Zo panted. "Or a woman with reddish blond hair?"

"No." Nix searched the grounds behind Zo. "Somebody after you?" He leaned in closer to Zo. "Is someone giving you a hard time about Iden? Tell me and I'll take care of it."

Zo stopped. His brow furrowed while he raised one eyebrow. "No. Why would you... Never mind. I've got to go."

Zo resumed his run for the mess hall.

"I'm here if you need me." Master Nix called after him.

Zo didn't have time to process Master Nix's weird reversal. His harsh treatment of Zo had started to change somewhere inside the Library tunnels. Zo had assumed it was because he got hurt, but now he wasn't sure.

When he reached the mess hall doors, they were locked and the windows dark. No one was around. Zo wondered briefly where Nix had gotten the clams, then did the one thing he decided was the only option left—he ran for the Curator's cottage and hoped Lar and Ryette had headed there. If they were still on the Library grounds it seemed the logical place they would go to get help.

Once he stood at the Curator's cottage door, he was completely out of breath. Light shone from inside, suggesting the inhabitants were up. Zo pounded on the door.

Yll answered it and Zo had to pace back a few steps to keep from taking her by the shoulders and shaking her. He took several deep breaths, struggling to control his racing heart and thrumming anger. When he turned back around, Regg had moved to Yll's side and put his arm protectively about her. That told Zo everything about where his brother stood in all this.

"Is Dad here?" Zo tried to control his voice, but even to his ears it came out a snarl.

Yll shrank from him.

"Yes," she said, turning her face away.

Zo pushed past her into the cottage. Lar was pacing, while Clayr sat at the table looking half awake, disheveled, and disturbed.

"Can I speak with you a moment?" Zo asked his father.

Lar's eyes seemed to be distant, thinking on something else, but he nodded and followed Zo outside.

When they were a few paces from the cottage Lar said, "Ryette's missing."

Zo stopped. "What?"

"We split up to look for Ryn. Yll had last seen her at the mess hall. Ryette went to check there while I came here. When Ryette didn't join me, I went looking for her. We can't find her anywhere. Clayr has people searching, but so far nothing," Lar said.

Zo's mind raced around this information. Ryette was missing? The one person who could possibly save Ryn from something awful. Lar barely knew Clayr. Zo doubted he could have the same influence on Clayr and the Library as Ryette.

Great. Can this night get any worse? Zo pounded his knuckles on his legs in frustration.

Zo's voice rose, "Ryn went into the Library. Master Wes asked her to retrieve something for him. She's determined to win that spot. One of the guards has gone to find her. When they do, she's going to be in a mountain of trouble."

Lar went very still. Exhaling, he placed a hand to his forehead covering his eyes. "This is all my fault. I shouldn't have let her talk me into allowing her to study with that man. I knew it would be dangerous."

"Doesn't matter now, we've got to help Ryn," Zo snapped. Sometimes he felt like he was the father in this relationship.

A guard rushed up the path toward the cottage, pushing past them to get inside. Lar turned to follow. Zo came after.

Zo's worst fears were confirmed by the news the guard brought.

"There's a disturbance in the Library," the guard said to Clayr. "You need to come quickly."

Clayr let her exasperation show. "Can this night get any worse?"

The guard hovered protectively by Clayr as they exited the cottage, followed by Lar and Zo. They passed Regg holding a sniffling Yll. Clayr seemed too distracted to notice, but Zo did.

Good, he thought, *she should be upset after what she did*.

Regg and Yll fell in behind them at a slower pace. The trek across the Library grounds felt long, but too short.

Zo let his anger loose with his tongue. He called Yll some ugly names.

Regg grabbed Zo's arm. "Stop."

Zo shook him off. "Why are you defending this person? If she'd stab her best friend in the back, think of what she'll do to you."

Yll let out a sob. It only made Zo angrier. He picked up his pace to catch up with his father. If he stayed there by the two of them, he would likely punch his brother.

When they mounted the steps to the Library front door, a couple guards emerged, holding a struggling figure. Zo's heart sank till the hood of the cloak slid back, revealing blond hair shining in the lantern light.

"Prym!" Clayr exclaimed. "What is the meaning of this?"

One of the guards held out a book to Clayr. Zo recognized the cover. It was the one he had helped Ryn take from the third floor. The book Yll had taken from Ryn and betrayed her with, giving it to Prym.

"We caught the Regent's daughter entering the Library with his keys, carrying this restricted book. She claims to be doing urgent research for her studies," the guard said. "We suspect she was the one who broke onto the third floor the other night, since she has restricted materials in her possession."

"She did it," Prym pointed at Yll. "She gave me the book, and told me I should use my father's keys to enter the Library."

Zo's eyes darted to Yll. Her eyes were still wet from tears, but she gave Zo an almost imperceptible smirk.

Clayr let out a tired sigh. "Somebody rouse her father. Please bring her to my office where we can sort this out."

Zo sagged in relief. The disturbance hadn't been Ryn. He hoped all the commotion over Prym had allowed Ryn to make it out past Fergus.

A guard burst through the doors of the Library at a dead run, drawing up short at the crowd on the steps.

"Man down!" he shouted.

The guards and Clayr surged toward the door, the guard holding Prym dragged her with them. Everyone else moved to follow, but one of the guards put out an arm to restrain them.

"Library workers or students only," the guard said.

"I work for the Library," Zo said.

The guard waved him forward, Yll surging forward on his heels. He gave one backward glance at his father and brother before turning to rush through the door. Crossing the threshold, he felt his magic strip away. He was dimly aware of lantern light glinting off white statues, before they plunged into the Library darkness.

Chapter Twenty-Six

I seen a pack of wolves once. Cursed dragon offspring. I hid in the trees till they passed. Good thing they weren't hunting me.

— As quoted to Cheryl de Muto in *Of Magic, Myth and Lore- Commentary and Anecdotes from the people of Waatch, the Library, and the Surrounding Area.* Ancestral Library, First Floor, Lore Room, Shelf 29, Shelfmark 33.

Ryn clutched Luc's journal to her chest. It was hers, it meant everything to her. It was going to tell her exactly what she needed to know about who she was. No one was going to take it from her.

"Ryn, please," Fergus' voice came from behind her.

She used the turn to confirm it was him to cover slipping Luc's book into her pocket. Once she felt its weight tugging at her waist, she put her hands up and backed toward Fergus.

When she reached him, he sighed, turning her around.

"What do you think you're doing?" His brow furrowed with worry as his sad eyes pled with her. "Do you know what they do to people they find sneaking into restricted sections? Didn't you listen to my warnings on your first day?"

Ryn's stomach buzzed with the sick feeling of trouble.

"I had to. Master Wes told me I had to do this to pass the test and win the Library Researcher position," she said.

Fergus gripped her arms tight. "Do you honestly think the Curator would give a researcher position to someone who *broke into the Library* and gained unauthorized access to its materials? It's a lie, Ryn. He's not giving you a position. I think he just wants whatever he sent you to fetch. What is it, by the way?"

Ryn hesitated, even now. She couldn't help it. They were trained not to speak of what they were looking for.

"It's just some materials on House Viator. There's some lost scion he is trying to find for them." It wasn't a complete lie. Master Wes was looking for her mother.

"Then why not just ask a Researcher to pull the material for you?" Fergus crossed his arms.

"He didn't want the person he's looking for to get wind of his search and flee." Also true.

Fergus shifted, running a hand through his hair in frustration.

"Ryn, I can't overlook this. Last time I was able to cover for you. You and Zo broke in the other night, didn't you? I have to report it this time. I'm sorry, it's my job and my life if I don't." Fergus looked miserable.

Ryn's heart sank all the way to her feet. This was bad, but the weight of the book in her pocket gave her confidence. She knew it was hers and hers alone, and she would protect and defend it the rest of her life. There was no way they were taking it from her. She would find a way to escape.

Fergus blew out a breath in frustration. "Let's go."

Holding firmly to her upper arm, Fergus pulled her out of the secret room, closing the door behind them. He picked up her lantern, pulled her through the third floor, passed a startled guard at the research desk, and down the stairs. The whole time Ryn calculated how to get away. When they hit the first floor and headed toward the back door, there came a cry for help in the dark.

Fergus stopped, head raised, listening. The cry came again, off toward the north end.

Fergus muttered something then turned to Ryn. "Stay here. I'll be right back, don't go anywhere."

He disappeared with the lantern, leaving her in pitch dark.

Ryn reached out a hand to feel for the closest bookshelf. If she could just feel her way back to the front doors she could leave and get to freedom.

A cold hand grabbed hers in the dark.

"Shhhhh. It's me, Thalya. Follow me, I'll get you out."

Ryn let Thalya lead her away, running and stumbling through the inky blackness. Ryn had no idea how Thalya was seeing where they were going. All she knew was she needed to get away as fast as she could, so she trusted in Thalya's lead.

Instead of finding herself at the front doors though, she saw them approaching a light coming from a research alcove.

"Why are we here?" Ryn asked. "We need to get away, they are going to arrest me."

"Just a quick stop," Thalya said. "It won't take long, then we'll be on our way."

Ryn didn't like the way that sounded, but let Thalya pull her into the alcove and the light. Ryn squinted at the brightness.

"There you are," Master Wes said. "Did you retrieve the book?"

Ryn took a deep breath, hugging her sides to keep from reaching protectively for the book hiding in her pocket.

"No. I'm sorry, I'm still working on it. I have a lead on the third floor. I need to go check it." Ryn turned to run from the alcove, but Thalya was blocking her way.

"Silly me," Master Wes said from behind her. "I forgot to inform all of you of a very important detail about Luc's book." He paused. "Legend has it the book has a strange effect on people. Once in someone's possession they can't give it up. They feel the book is the most important thing in their life, and they will defend it to the death."

Ryn turned, giving him a startled look.

"I'm sure at some point someone from House Vivus put animate magic on that book to protect it," Master Wes gestured with his fingers and Thalya herded Ryn closer to him.

Master Wes closed his eyes and took a deep breath. When he opened his eyes, he fixed Ryn with a hard stare.

"I can feel the pull of the book from here. It's calling me to take it." He held out his hand. "Give it to me. You'll get your reward."

Ryn clutched her hands to her heart as if she was holding the book there and backed away.

"No," she said firmly.

It was hers and hers alone. It was the key to knowing who she was, she could feel it.

Master Wes' face was hard as stone. "I was saving this reunion for later, but..." He snapped his fingers.

Two men dressed in House Viator colors entered the alcove, dragging someone with them. It wasn't till they shoved the person into a chair that Ryn realized who it was.

"Mother!" Ryn tried to go to her, but Thalya grabbed her arm, holding her in place.

"Now then, dear..." Master Wes looked to Thalya. "What's her name again?"

"Ryn," Thalya said.

"Right, right. Ryn. Hand over the book," Master Wes' voice was hard and impatient.

One of the men standing behind her mother pulled a long knife from his belt and held it near her mother's neck.

Ryn swallowed. The threat was clear, but the book pled with her not to give it to these terrible people. It was hers. It would tell her everything she needed to know.

Her mother's face was drawn in determination. "Don't give it to him, Ryn. The power that book will unleash in the hands of the wrong people is staggering. He won't hurt me. He needs to give me to your grandmother."

Master Wes turned to give her mother his full attention. "It appears, dear Matriarch-in-Waiting, that not only have you been hiding from your family, but you've been actively working to deny your children the access they deserve to the most powerful Ancestor House."

Ryette's mouth pressed into a flat line, but she said no more.

Master Wes gave an exaggerated sigh, waving his hand. "No matter. You have the book on your person, and the pull of it confirms that fact. Our time is up here in the Library. We'll simply take you along with your mother someplace where we can forcefully remove it from you."

Thalya grabbed Ryn's arms.

"No!" Ryette started to rise from her chair. "You promised me you would only take me and leave my children alone."

Master Wes threw an arm out toward Ryn. "Get her to give up the book and I'll leave her here."

Ryn crossed her arms in sheer stubbornness. Her mother bowed her head. Ryn imagined her mother was thinking the same thing she was—the longer they kept the book from him, the more likely they had a chance of permanently keeping it from him.

"That's what I thought," Master Wes said. "Let's go."

Master Wes stood to leave. Thalya pushed Ryn ahead of them.

Something moved in the dark beyond. It resolved into Zo as he burst through the door, spinning Ryn around and pressing her behind him.

Clayr appeared in the doorway, flanked by two guards. The man holding the knife to Ryette's throat put it away.

"Madame Curator," Master Wes said. "So nice of you to join us."

"What's going on here?" Clayr demanded.

"Nothing out of the ordinary. My young pupil here has done excellent research work, finding something I've searched for decades, and locating it in a short amount of time. I was just discussing with her parent how I will be recommending her for the Library position."

Clayr's eyes narrowed. She reached behind her and pulled a very pale and trembling Prym into the room.

"We found this student with materials from the restricted section on the third floor. She claims it was retrieved on your orders with blatant disregard to Library protocol for examining such materials."

Master Wes frowned. "Me? I would never suggest to my students that they break Library rules in such a way. I am a professional."

Clayr's eyes flicked at the Viator man behind Ryette. "Not to mention the assault on a Library guard tonight."

Yll squeezed into the room past Clayr and the guards.

"These are serious accusations, and punishable offenses." Clayr said.

Yll caught Ryn's eye, giving her a small, sly smile. Then bowed her head as if in apology. Ryn looked back and forth between Prym and Yll. Had Yll actually set Prym up to get into trouble for the stolen book? Ryn's head was reeling. She couldn't quite process it all.

"I'll need you and all your students to come with me while we sort out this breach of Library security," Clayr said.

At those words, there was a long pause. Then the room burst into chaos. Master Wes' man behind her mother vaulted over the table, kicking Zo in the chest and pinning him to the ground. The guards behind Clayr tried to shove past her, but got tangled in the doorway. Thalya grabbed Yll, twisting her arm around her back and holding a knife to Yll's throat. Ryn backed as far into the alcove walls as she could get, but Master Wes crossed faster than he seemed capable of, pulled out a knife and pressed it to Ryn's throat.

"Now, we'll hear no more talk about my teaching methods." Master Wes growled. "We are all going to walk out of the Library and off the grounds. I will be taking all the children with me as a guarantee against any magical attacks till we're safely at our destination. Understood?"

Clayr's mouth hit a flat line. She stood firm till Thalya pressed her knife right up against the skin of Yll's neck. Clayr and the guards backed off at Yll's sharp intake of breath, making way for them to be dragged into the pitch-black Library.

Chapter Twenty-Seven

I had this dream once that this girl came to me, slipped out of her seal skin and spent the night with me. Strange thing was, I woke up the next morning and there was water all over my fishing cabin.

— As quoted to Cheryl de Muto in *Of Magic, Myth and Lore-Commentary and Anecdotes from the people of Waatch, the Library, and the Surrounding Area.* Ancestral Library, First Floor, Lore Room, Shelf 29, Shelfmark 33.

Zo had Viator Muscle's boot embedded in his back, pressing him into the warm stone floor. He noted the heating system was working—always a good thing. While Master Wes and Clayr had their little standoff, Viator Muscle yanked Zo's hands behind his back and bound them with cords. Zo scoffed. That would only last till he got outside and his fire magic returned, but as Viator Muscle pulled him to his feet he saw Ryn's teacher holding her at knife point. There were knives all around. Zo's mind began to work out how to throw a fireball at the master, but avoid Ryn. Because it was coming.

At a word from Master Wes, they all moved toward the door. Anger that normally would have brought flames so easily to Zo's fingers, burned in his chest. He needed to keep it together as he watched Master Wes usher Ryn forward, knife dangerously close to her throat. The Lazy Viator holding Ryn's mother hardly had to do anything, Ryette was watching Ryn closely, hands up in surrender, doing exactly what she was told to do.

Thalya led the way with Yll at knife point, Lazy Viator escorting Ryette beside her lighting the way. Yll seemed to be dragging her feet, walking as slow as possible. Every time a Library guard came charging up to them, Clayr would gasp as Thalya yanked Yll's head back, knife flashing in the lantern light. The guards would melt back into the darkness. It was taking too long. Zo chafed at the cords binding him.

"Get on with it, get on with it," he whispered under his breath, silently grateful Master Wes and company couldn't travel magic away as soon as they hit the Library doors.

At last, the archway to the foyer came into sight. Just a few more steps and Zo would be out of the Library and free to burn.

In the foyer was a battered and disheveled Fergus, sword drawn and blocking the front door. The red pre-dawn light shining through the windows turned him into a formidable apparition. Even Zo, who was anxious to get outside and restore his magic, paused.

Master Wes dragged Ryn a long step in front of Thalya. "Try me."

Ryette took a step but was pulled back. Fergus eyed the knife Master Wes held up, next to Ryn's face.

Blood dripped from Fergus' nose, but he stood tense. His knuckles white on his sword.

Yll cried out as Thalya made a quick cut on Yll's shoulder.

"Fergus, stand down!" Clayr yelled.

Fergus held, looking like he was about to sacrifice all of them for the good of the Library.

"Move, move, move, move," Zo chanted under his breath. He didn't need Fergus getting them killed, he needed him out of the way so he could use his fire magic to do the one thing for which House Ignis did approve of its use—taking down the enemy.

"You heard the Curator," the Library guard next to Clayr said.

Fergus finally relented, moving to the side, but not putting up the sword.

Master Wes turned to address them. "Hold tight to your charges. They're our ticket out of here. Thalya and I go first. The rest of you follow close behind. They won't touch us, not with who we hold."

Master Wes found Clayr lurking behind them and gave her a pointed look.

Lazy Viator holding Ryette opened the door. She was the most submissive, eyes still locked on Master Wes and Ryn.

In a rush they surged forward. Outside the door, the grounds were growing brighter with the rising sun. Master Wes put his fingers to his lips and gave a loud whistle. Zo heard a carriage rushing down the drive toward them. Over Ryn's head, Zo saw what he had hoped to see—his father and Regg standing at the foot of the stairs. As he got closer to the door, he saw what was the majority of the Library guard flanking the stairs. Behind them he thought he saw Master Nix, and possibly Iden in the mix.

Zo passed through the threshold of the Library, and breathed in his magic. Immediately he burned through the cords holding him. Once they broke, he caught Regg's eye, then his father's. Giving them a subtle nod, flames exploded into their hands.

"Water!" Master Wes screamed, and Lazy Viator reached a hand toward a fountain, directing the water at Regg and Lar.

At that, Yll transformed into a sharp taloned eagle, flying into the face of Thalya. Viator Muscle holding Zo started. Flames leapt into Zo's hands as he grabbed Viator Muscle's knife hand, while pushing fire into the man's chest. He howled in pain, punching Zo away with a burst of Air magic, which worked against him, only serving to fan Zo's flames. One of Clayr's guards rushed them from behind, grappling the man to the ground.

Zo looked up to see Fergus wrestling Ryn away from Master Wes. Zo took two stairs at a time toward them, as a damp Lar launched a fireball at Master Wes, who dodged it by tackling Ryn and Fergus to the ground. They rolled down the steps in a jumble of arms and legs. When they hit the bottom of the stairs, Master Wes knelt over Ryn. His hands searched her clothing, tearing her skirt apart. Zo and Lar converged toward them, both dripping flames from their hands. Lazy Viator sent another volley of water from another fountain, this one too far away, and the wave fell short.

The carriage rolled to a stop right next to Master Wes. He gave up searching Ryn and hauled her up by her collar, opening the door to shove her inside.

Ryette reached her hand toward the guard holding her, and he shimmered, then collapsed to the ground.

Fergus shook off the tumble down the stairs and pounced on Master Wes. He grabbed Master Wes by the collar, yanked him away from Ryn, slammed him against the side of the carriage, then brought his sword up to the man's throat.

Zo didn't care that Fergus had Master Wes. Into his hands sprung a fireball he was still learning to produce, but anger was fire's ally. Just as he was about to launch it straight at Master Wes' chest, Library guards swarmed the man and moved him out of Zo's sight. Lar hugged Zo's middle, swinging him around so the fireball shot off harmlessly into the nearby, now empty, fountain.

A blurred fluttering of wings in the corner of Zo's eye reminded him of Yll's struggle with Thalya. He started up the stairs to help when Thalya grabbed Yll's taloned leg and swung her toward the ground in an attempt to bash her eagle head on the steps. Regg was already there, hands alight with fire. He grabbed Thalya's arm, making her release Yll, who flew off in a flutter of wings. Thalya turned in one fluid motion, stabbing Regg in the stomach right up to the hilt of her knife. Regg's face dropped in surprise.

"NO!" Zo shouted.

Racing up the stairs toward his brother, throwing people out of his way as he went, he saw a guard tackle Thalya, slamming her to the ground. In a flutter of wings Yll landed next to Regg, Shifting back to herself, her hands roamed all over him, like she wanted to help, but didn't know where to start.

Zo was ten long steps from his brother. It felt like an ocean away.

Regg gripped the hilt of the knife.

"Don't pull it out!" Zo shouted. Five more steps.

Regg pulled out the knife.

Zo swore a long string of obscenities he didn't even know he knew.

His brother dropped to the ground right before Zo reached him.

"Idiot! You don't pull a knife out! What are you thinking?" Zo shouted at his brother.

"Can't heal...with it in," Regg said, passing out.

"You can't heal if you're unconscious either!" Zo yelled at his limp brother.

Zo stripped off his shirt, wadded it up, and plunged his hands into his brother's stomach wound.

Yll held Regg's head in her lap, begging him to be alright, her hands covered in blood.

All was a fog. Dimly, he was aware of someone lifting Regg and Zo following, still holding pressure to Regg's abdomen.

Ryn, torn and battered, and Yll, covered in blood with feathers sticking out of her hair, were clinging to each other off to his side. Fergus roughly dragged away Master Wes,while other Library guards took control of the carriage. Zo spared a glance at Thalya, Viator Muscle, and Lazy Viator being led away. To his surprise, the person carrying Regg turned out to be Iden.

Zo watched Master Nix swing into the carriage driver seat as they loaded Regg carefully inside. Zo maintained pressure on the wound through the process. Lar climbed in after them and the carriage horses took off at a full gallop.

Zo watched his brother grow paler and his breath become shallow. Lar sat holding Regg's hand, his face impassive, saying nothing. For once his father didn't berate him, but his silence was more condemning.

He put as much pressure as he could on the wound, though he knew it was a losing battle. There was no way to stop the internal bleeding from the outside.

Zo swore again. "Why didn't you listen to me? We could have gotten you to the Healers. They could have healed you quickly."

Zo swam in anger. It burned with everything that had brought him to his moment, watching his brother's life slip away beneath his fingers. He was angry with his mother, with House Sano, with his brother for being such an idiot...

Next to him his father began to hum. Zo recognized the song. It was one his mother, then his father, used to sing them to sleep. A flood of good memories filled Zo's head. The comforting ones. The times his mother had taken care of him, when he was small and scared. The times his dad had played ball with him, or the first time they used fire together. The times he had played with Regg in the garden.

Zo's breathing became soft and regular. He breathed deep the scent of blood and injury and his mind traveled down toward his brother.

"Well, it's about time!" Madame Sano's voice came into his mind loud as a thunderclap.

Zo started at the sound of her voice. Taking several deep breaths, he fought every ounce of his pride and stuffed it into a box.

"Help me!" he cried to her.

"Right. Let's get started."

Seizing his mind, they dove into Regg's body together.

Chapter Twenty-Eight

I heard a rumor once that each Ancestor magic can be reversed. Wouldn't that be interesting.

— As quoted to Cheryl de Muto in *Of Magic, Myth and Lore- Commentary and Anecdotes from the people of Waatch, the Library, and the Surrounding Area.* Ancestral Library, First Floor, Lore Room, Shelf 29, Shelfmark 33.

The bench outside Clayr's office was hard. Ryn's feet didn't quite touch the ground, so her legs were growing stiff and numb. Inside the office were all the adults, including Ryn's mother, with Prym and her father. Ryn couldn't take much pleasure in Prym getting into trouble, knowing she was next. Through the spot where Master Wes had torn her skirt, she could see a bruise developing on her shin from where she banged it in Clayr's cottage. Fergus stood guard next to her. His eye was black and swelling shut, his hand had blood on it—Ryn wasn't sure whose—and he was favoring one leg. One of those House Viator men had lured him away from Ryn with cries of help and attacked him. Ryn could see now how it had all been a set up to get Luc's book, and take it from the Library. Master Wes had used all of them. He couldn't steal the book and take it from the Library, but his "students" could—and then take the fall for it. It was all very clever and would have worked if Ryn hadn't stolen the other book from the third floor and Prym hadn't gotten caught with it. So really, if Yll hadn't framed Prym for the theft of the book, Master Wes would have probably gotten away. Well, and if Ryn hadn't gotten stubborn about handing it over.

After whisking Zo and Regg away to the Healing House, Ryn wondered why her mother didn't just travel magic them, but vaguely recalled Thalya saying something about not being able to use travel magic on Library grounds when she brought her here earlier—today? Yesterday? She couldn't recall what day it was anymore. Once the boys were gone, Fergus had escorted Ryn here to wait while the Library guards handled Master Wes and his crew. Ryn had asked Fergus what was happening, but Fergus was as stoney and distant as all the other guards had been. Time dragged on, and the adrenaline began to wear off. As Ryn sat contemplating, she slumped. Regg was severely injured. Ryn was in deep trouble with the Library. She'd be lucky if they only banned her for life from the Library. Loads of people were angry with her. She glanced up at Fergus' face...*and* Fergus wasn't speaking to her. As fear and anger drained away, her emotions welled up inside. Tears slid down her cheeks as she fought to keep her breathing even so no one would notice.

Fergus reached into his pocket and handed her a handkerchief, which completely undid her. She fought to keep it quiet, but couldn't avoid the occasional sniffle.

The door to Clayr's office jerked open. Prym stomped out. Turning, she shot Ryn the sharpest withering glare Ryn had ever seen, then stalked off. Her father the Library Regent followed, but in a way that suggested Prym was not leading. More like he was herding her to something awful.

"Next," came a hollow, tired voice from the office.

Fergus reached down and took Ryn by the arm, pulling her to her feet. Fear dried her remaining tears. She tried to give Fergus his handkerchief back, but he ignored her. Fergus led her into the office and sat her in the chair opposite Clayr's desk. Yll was there in a chair off to the side, along with Ryn's mother. Fergus once again stood stiff and formal next to Ryn's chair. Clayr moved to the windows overlooking the Library grounds. She stared out at them for a long time. Sweat dripped down Ryn's back as she waited in the silence.

At last, Clayr spoke.

"Leave us," she said.

There was a gasp of dismay, but Fergus turned to go, and Yll stood. On her way out, Yll stopped to kneel before Ryn.

"I'm sorry," she said. "I know I hurt you. It was a terrible choice I made. I won't ask you to forgive me, but..." Yll turned to look at her mother's back. She leaned in to whisper in Ryn's ear, "Prym didn't get punished, but she didn't get the Researcher position either. Daddy's furious."

Ryn's heart wanted to forgive her, just as she had after they fought when they were little, but the pain was still sharp. Yll had saved the day, but Ryn's heart still hurt. Best she could do was a slight nod.

Clayr cleared her throat. A tear slid down Yll's cheek as she rose and followed Fergus out.

"I wish to stay," Ryn's mother said. "I should know my daughter's fate."

Clayr turned to look at her best friend. She nodded and a Library guard shut the door behind him, leaving Clayr, Ryette, and Ryn alone. Ryn's mouth went dry as she tried to swallow.

Clayr turned back to the window. "The book, please Ryn. On my desk."

Ryn stood. Her shaking hand reached into her pocket to pull the book out. Even now it begged and pleaded with her to flee with it. She'd read the book while waiting. Despite the book's promises, and to Ryn's great disappointment, it didn't say anything about who Ryn was and where she came from. There was no lost orphaned girl in the story. No parents who lost a child. Just the tale of Luc and Praedo's company. It was the tale they'd all heard, the one every history book told, plus quite a few nursery tales about Praedo and the slaying of the dragon. She hated the book for lying to her. The things she had done to obtain it would probably put her in jail, but the book cared nothing about that. All it wanted was to be free.

Pulling the book from her pocket, she laid it carefully in the middle of Clayr's desk. Then she withdrew to her seat, shoulders hunched against the onslaught of what was coming.

Clayr crossed to her desk and sat. She picked up the book and inspected it, as if confirming it was the right book and checking for damage. She gave Ryette a hard look as she passed it to her to inspect.

Ryn's mother took it and thumbed it open. "It's been a few years since we've seen this."

Ryn gave her mother a sharp look.

"How in the name of the Library did you find it?" Clayr asked.

Ryn pulled the Library guidebook from her other pocket. "I followed the clues here and just got lucky."

Clayr looked incredulous. "But there's no directions in the reference book to where to find it on the shelves. It would take hours to go through all those books."

Ryn shrugged. "I don't know. It was just a feeling I had."

"And how in the name of the Ancestors did you open that box?" Ryn's mother asked.

Clayr's gaze intensified. "Yes, only the Curator can open the box."

Ryn showed them her palm with the small bloody slit. "I don't know. I set my hand on the box, it poked me somehow, and the next thing I knew the box opened."

Clayr held up her palm with a barely visible silver scar in the middle of her palm.

"The box is supposed to only open for the Curator," Ryn's mother said.

"I can't tell you why it happened, just that it did," Ryn said.

Ryn's mother handed the book back to Clayr.

"We believe you." Clayr held up the book. "This is the proof."

"So, what happens now?" Ryn blurted out. She couldn't stand her unknown fate any longer.

Clayr's fingers drummed on the book, her face thoughtful. "I've interviewed all of Master Wes' students, and one thing is clear—you certainly have a way and a talent with the Library, but that doesn't excuse stealing my keys, breaking into my office, and taking a rare and precious book that's *supposed to be impossible to retrieve* from the Library. Let's be frank here, you've broken a whole host of Library rules, many of which have jail time sentences attached to them as punishment."

Ryn opened her mouth to explain, but Clayr held up her hand to stop her.

"I understand Master Wes had you all convinced secrecy was the only way, but I know we've raised you better than that. You knew full well what you were doing was wrong. You should have come to us. You've betrayed my trust." Clayr folded her arms.

Ryn bowed her head. "I just thought for once I was special, and could win a spot doing something I seem to be good at. I thought I finally found where I belong."

Clayr put her elbows on her desk and dropped her face into her hands. She sat that way for a long time. When she finally stirred, her face was composed and stern. Ryn's stomach dropped in fear.

"Ryn, you are hereby expelled from class and the Library. You are not to sign up or take any more classes from tutors teaching in the Library."

Ryn nodded, fighting hard to keep the tears from her eyes.

Ryn's mother let out a sigh of relief. Clayr gave her a sharp look.

"Consider yourself lucky," Clayr said, "The Board of Regents was demanding jail time."

Of course Prym's father was, Ryn thought.

Clayr rang a bell on her desk. The door opened and Fergus stepped inside.

Clayr nodded to him. "Show them out."

Ryn stood, numb and in shock. Strangely over the past days the Library had quickly come to feel like home to her. She curtsied to Clayr, then Fergus took her arm and escorted her out of the office. Pressure started to build in Ryn's chest. A pressure she kept bottled in until Fergus opened the front door and ushered them out. When he closed the door Ryn burst into tears. She couldn't walk, so she sat down hard on the stairs. Stairs that just a few hours ago she had been led down at knifepoint, the focus of so much, and now she was back to being nothing.

Ryn's mother sat down beside her on the stairs, putting an arm around her. Both of them watched as cleaning crews worked to clean blood from the stairs.

"Is he alright?" Ryn asked when she could control her voice again.

She dabbed her eyes and blew her nose into Fergus' handkerchief.

"I don't know," Ryn's mother said. "Hopefully they made it to the Healing House in time." Her voice sounded grim.

"You haven't heard?" Ryn asked.

Ryn's mother stood. "Let's get you home."

She held out her hand to Ryn, who took it and let her mother lead her down the stairs. They wandered down the path that led to the east gate. The fall mums of bright yellow and orange dancing in the breeze. The Library's world had returned to normal, but Ryn's had not. When they stepped through the east gate, her mother put her arms around her. The world began to swirl and the next thing Ryn knew they were standing in front of their little cottage in Sooke. It was fast. Much faster than Thalya was. Ryn couldn't get over the thought that her mother had just travel magicked her home. There were so many times in her life that would have been such a convenience. Ryn had done so much needless walking. She wondered how her mother had known what she could do, yet put up with the Ordinary ways of doing things.

Her mother kept one arm around Ryn and led her up the steps. Once inside, Ryn took in her world and her life. It had all been a lie.

"Why don't you put your nightdress on, and I'll put on some chamomile," Ryn's mother gave her a sad smile.

Deep inside Ryn wanted to yell at her mother, but all the fight had drained out of her. She simply nodded and trailed off to her room. Passing Jett's room, she was startled to find all of Jett's things, except a few shirts he'd grown out of and an old holey pair of boots, gone.

Ryn couldn't even begin to process it. She went to her room and pulled off the dress she'd been wearing since...she no longer remembered when, and put on her comfy night things. Toddling back out to the table in her stockinged feet, she sank into her chair. Her mother put a mug of tea in front of her. Ryn stared at Jett's empty chair.

"Where is he?" Ryn asked.

Her mother sat with her own mug. "I don't know."

The look on her mother's face made Ryn want to reach out to her, but she couldn't. Her heart hurt. She wished again she could rage at her mother, but the chamomile had calmed her.

"Why?" Ryn asked. "Why didn't you tell us? I thought you were the only person here who was just like me, and now there's no one."

"Except Clayr," her mother said.

She glared at her mother. The thought of Clayr at the moment made Ryn embarrassed and humiliated.

Ryn swallowed a new lump in her throat. "Does Dad know?"

"Yes, he knows. As for you and Jett, well there were lots of reasons to keep you in the dark. One of those is that young children are so sweetly open and honest, it would have been hard for you to keep that secret, and it is a dangerous secret. Clayr will try her best to keep Master Wes from sending word to the Matriarch of House Viator, but the truth is he probably already told her. Soon we will not be safe here."

"But why? What's so terrible about being a part of House Viator?"

Her mother sipped her tea. "It has everything to do with the control and expansion of power. Did Master Wes tell you why he wanted Luc's book?"

"Something about Praedo's beads of power. Or that's what we guessed." Ryn remembered her mother's comment in Clayr's office about seeing the book before. "How do you know about it?"

"It's a project your father and I have been working on together." Her mother got a far-off look on her face. "We located the book some years ago. Your father was anxious to follow the clues to finding the beads. I was not."

Ryn's eyes widened with understanding. "That's why he left."

"Yes. And in that path lies madness. My family is hungry for more power. The Ancestors may have started out as beloved companions, but their descendants are not. They fight, and they guard their magics jealously. My grandfather had the idea to harness the power of all the magics under one house. He struck a bargain with House Pentral to arrange a secret alliance with the second most powerful house—an arranged marriage of his daughter to the heir to the Patriarchy of House Pentral. Once I was born, my House Pentral father arranged to take me from my crib in the middle of the night. He did not succeed, and was sent home to Inispentral in pieces."

Ryn gasped.

Her mother gazed long into her mug.

"But Jett—he's House Pentral," Ryn said.

"Apparently House Pentral doesn't learn easily. Another arrangement was made, to the next heir—the seat had passed to my father's brother." Her mother's shoulders sank. "He was handsome, and I was young. When Jett was born, my mother and my uncle, the Patriarch of House Viator, feared another kidnapping attempt. Jett is a rightful heir to the Patriarchy of House Pentral."

Dread weighed Ryn's heart. She almost didn't want to listen to the rest.

"They came to our room in the middle of the night and took Jett's father away. I don't know what happened to him, but a cousin has assumed the role of Patriarch-in-waiting for House Pentral."

There was silence for a while. Ryn watched the bits of chamomile flower float around in her tea.

Her mother sniffed. "I got out as soon as I could, and brought Jett here. We've been hiding ever since. When your father became obsessed with the same project. It was too much, Ryn. I have hid from them for so long. Now I will have to fight to keep them from obtaining the power that will destroy the balance the Ancestral Houses enjoy. It's a fight Clayr and I—and I thought your father—were committed to." Her mother sighed.

"Is Lar committed to this cause?" Ryn asked.

Her mother nodded. "It's how we met."

"But I don't understand..."

"That's enough for now," her mother said. "You've been up all night, you need to go get some rest. We'll talk again later."

"But I don't..." Ryn started, then noticed how old her mother looked.

They had all been through something today. She vowed she'd find a way to make her mother open up again. Her mother never spoke of the past except in cute, funny anecdotes, she had never spoken to Ryn of the past like this before. She felt an opportunity was slipping away, but her mother was already closed off and withdrawn.

Ryn stood. Her mother normally wore a high buttoned collar like all Ordinaries, probably to hide her bead scars. Now it was unbuttoned and Ryn realized the scarring on her collarbone did match where beadscars should be. Ryn had always believed her mother when she said it was an injury from when she was a little girl. The tale she told was of someone putting a river rock in the fire and how the super-heated rock had exploded and hit her in the chest. Her mother always talked of being embarrassed by the ugly scar so Ryn had only seen it maybe once or twice. No one had ever dreamed of masking and hiding their Ancestral heritage, so the story was believable.

Ryn rubbed her eyes. The chamomile was working. She slumped to her bedroom, and laid down in the bed. Her mind went to Jett's empty room, and how he might have stayed if he only knew their mother's story. Now Ryn was truly alone. Who knew where she would end up if they would have to move away to protect themselves. She hated that she didn't fit in Sooke, but at the same time, she had lived here all her life. This was her home. Outside was the trail leading to the log fort where she had played as a little girl, and the river where she skipped rocks. How could she ever feel at home anywhere else? And now without the prospect of making the Library her home, she had nothing. No hopes or prospects for the future. No hope of finding her heritage.

Tears slid onto her pillow. She rolled over and fell asleep.

Chapter Twenty-Nine

To fall in the wrong hands is forbidden.
From the start where the mountains rise,
The treasure was hidden neath azure skies.
Seek the glade where whispers of pines,
Guard the secret that time defines.

— Excerpt from Luc's Poem as recorded in *On the Legend of Luc, Praedo's Scribe*. Ancestral Library, Third Floor Restricted Section.

Zo was aware of them taking his brother from him, though his hands never felt like they left him. Half carrying, half dragging Zo out of the carriage, they placed him in a sparse patient's room. He recognized the smell and feel of the Healing House, but had no choice. He was only partially aware of his surroundings, because Madame Sano had decided she was taking advantage of the situation and making up for lost time, hitting him with what felt like every lesson he had missed over the past five years. When she finally left him, it was dark again. His head pounded, he was incredibly thirsty and hungry, but his body refused to move. The bed on which he laid was incredibly soft and comfortable. He drifted off into a troubled sleep filled with nightmares of blood and deaths and funerals.

When he woke, the sun was bright in the windows, inviting a new day, but Zo's body and mind felt like it'd been stomped on by a horse—repeatedly. His grumbling stomach made him move. His hands had been cleaned of blood, and someone had dressed him in a nightshirt. Searching for his pants, all he found was a neatly folded soft pair of patients' pants, the kind that tied at the waist. He pulled those on, then left the room in search of his brother.

A healing student passed by him carrying a bucket. When he asked, she directed him to a room at the end of the hall. Zo ran to the sound of the girl's protests about rules and running. He didn't care, he flung open the door—

to find his brother sitting in bed reading. He was a little pale, but looked for all the world like he was enjoying a lazy day reading in bed.

Zo shut the door hard behind him, and leaned his back against it. Regg looked up from his book.

"What?" Regg said.

"You almost died," Zo said,

Regg shrugged. "I didn't." He went back to his book.

"Why you little..." Zo advanced on his brother. "I'll stab you myself."

Throwing up his hands, Regg dropped the book. "I kid, I kid!" He gave Zo a huge grin.

Regg stared down at his abdomen. "They say you used your healing." He looked up into Zo's eyes. "I know how hard that was for you."

Zo thought about all Madame Sano taught him since the day before. It made his head spin. He was still hurt and angry, and being in the Healing House made him want to flee across town, but he couldn't deny how grateful he was to have saved his brother.

Zo gave a curt nod, not trusting his voice with his feelings.

Regg came to his feet.

"Thanks brother," he said, pulling Zo into a fierce hug, squeezing him tight, as if to emphasize his words.

"Don't ever do that again," Zo whispered, fighting to keep emotion from his voice.

"I'll try to avoid crazy girls with knives," Regg said, there was laughter there, but also a soberness. It had been a close call.

When Zo finally released him, Regg sat gingerly back on the bed.

"When do you get out of here?" Zo asked.

"I still need a couple more healing sessions. They need to help my blood cells regrow and double check for infection, stuff I haven't learned to do yet. I should be able to get out of here by tomorrow."

"Good, because I'm not staying a second longer in this Healing House. I'll check on you when you get home," Zo said.

A knock at the door was followed by a healing student flinging it open. There was something striking about him. He had midnight black hair, nearly as tall as Zo, dressed in a finely tailored black suit and shirt, which dipped low to show off his beads. Every one of his fingers contained a silver ring. There was something about him that drew Zo's focus instantly.

"Zo, son of Fyri?" the student asked.

"Possibly, who wants to know?" Zo asked.

"The Headmaster of this Healing House wishes to speak with you," Mr. Mysterious said.

Zo turned, clapping his brother on the shoulder. "Get better or I *will* come back and stab you." Then pushed his way past Mr. Mysterious, letting his angry feet carry him down the hall. Veering toward the main entrance, Zo strode toward it, reaching for the door.

"Wait!" Mr. Mysterious said, "The headmaster's office is this way."

"That's nice," Zo said, yanking the door open and marching down the stairs and across the street.

Flinging the door to Wilmar's exam room open, he almost jumped back outside at the sight of Master Nix sitting having tea with Wilmar. The cookies on the plate next to them made Zo's stomach grumble.

"Well, well, well. Were your ears burning?" Wilmar asked Zo.

Zo looked around behind him. "What?"

"He means we were just talking about you," Master Nix said. "Pull up a seat."

Wilmar bustled into his living quarters and came back with another mug of tea and a plate of sandwiches. What *kind* of tea was difficult to determine given the abundance of herbal smells in Wilmar's work room. Zo didn't care, he sipped it, and the herbs soothed his scratchy throat, then he picked the sandwiches off the stack one by one.

Master Nix chuckled.

When Zo was done with the plate of sandwiches, and happily munching a cookie, Wilmar and Master Nix turned to him.

"What?" Zo asked again around a mouth full of cookie.

"I invited Nix here for tea and a discussion. We have reached an agreement, if you find it acceptable." Wilmar said.

Zo's eyes went from Wilmar then to Master Nix and back again. He set the rest of the cookie on the plate.

"I'm not going to like this, am I?" Zo asked.

Master Nix chuckled.

"Don't be hasty," Wilmar said. "Hear us out."

Master Nix gestured to the physician. "Wilmar here has proposed a little apprentice sharing. You work for me a few days a week, and the rest of the time you spend here with Wilmar, learning to be a physician. You can remain in the Library dorms, and we'll still feed you, but you will spend half your time here."

"I need help." Wilmar's eyes were pleading. "You've seen my caseload. I could really use you here."

Although Zo suspected a trap to get him to accept his healing side, he couldn't help but feel the warmth and care that filled the room. It rolled off Wilmar, leaving Zo feeling at peace. Yet he felt obligated to push back, just a little.

"I don't know. Fire is my primary magic, and I do love a good fire." Small flames came to Zo's fingers.

Wilmar's eyes got wide.

"You'll accept this arrangement, or I'll put you on the boiler line till you pass out from heat exhaustion," Master Nix huffed, face turning red.

The flames left Zo's hands as he held them up in submission.

"Alright, alright." Zo gave them a mischievous grin.

"Oh dear." Wilmar wiped his brow.

"Good luck with this one," Master Nix said. "You sure you still want him?"

Wilmar's chuckle filled the room with more warmth than Zo's flames.

Zo stretched his feet under the table—and encountered Wilmar and Nix's feet playing footsie.

At his touch, their feet withdrew. Zo jerked up, his gaze passing between the two of them. Nix's eyes twinkled over the rim of his teacup.

A single knock at the door, and Iden stood in the doorway. Zo felt like he was reliving the scene from a few days ago, with Iden's same worried expression. The concern on his face made Zo's heart beat faster.

Iden let out a long breath. "Can we talk?" he asked.

Master Nix drained his tea and stood. "I need to be on my way anyway. The grunts'll burn down the place if I leave them too long."

Master Nix took Wilmar's hand. "Good doing business with you."

Wilmar batted Master Nix's hand away and stood to pull him into a hug, then a kiss on the cheek to deliver a threat in his ear:

"If you send me any more heat exhausted, blistered kids I'm charging you triple," Wilmar said.

"Not according to this new agreement." Master Nix grinned. "Good to see you, Iden." Master Nix looked at Zo, then turned to Iden, squeezing him on the shoulder he said, "Make good choices."

Wilmar gave a grunt of frustration as Master Nix closed the door behind him. "If he wasn't so cuddly, I'd kill him... slowly..." He gestured to his shelves full of potions.

Zo blinked at him for several heartbeats trying to process what he'd just witnessed. This was intriguing. He needed more information.

Iden cleared his throat, and Zo came back to the moment. The open door that led to Wilmar's garden looked inviting.

"May we?" Zo pointed out the door.

Wilmar looked up from clearing the tea mugs. "Oh, sure, sure." He waved them out the door.

Zo led the way like he knew where he was going, but almost tripped Iden when he froze a few steps into the garden. It was like entering organized chaos. There were plants everywhere, some looked to be growing wild, but every one was carefully labeled. Zo wandered the narrow path till he found a bench under a huge pear tree. He sat, but Iden didn't join him. Zo's heart sank.

"How's Regg?" Iden asked.

"He'll recover, thanks to the Healers."

"I heard it was because of you," Iden said.

Iden looked him full in the eyes. Zo swallowed nervously at Iden's intensity.

"What's going on?" Zo asked.

"I returned my promise necklace to Prym."

Zo's stomach fluttered. "Oh?"

"She's furious, but my parents were scandalized by her behavior, so they called the arrangement off."

Iden started to pace. "And I've been thinking, before my parents find another poor unsuspecting girl to promise me to..."

Zo's heart leapt. Then realization sunk in.

"You should go," Zo said. He wanted to say it first. As if it was his idea, because it sounded better that way. Maybe it would hurt less.

"This is my chance." Iden kept going. "I just got word of an opening in that community on Oydico I talked to you about. My parents won't be happy, but they have my little sister. She's a better choice to inherit the family business. She carries notebooks around pretending they are reference books, and..." Iden stopped. "Wait what?"

Zo gazed long into Iden's face. His high round cheekbones, and the sweet dimple in his chin, and he knew he would never see that face again.

"You should go," Zo said. "I'm happy for you."

Even as he said it, his heart sank into the hard pit of his stomach. He wasn't sure what was worse—having Iden promised to Prym and having to sneak around, or never seeing him again. He decided on the latter.

Iden pulled Zo to his feet and embraced him as hard as Zo had embraced the brother he had thought he had lost. Zo tried to return the enthusiasm, but couldn't quite match it.

Releasing Zo, Iden cupped his hand to Zo's face. Tears sprang into Iden's eyes. "Thank you, my friend. I knew you would understand me."

Zo didn't trust his voice. He only nodded.

Zo sank back onto the bench, as Iden left the garden. He tried to forget, tried to shove the feelings someplace else. In the end, he let them overwhelm him for a time. Until the sun started to sink low, and banging came from Wilmar's workroom.

Zo wiped his eyes and went to see what was happening.

When he entered the exam room, he heard a little girl's squeal of delight and the clomping of feet and a cane on the floor. Next thing he knew the little girl from a few nights ago was there, embracing his middle.

"You're here," she whispered into his shirt.

Zo knelt down, looking her over, examining her leg. "And how are you?" he asked.

"Good! Wilmar needs to put a new splint on my leg. I had a small accident, and the last one came off," she said. It was more words than Zo had ever heard her speak.

"Can I help?" Zo asked her.

He thought her enthusiastic nodding would shake her head right off.

"Good." Zo scooped her up and carried her to the exam table. "Let's get you all fixed up."

The door to the street burst open, startling Zo and the girl. Apparently, Wilmar was used to his door flying open.

Iden stood in the doorway.

"What are you..." Zo started.

Iden took two long strides across the exam room, swept Zo up in his arms and kissed him, long and hard. Zo could scarcely breathe as his hands wrapped into Iden's shirt, pulling him closer.

Little girl giggles brought them back.

Zo looked into Iden's face. "I don't understand."

Iden ran a hand down his face. "I don't know. The further I walked away, the heavier my heart felt. I kept hearing Nix say, 'Make good choices.'" His eyes held Zo's. "I still want to live on Oydico someday, but now doesn't feel like the right time. I think I'll apply as a Docent in the Library for a while...maybe find someone I can eventually take with me." Iden gave Zo that mischievous look he couldn't resist. "What do you say—shall we defy the Ancestors and be like Wilmar and Nix here?"

Zo's gaze swung between Iden, who looked hopeful, and Wilmar, whose face was impassive. "I'm still not sure what it is they have, but...yes!"

Iden kissed Zo again.

The little girl squealed in delight.

Wilmar clapped his hands together. "This calls for a celebration!"

"Cookies!" The little girl looked hopefully between all of them.

Zo laughed as he slipped his arm around Iden, who cupped Zo's head in his hands and kissed it.

Chapter Thirty

The Library holds many mysteries, and that's not including the books and records.

— Myra de Lux. *A Comprehensive History of the Library*. Ancestral Library, First Floor, History section, Shelf 82, Shelfmark 43.

The breeze blew leaves of red, orange, and yellow past Ryn's window. After nearly a moon cycle, autumn was full upon Sooke, but today was sunny, warm, and bright. Ryn leaned her broom against the bed and flopped back onto it. Today was her birthday. The big one, the one where she should be having her Debut party, just like Prym—*if* Ryn was an Ancestor descendant, which she wasn't. It had been a nice day—so of necessity it needed to be chores day. The break from the rain provided a much-needed opportunity to get things done. Her mother made her favorite breakfast, then the two of them had worked to pull the dead plants from the garden, and turn under the soil. Restless, Ryn had cleaned and swept her room. She still missed Jett. She'd lived her whole life with his presence and not having him was strange.

Everyone else was gone as well. Clayr had given Master Wes' promised position to Yll. Ryn supposed she deserved it. She was the best of the class next to Ryn, but it did feel unfair. Perhaps Yll still hadn't escaped the stigma of getting the job because of her mother as she'd hoped. Given how their training was truncated, Yll's mother hadn't given her the promised Assistant Researcher job. Still, a Docent position at the Library was nothing to sneeze at.

Ryn hadn't seen much of Zo. She heard he was excelling in Library temperature as well as assisting the physician. Lar was a regular visitor to the cottage, her mother and him often bent in hushed conversations about moving and dealing with House Viator. Ryn wasn't sure why they hadn't left yet, but they had bags packed by the door in case they had to leave in a heartbeat.

Regg was still in Sooke. Well, he technically still lived in their cabin, but he spent most of his time in town hanging out with Yll. Ryn got most of her news from him, but something he said when she'd seen him last hinted that he would be leaving permanently for Waatch soon. She wasn't sure what he was planning.

Ryn's eyes drifted up to the portrait of the orphaned flower girl over her bed. Ryn related, a little too much. Maybe she really was that orphaned girl, forever bound to selling dying flowers in the cold, wet street. Heaving a huge sigh, she picked up her broom.

A loud knock came at the front door. Ryn stuck her head out of her room, expecting her mother to answer. Her mother, who stood next to the table pouring over some documents, gestured for Ryn to answer it. Grumbling, Ryn went to the door.

"We heard there's a birthday girl here—have you seen her?" Zo stuck his head in the door making a show of looking around.

"You think maybe it's this maiden here?" Regg gestured to Ryn, trying to arrange his face seriously, but there was laughter in his eyes.

They were both dressed in fine coats, embroidered with flowers down the front and around the cuffs—the very latest fashion. (Or so Yll had once said.) Both wore shirts that covered their beads, making them look Ordinary, but extraordinary.

Regg waved a hand in front of her face. "She's just staring at us. I think we broke her."

"No," Ryn started. "I mean yes. I mean—it is my birthday."

"Well don't just stand there, girl, go put on that fancy dress of yours, we have places to go, people to see." Zo spun her around and pushed her back toward her room.

"I...What?" Ryn started.

"Just go get ready," Zo laughed.

Ryn was startled to find her mother standing by Ryn's bedroom door with a dress in her hands—a dress Ryn had never seen before.

The boys took seats in the living room as Ryn's mother pulled her into the bedroom.

"What's going on, mother?" Ryn asked.

Her mother just smiled, helping her undress from her chores day clothes. Pulling Ryn's hair into an elaborate braid, she stuck tiny flowers into each feathery turn of the braid. Then her mother used some of the potions she had to make Ryn's lips redder and cheeks more blushed.

The mirror on the wardrobe door showed Ryn someone she'd never seen before. She stood there in a midnight blue dress, the same color as the boy's suits, with the exact same neckline. There was no embroidery on the dress, but it shimmered in the way only fine fabric did. It fit perfectly through the bodice, then flared out from her waist in a pleasing way. It seemed to make her look taller.

"You look lovely." Her mother placed her hands on her shoulders.

"Thanks Momma." Ryn squeezed one of her mother's hands.

A gentle tapping came on her bedroom door. "Are you ready to go?" Zo's muffled voice asked through the door.

Ryn's mother gave her a hug then opened the door.

When the door opened Zo froze in place for a long heartbeat, Ryn couldn't tell if that was good or bad till he composed himself, and offered her his arm. When she took it and entered the room, Regg jumped to his feet.

"Wow..." Regg said. "I mean... Wow."

Then he looked around him. "Don't tell Yll I said that."

Ryn giggled.

Regg offered her his arm and the boys led her out the door.

"Have a good time," Ryn's mother called after them.

Once they were down the porch steps and across the yard, Ryn looked back at her mother in the doorway. She looked tired, but happy. Ryn didn't understand what was happening, but it felt good to at last be doing something for her birthday.

A few steps further, however, and she discovered there was no carriage at the end of the lane.

"Where are we going?" Ryn asked.

"So bossy," Zo said.

"It's like she thinks we don't know where we're going," Regg said.

"Didn't you always dream of a walk in the woods in a fancy dress for your birthday?" Zo asked.

"Well, I mean, not really, no, but it is nice to be with you two." Ryn pulled on both their arms, bringing them closer to her.

Zo stumbled a bit from the tug. They entered the woods down a path just barely wide enough for the three of them to walk arm in arm.

"It is good to see you," Zo said.

Ryn sighed and touched her cheek to his arm. "I've missed you."

"Me too," he said.

"I miss me too," Regg said.

"Shall we leave him in the woods?" Zo asked.

Ryn tightened her grip on Regg's arm. "I think not. He's growing on me."

Zo gave an exaggerated sigh. "Fine. If we have to."

Ryn laughed out loud.

Taking a deep breath, she asked Zo what he'd been up to. He regaled her with loads of fun stories of how he'd managed to drive Master Nix and Wilmar crazy. Ryn laughed till tears rolled down her cheeks, but deep inside, she wished she could be a part of it. She hadn't appreciated those few short days in the Library enough. Now she was barred from studying there. The Library, dark and mysterious as it was, had taken hold of her heart and Imagination. She craved to return, and Zo's stories only made the feeling more desperate.

The boys suddenly stopped on the path. Ryn hadn't been paying attention to where they were going. Somehow the path had led them to the archways Prym had for her party. Ryn didn't understand why Prym's family hadn't taken them down—and why were the flowers on them fresh? How did that happen?

The blowing of the shell horn sounded out from across the water.

Ryn's eyes darted between Zo and Regg. They had both turned serious. They shifted her slightly to reveal her mother, somehow dressed in a lush gown the shade of a deep red rose. How her mother had changed that fast and gotten here, she could not fathom. Had they really been walking in the woods that long?

Ryn's mother nodded to the boys, and they pulled torches from the ground. Lighting them with the snap of their fingers, they took their place in front of Ryn and her mother.

"Wait..." Ryn started.

They all moved forward in solemn grace through the arches.

Are they actually...no, Ryn thought. *It can't be.* She wasn't Ancestor born. No one wished to be promised to an Ordinary—not in Sooke anyway.

The boys led the way through the arches, backs straight, heads held high. About halfway down the arched path a gathered crowd came into view. How could there be people here? And for her? There were a few villagers, but she recognized many of the market day vendors, including Brynd and her apple farming family. Iden was also there, and Yll.

When they reached the end of the arches, someone trumpeted a fanfare. Ryn was in shock to see all the faces smiling at her. She would have cried, but she was so surprised no tears came.

The boys parted to stand one on each side of Ryn and her mother.

"Our dear family and friends. On this lovely autumn day, I present to you my daughter, Ryn, the brightest researcher to come along in decades, if not centuries."

What? No. Ryn certainly did not agree with that statement. A few days in the Library did not a great researcher make.

"She's beautiful..." her mother continued.

Ryn choked a little on that one.

"Occasionally stubborn, but fiercely loyal and loving. Most of all—very patient with all of us."

Everyone clapped. Ryn blushed deeply.

Lar stepped up to her and pressed her hand to his forehead as he did when they'd first met.

"Would it be alright if I filled in this evening?" Lar asked her, eyes hopeful.

Ryn looked at him, wishing with all her heart that it was her own sweet father standing in front of her, but her love for Lar's sons spilled over onto him and she gripped his hand with a smile.

A band Ryn hadn't noticed began to play, and Lar danced her gracefully around the dance floor, showing her off as if she was his own daughter. His chest puffed out in pride. Ryn was trembling with nervousness. She couldn't believe she was here in this moment. A moment she never thought she would have.

Next, it was Zo's turn to dance with her.

"Don't fall for the same guy as me tonight," he said.

Ryn chuckled. "Tell me which one you're thinking of, and I'll avoid him."

"Hmmmm—maybe since it's your day I should let you pick first," he said.

"That's very generous of you."

"I'll steal him later." Zo winked.

"Whatever. I saw Iden. I know he's the only one you'll be in the bushes with."

Zo opened his mouth to say something then shut it.

Ryn threw her head back and laughed. She relaxed into the rhythm of the dance and Zo's presence.

Regg came next. He spent the whole dance peppering her with questions about Yll, and her preferences. Then he told her what she had suspected for a while.

"I'm leaving to study at the Healing House." His eyes flicked to Yll. "Apparently there's some very outdated rule about fire magic only being allowed to work in the boiler room of the Library, so I can't study to be a researcher. I don't want to work in the boiler room."

"Understandable," Ryn said. "At least you'll be in Waatch."

Regg's grin showed off his teeth. "Yes! That's the plan."

Next to dance were some boys from the village who weren't firmly in Prym's camp. Each boy presented Ryn with a rose before dancing with her. Brynd's brother was next, making Ryn blush from the top of her head to the tips of her toes. As he spun her around, she caught Zo winking at her.

At the end of the spin, she found herself looking up into the face of Fergus, in full dress uniform, holding a rose.

Ryn stopped. Unsure what to say.

He held out the rose to her. "May I?"

Ryn nodded, adding the flower to her growing bouquet.

Fergus' embrace led her back into the dance.

"How've you been?" Fergus asked.

"Sad, lonely, depressed," Ryn answered.

Fergus frowned down at her. Pulling her a little closer he whispered, "I think that might change soon."

When the dance had finished, they all sat at a long table with Ryn at the head. As dinner was served, Ryn looked down the table at all who were gathered there for her and marveled. The evening was a delicious warm fall night, and the torches kept any creeping autumn chill at bay. How had she managed to get so lucky to have Clayr, Brynd's family, Fergus, Zo, her mother, Lar, and the others here for her?

Then she felt guilty about what they'd done to Prym's party. It was her night and Ryn had ruined it. No matter how awful Prym was, she didn't deserve that. Ryn stared at her plate in shame.

The clanging of a fork on a glass brought her attention back.

Lar, who was seated next to Ryn's mother to the left, stood and raised a glass.

"To Ryn, on her special day," Lar said, "and if she will permit me."

His eyes held hers with such intensity she had no other thought but to nod, having no idea what she was agreeing to.

Lar knelt in the grass in front of Ryn's mother and pulled out a promise necklace. "I would like to ask your beautiful mother if she would do me the honor of becoming my wife."

There was a small gasp from the crowd.

Ryette pressed her fingers to her lips. Clearly, she hadn't seen this coming, or at least not so soon.

The "yes" Ryette whispered was choked with emotion.

Lar's gaze shifted back to Ryn.

Her brain had stopped. She looked to Zo and Regg who both had silly grins on their faces. They could be a real family? Ryn hadn't considered this before.

Returning the boy's grin she said, "Yes."

A cheer went up from the table as her mother leaned down to kiss Lar while he slipped the necklace around her neck. There was a bit of fumbling with the clasp till it hung proudly in place.

Another fork began tapping on a glass. Ryn's gaze drifted down the table to the sound. It was Clayr seated at the other end.

"With that out of the way, I would like to make another proposal. I had the opportunity to look over the documentation Master Wes left, which included student applications." Clayr stared down the table directly into Ryn's eyes, even from that distance, a shiver ran up Ryn's spine. "I have to say that yours was exemplary." Clayr's eyes shifted to Brynd further down the table. "I was then informed exactly what research was done, and how it all came together. It's true what Ryette said about you Ryn. In just a few days you proved yourself a master of the Library." Clayr lifted her glass high. "After much discussion I have managed to convince the Board of this fact. They agree with me that you are much more valuable working with the Library than against it. The Library would like to offer you the position of Assistant Researcher, starting day after tomorrow." She paused. "Do you accept?"

Ryn couldn't process what Clayr said.

Ryn turned to Zo, who appeared to be clapping and cheering, but Ryn didn't hear a sound. "What did she say?"

"They're offering you a job in the Library!"

Regg leaned in, "You're moving to Waatch and we're becoming family." He turned to Zo. "We've never had a sister before, this is going to be interesting."

"Well," Clayr said, "what do you say?"

Ryn's jaw worked until she could find her voice. "Yes! A thousand times yes!"

From somewhere down the table, two chairs scooted back and Yll and Brynd came running to throw their arms around Ryn.

There was a jumble of "I can't believe it" and "we could be roommates," and "I can't wait," and "the Library's never going to be the same" before they finished hugging, and the cake came out, and everyone sang to her, and she cut the cake.

***

Later, Ryn was walking around bidding people goodbye and thanking them, when Yll approached her.

"Let's walk," Yll said.

Ryn noticed most everyone was either leaving or helping clean up. "Sure."

Yll linked arms with her and led her away from those picking up. "I want to explain..."

"You don't need to," Ryn said.

"But I do. I'm sorry I got so caught up in getting back into Prym's good graces. I got a taste of the popular life and was desperate to get it back. In the process, I lost sight of the one person who's always been there." Yll stopped at the edge of the forest. "I'm sorry."

"I get it. I know how it feels. It hurt more than you can imagine when I found the book gone, but when I saw Prym get into trouble—why did you do it?"

Yll shrugged. "To be honest, I was being selfish at the time. I figured if Prym used it and got what she wanted it was a win, and if she got caught—it was still a win."

"Well, even unintentionally brilliant, it was brilliant. If you hadn't done that, Master Wes would have gotten away with Luc's book."

Yll's gaze shifted to her mother helping pull tablecloths off the tables.

"Things are different in the Library. There are better people to ally with than Prym." Her eyes met Ryn's. "I'm excited we're going to be there together."

Ryn gave her best friend a huge smile then a hug.

"Always," Ryn said.

Clayr called to Yll to come help. Ryn moved to follow her, but something white shifted in the bushes. She tried to ignore it, but she swore she heard her name called. Trying to see into the dark, she was sure it was Zo or Regg out there trying to scare her.

"It's not funny guys," she called into the dark.

A shadow emerged from behind a bush, and she found herself face to face with a man. His hair was wild, tangled with leaves and twigs, but his posture was tentative and unsure.

"Mistress Ryn, I must speak with you." He tapped at his temple with his fingers.

Ryn took a cautious step backward.

"Who are you?" she asked.

He bowed his head. "I am Schiz of...of..." The man looked up, confused. "I am Schiz." He said again. He knocked his fist against the side of his head a couple times.

Alarm rose inside Ryn. She wanted to run. The man seemed to sense her distress and panicked.

"I am...very sorry mistress, I come from Shimamare. Shimamare and...and. Shimamare. I've come to..." He knocked his fist against his head again. "I've come to warn you."

Ryn backed away a few more steps. He closed his eyes and took two deep breaths. When he opened his eyes, he seemed more normal. He held his hand up in front of him in a calming gesture.

"It's alright, I'm alright. I don't want to hurt you. I have important information for you."

Schiz gave a slight shake of his head. "I have...come to warn you...information about you and your mother...it was passed on to...to *Them*," he said.

"*Them*?"

"Them...Them..." He knocked at his head. "The ones who made me as I am...*Them*."

Ryn sifted her eyes toward the party. Zo was heading toward her. Silently, she wished him to move faster.

Schiz followed Ryn's gaze to Zo, then shifted back into the trees.

"I cannot stay," he said. "Can I... Can I meet with you again?" His look was earnest. "Please?" Those blue eyes stared into Ryn's eyes.

"Sure." Ryn found herself saying. Terrified, she hoped she wouldn't see him again.

"Thank you!" Schiz's clear blue eyes stared into hers. "I made a promise long ago to your father that I would look after you. I take that promise seriously." With that Schiz bowed to her, and disappeared into the woods.

Epilogue

Rain pattered on the great windows of the Library Docent Hall. Despite the daylight the giant windows let in, it was dark and gloomy. The trees outside had lost most of their leaves. Autumn was nearly over, and winter was close upon them. Ryn sat at her desk, carefully recording new acquisitions into a reference book. The documents she worked with were the ones brought to the Library by her mother at the end of summer, when all the craziness of Master Wes had happened. Ryn had been working in the Library for over a moon now. She held the title of Assistant Researcher, but so far all she and Yll had done was Docent work. It sort of made sense, as both her and Yll really didn't know much about the Library. Studying with Master Wes for a few days hadn't taught them much, despite their early success. Still, Ryn longed for the chase. The small taste of hunting down records and books had given her a thrill that logging entries just didn't achieve. She couldn't help but wonder when she could get back to it. Pulling reference books only tempted her to yank random books off the shelf and run with them down whatever rabbit hole they would take her.

She also longed to resume her pursuit of orphanage books. At the moment though, her mother was caught between dodging family and trying to find Jett. Living here in the Library dorms, Ryn was unaware of the whereabouts of her mother on any given day, but she came to check on Ryn often, so she knew her mother was around. She was also aware of how much stress her mother was under, so Ryn had set aside her orphanage book search—at least for now.

The clouds outside darkened, and a crack of thunder accompanied a downpour of rain. At the pounding of drops on the window, Ryn looked up, jumping almost out of her skin to find Yll hovering over her. She hadn't heard her approach.

"Gracious Yll, are you trying to scare me to death?"

Yll sparked a huge grin in the dark. "The acquisitions department has a new stack ready for us. They sent a note to come and retrieve it." Yll held up a piece of paper in her hand.

"I'm not done with this stack." Ryn thrust out her hand to the papers and books on her desk, her hand almost knocking over a pile.

Yll lifted one shoulder in a half shrug. "Sandy is insisting we pick it up now."

Ryn held back a growl of frustration. Sandy was the Collections Manager in charge of Docents—as well as Ryn and Yll's training. Sandy openly displayed her thoughts about Yll only being here because of Clayr's position as curator. She also made it clear exactly how she felt about Ordinaries, and their working in the Library. Being assigned Sandy as their supervisor had been a challenge for Ryn and Yll. Their load of long, boring, tedious assignments just kept growing. It was almost as if Sandy were trying to get Ryn and Yll to quit, but Ryn and Yll loved the Library too much. They would outlast Sandy and her mountains of paperwork if it killed them.

"Fine." Ryn put away her pen and stood.

Yll grabbed the lantern off Ryn's desk and headed for the stairs leading to the Library's basement. The pitch darkness of the stairwell enveloped them. It was like descending into a pit, yet Ryn knew the basement was not the bottom. She had been to the underbelly of the Library. She shuttered thinking of the dark something that had chased her and Zo down there. She didn't know how he went there day after day, but he seemed a lot happier and healthier since he took up the added responsibility of physician's apprentice.

At the bottom of the stairs, Yll turned right into the acquisitions office. Here in the basement, new documents and books were brought to be assessed for damage and providence, then categorized. There were tables with stacks of books, scrolls, and loose documents everywhere. It was organized chaos. Today though, a light at the end of the hallway leading to a room Ryn never noticed before, captured her attention.

"Do we know what room is down that way?" Ryn asked.

"Repairs and Restoration," the Researcher at the acquisitions desk answered.

But Ryn barely heard her. She was moving down the hall, drawn by the light.

Once in the doorway, she was overwhelmed at the sight. Shelves and tables held damaged scrolls and falling apart books which were tattered, and crumbling. Some books were scattered in pieces, or just plain missing parts—like the cover or the binding. It looked like the aftermath of a battle, if books went to war.

In the back, a man sat at a desk with a huge magnifying glass before him. Several lanterns were trained on the subject lying on the desk in front of him. It appeared from Ryn's distance to be an enormous document he was painstakingly piecing back together with tiny tweezers.

On the far wall was a normal shelf of books. Ryn moved among the rows of book carnage. All the manuscripts smelled of ancient decay. Ryn's black Assistant Researcher dress brushed against a table, coming away with crumbs of paper and leather.

"Careful, I need every last piece to put that back together," the man said, without looking up from his work.

"Sorry," Ryn said.

Not knowing what to do, she guiltily brushed the dusty bits from her dress.

Ryn turned back toward the far wall. She was intrigued by how out of place it seemed. When she reached the shelf, she took one of the books down. There were no identifying marks on it anywhere. Not on the cover, nor on the inside. The contents looked to be some sort of journal, but it also contained charts and accounting tables. It seemed to be some sort of annotated business log, yet Ryn couldn't determine what kind of business or where it was located.

"That's the mystery wall," the man behind the glass said. "Books for which we have no provenance."

"Interesting." Ryn replaced the book on the shelf.

They did seem to emit the energy of mystery. She ran her fingers down their spines, walking the length of the shelf while absorbing the tingling thrill they gave her. When she reached the end of the shelf, she had a strange thought.

"Excuse me Master, I've been rude. My name is Ryn, and you are?" She asked the man.

"Walt, Master Restorer. Good to meet you." He lifted his tweezers at her.

"Walt, would you happen to have any orphanage books on the mystery shelf?"

Yll's appearance in the doorway drew her attention. Eyes wide, her hands went to her mouth in surprise. She said something Ryn couldn't make out.

"What?" Ryn said.

Yll put her hands down. "Orphanage books here? Looks more like a battle zone."

Walt chuckled, "Only the time-honored battle with age and decay." He rubbed his shoulder. "I believe there's a book that could be an orphanage record. Fourth shelf down, shelf mark fifty-three." Walt turned back to his magnifying glass.

Ryn stared in wonder for a minute at how Walt could know that off the top of his head without looking in a reference book.

Yll joined her as Ryn shifted to the fourth shelf and counted down fifty-three books. The spine seemed fairly new compared to the rest of the room. When Ryn pulled it from the shelf, she almost dropped it in shock. She knew that binding. She had seen it before...in that room...on that cliff...

"It can't be," Ryn whispered.

Her knees buckled beneath her, but Yll was fast on her feet and caught her before she fell to the floor.

"What's going on?" Yll asked, as she pulled a chair over with her foot and deposited Ryn in it.

"I've seen this book before...in a dream."

"Can't be," Yll said.

Though she had never read the contents, she recognized the leather binding with its unusual tree shape pattern. Ryn set the book on a table close to her. The binding creaked as it opened. Her breath caught in her throat. The first few pages of the book were missing, exactly like in her dream.

"I can't believe it," Ryn said.

"What?" Yll said again, impatience in her voice.

"It's real!"

"Ryn..."

She turned her face up to Yll. "I've had...I keep dreaming about a library. It's on a cliff. It's filled with books and the curtains...and a potted plant..."

"You're not making any sense," Yll folded her arms.

"My father is there, and he shows me this book. He keeps telling me to find it. Here, in the Library!"

Yll's lips pressed together. Ryn could tell she didn't believe her.

Ryn took a deep breath and started turning pages. She knew at once from her experience searching orphanage records, that this book indeed came from an orphanage. It listed children, their approximate ages, and the date the orphanage took them in, with notes on the person who left them, and the child's ancestry if it was known.

Ryn flipped to the fall of the year she was born. No babies were taken in during the harvest moons. She turned the pages backward. Nothing. Nothing until she reached the day after the summer solstice. There—a little girl left by a man with pure white hair. She was listed as an infant, barely a day or two old.

Yll gasped. "Do you think that's you? It's not in autumn."

"My parents did adopt me when I was a few months old. Perhaps they are marking my gotcha day as my birthday."

Yll nodded absently.

Ryn flipped forward and backward through the book. There were no identifying marks on it anywhere. She turned to the front and ran her fingers over the stubs of the torn pages. Then she turned back to the page where the little girl was dropped at the orphanage the day after solstice. She stared at the entry, trying to absorb it into her brain, every last detail from the curl of the handwriting to the description of the man who left her. In her mind, she faintly heard a man sob. She put her hand on the entry.

"I think this is me. I mean, it's hard to tell for sure, but my heart just—I don't know why, but it's me." Ryn's eyes blurred as she looked into Yll's pale face.

Yll nodded slowly. Ryn could no longer see through her tears, but she closed the book and crushed it to her chest.

Yll placed a gentle hand on her shoulder. "Well...let's find that orphanage!"

Appendix I: The Ancestral Houses

House Terr
Earth Magic. House seat located on Daoterr

House Mare
Water Magic. House seat located on Shimamare

House Venti
Air Magic. House seat located on Kohventi

House Ignis
Fire Magic. House seat located on Ignisapan

House Lux
Lightning Magic. House Lux is located on Luxpulau

House Viator
Travel Magic. House Viator is located on Viatoro

House Dico
Mind Magic. House Dico is located on Oydico

House Muto
Shape shifting Magic. House Muto is located on Saarimuto

House Sano
Healing Magic. House Sano is located on Eileansano

House Pentral
Spirit Magic. House Pentral is located on Inispentral

House Vivus
Animation Magic. House Vivus in located on Ynysvivus

House Illusio
Illusion magic. House Illusio is located on Iegillusio

Appendix II: Luc's Poem as recorded in *On the Legend of Luc, Praedo's Scribe*

In shadows deep, where ancient echoes sing,
Shores were cursed by the serpent's wing.
Where the beastly dragon ruled the land,
The most majestic mountains stand.

Citizens cowered, afraid for their life,
When Praedo came to end the strife.
Holding great power he set on the quest,
To conquer the dragon, to vanquish the test.

With twelve companions to fight at his side,
The dragon had nowhere safe to hide.
His fierce evil eyes glowed of embering flame,
Praedo outsmarted the dragon with magical game.

Flashes of lightning and roaring thunder,
The earth moved and rocked asunder.
The dragon fell and crashed in the deep,
Where the waters devoured and his corpse sleeps.

Injured our hero fell to the ground,
To aid his needs his friends gathered round.
Alas it was late, as his dying breath whispered,
They drew near to him to help and they heard.

Take ye my bones and turn them to beads,
My magic will guide and protect your needs.
As long as it's used for the good of the land,
Ye shall hold great power within your hand.

Pass this gift down through each family line,
To guard this place throughout all of time.
So they crafted beads from his magical bones,
And wore them round necks like tiny white stones.

What's left must stay safe and must be hidden,
To fall in the wrong hands is forbidden.
From the start where the mountains rise,
The treasure was hidden neath azure skies.

Seek the glade where whispers of pines,
Guard the secret that time defines.
By rivers winding through emerald lands,
Where the eagle soars, the seeker stands.
Follow the call of the owl at night,
To a secret passage where ye will find light.

Appendix III: Gesta Praediana

In the verdant fronds of my solitudes,
My verses flourished with a mountain voice.
I sang the archaic echoes of the earth,
In the growing poppies, and the grassy herbs.
In the streamy waters, I sipped the sweet truths,
That the mountain gives to those who love them.

My lyre was foraging for the perfect cadence,
In the vitreous rhythms of a full, cold rain,
And under the moonlight, between sea and sand,
I searched the sonorous accents of the waves.

But alas! My verses turned into a lament,
Under the bright flashes of the traveling star,
Who would have thought that a radiant sky,
Omen would be of such pain and despair?

Sweet melodic accents dying in the ash,
Great agrestal anthems profaned in the flames,
Fire in the forest, trees becoming blaze,
And a solemn requiem left in the night air.

When the somber fumes invaded the skies,
They spread in fields, through cities and towns,
Becoming the voice, the herald, and sign,
Of pain and calamities, misery, and mourn.

But what was the cause of so much commotion?
What turned all my odes into burial hymns?
What tinted the lights of the day with black shadows?
The old vicious dragon and his conquest thirst.

The burdens of servitude fall on our backs,
Where freedom existed, bondage came to be,
Where joyfulness flourished, bitterness remained,
Where beauty and grace blossomed, only rot was seen.

What will bring joy back to the chants?
Who will deliver from the iron yoke?
What will scourge the draconic lord?
The strong arm of Praedo, his power and sword.

ACKNOWLEDGEMENTS

I wrote a book once. Twenty plus years ago, I sat at a computer every morning before my kids woke up and wrote. Nobody could finish it. I gave up. I was sad for many years. I still wanted to write a book. Things changed in the world. My kids grew up, and the internet became a thing. One day, I happened upon Brandon Sanderson's university lectures and I discovered: I am a writer! So, the first person I want to thank is Brandon Sanderson, for paying it forward and encouraging us all to write—because it's good for you! He's my hero who saved me. Thank you!

Way back almost four years ago, I nervously handed my first draft of what would eventually become this book to three people hoping that they would be able to read it. Thank you to my lovely first Alpha readers: Joyce Holt, Angela Snedaker, and Kristina Yuen. I can't tell you how much your positive feedback helped keep me going. I owe a lot to you.

Next there's a huge group I need to thank for getting me where I am today. By the Potted Plant, The Potted Plant, Plont Folk–whatever you like to call them. Forged in the fires of the pandemic during a virtual SIWC, the Plont has been with me through many ups and downs, and has never failed to help me when in need. They are all fabulous writers themselves! In no particular order: Alissa Leonard, Caleb Huitt, Erica Collier, Jamie Pedersen, Jason Lowrey, Kevin Mack, Cara Hamborsky, Gina Fabio, Spencer McTavish, Keith McCormick, Marie Parks, Jessi Honard, Shantel McDonald, Cedan Bourne, and Sweth Chandramouli. Special thanks go to the following plant folk: Eva Doherty Gremmert, Kristi Jenkins, Cole of the Absent Lastname, Morgan Cameron, Jen Mandeno, AG Angevine, Rebecca Wright, Laura Blegen, and Timothy Forner for being amazing conference buddies, and for giving the best group hugs. To Joseph Hartman, Kim Aippersbach, and Roselyn James for all of the above, plus beta reading the second manuscript for me. Thanks for poking at my worldbuilding and pushing it further. To Michael Roth for spending hours on the phone with me helping me plot and plan, this story is what it is because of you. To Dan Eavenson for giving me the opportunity to be a part of your anthology, and for introducing me to William in the process. Most importantly to Lynda

McCarty for reading, editing, commenting on, etc. my manuscript, multiple times, in all its iterations, and for listening to all my doubts and fears, and for cheering me on. I appreciate you so much!

To my amazing cover artist, Amy Maker, who read my book, and with zero direction from me, managed to come up with a stunning piece of art. The cover never fails to dazzle. Thank you so much for your hours and hours of hard work, and for believing in my book.

Poetry and I are not friends. Fortunately, I have some really fabulous award-winning poets in my life! Emily Gearheart Lim has written me some amazingly beautiful and touching poems in the past and when I wrote myself into needing some poetry, I called upon her immediately. Lehonti Pérez Ovalle and I spent a year together discussing writing at my dinner table. He's won some fancy awards for his poetry in Guatemala. I'm so grateful he said yes to writing an epic poem for me.

To my family and dear friends who are family. What can I say? You are the pillars that keep me standing. I love you all so much!

To my mom and dad, Noreen and John Hosack, for always telling me I was wanted, loving me and spoiling me. I am so grateful to be a Hosack!

To my husband, Benjamin Lim, for letting me shut myself in my office for hours on end, cooking me dinner, going to social things alone when I feel the pressure to get something done, and for providing for me so I can have a no-brainer day job and come home to write. I couldn't have done it without your support. I love you!

We're getting toward the end of the list, but this book wouldn't be in anyone's hands without William C. Tracy who looked at my steaming pile of mush and saw something with potential that no one else saw. I'm so grateful to him and Space Wizard Science Fantasy for giving me this opportunity.

At the end here I want to thank the two people this book is dedicated to: To my aunt Linda Everett for talking writing with me for hours, and being my cheerleader way, way back over twenty years ago. I was so devastated when she passed. As this book goes to print, I miss her terribly.

Lastly, but certainly not least, to the man who inspired the idea for this story, Lorenzo Frazier. At first, I was nervous to show you this story, and I was so relieved when you loved it. I'm grateful you read over my shoulder and helped me get it right. From the kernel of the idea to the final product, this book doesn't exist without you. You're the best brother and I couldn't have done without you.

ABOUT THE AUTHOR

CJ grew up in Southern California loving fantasy and science fiction. She is married to her husband of thirty plus years, has four children, and an ever-growing number of grandchildren. Adopted at eight months old, she recently found her birth parents. She has a Master's Degree in Public History from Southern New Hampshire University, and if she's not writing you can generally find her quilting, costuming, or traveling to spend time with those she loves. She's a wannabe dress historian and has worked with museums on historical dress recreation. *The Slayer's Magic* is her first book in *The Beads of Bone* series. You can find CJ at her website cjhosack.com and on Instagram @cj_hosack

Please take a moment to review this book at your favorite retailer's website, Goodreads, or simply tell your friends!

Made in United States
Troutdale, OR
09/05/2024

22323851R00181